DEBT

A NOVEL

DEBT

a novel

RACHEL CAREY

SILVER BIRCH PRESS
LOS ANGELES, CALIFORNIA, USA

ISBN-13: 978-0615702278

ISBN-10: 06157022879

FIRST EDITION, February 2013

Email: silver@silverbirchpress.com

Web: silverbirchpress.com

Cover Photo: ©Jeff McCrum, Used by Permission

Mailing address:
Silver Birch Press
P.O. Box 29458
Los Angeles, CA 90029

I owe this book
to the Sallie Mae Corporation.

—R. C.

1

LILLIAN FITZGERALD WAS AN IDIOT.
But she had the redeeming quality of knowing that she was. Anyone who went into debt—anyone who went into student loan debt—for a master's degree in a field as unpromising and competitive as creative writing deserved what was coming to her.

Lillian was aware, as she sat in her rented graduation robes on a bright spring day in May, that she didn't deserve sympathy. She had picked up her packet at the financial aid meeting for departing MFA students that explained the various monthly payment plans she faced for the next fifteen to thirty years, and she couldn't pretend—and didn't pretend—that she hadn't known ahead of time how bad it would be, how much her decision to attend grad school would feel like a stupid, bad, life-damaging choice. She couldn't understand why her fellow classmates acted so surprised. "Wha-at?" they were groaning. "Nine hundred and twelve dollars a month?"

They had borrowed a hundred thousand dollars. What did they expect? Some magical patron of the arts to descend from the heavens and pay it back for them? But she sympathized with the collective delusion that had allowed them to put their heads in the sand, because she knew how it had happened to her and why, and the irony was that it had started from feeling poor.

"Jesus," her friend Nadya was saying as they lined up behind a pert pink woman in a long robe and puffy Ph.D. cap. "I should never have let them graduate me. If we were still in school, we'd still have access to the dorms, and the library, and the gym…"

"We should have lied and said we had writer's block," Lillian said, "and never finished our thesis novels."

"Forget thesis novels. We should have done that with every assignment. We could have dragged this out for years and years."

Nadya lit a cigarette, which was what she did when facing a life crisis, and Lillian stole one of Nadya's cigarettes, which was how she told herself she wasn't a smoker.

"If we were really smart," said Lillian, "we would never have written anything at all."

When Lillian had applied to Fortuna three years ago, when she had sought entrance to that prestigious university on the island of Manhattan, she had done it almost as a joke. She hadn't known whether her writing was any good. She hadn't been able to find a publisher for her first two impassioned attempts at novels, and she had sent in her Fortuna application on a whim, as a way to motivate herself, knowing all the while that the whole attempt was pointless. Who was she kidding? It was Fortuna, after all, home of Big Names, Pulitzer Prize winners, Voices of a Generation. Then they had accepted her.

Even then, at first, she'd had no plans to go. It was a hundred thousand dollars, and she was a realist. She was poor. Her parents had died when she was a teenager, and she had spent her final high school years in the hands of a series of well-intentioned but awkward relatives, all of them a bit ashamed of their inability to connect with her. She had put herself through college, in part, by selling her parents' house—not even a big one—and she knew there was no money or support to be had, if things went downhill for her. There was no one she could ask for help.

"All 2008 graduates. This way, please. Can you put out that cigarette?" Lillian blushed at the pink woman and rushed to stub out her cigarette, and then felt bad that she'd stubbed it out in a flower urn, looked for somewhere else to put the crumpled cigarette butt, and ended up tucking it inside her change purse wrapped in a napkin.

Nadya moved her cigarette to her other hand.

"This way, 2008 graduates. Through these doors…"

8

Even after being accepted to Fortuna, Lillian had told herself that she wouldn't go, that an expensive grad school was not for people like her, that only wealthy students could afford to take advantage of the fabulous teachers and networking opportunities and veneer of prestige afforded by such a degree, that she must muddle along and apply to a state school and keep working at her day job at a small publishing house in Baltimore. She had told herself not to pretend to be something she wasn't, part of the circle of Powerful and Meaningful Novelists. She should know her place.

But something about "knowing her place" struck a nerve. This was America, wasn't it? Where everyone was supposed to have the chance to make good? It was creative writing—a field where people should share their voices with multitudes, not curl up in obscurity because they couldn't afford the entrance ticket. She'd started to feel that turning down Fortuna would be admitting that she would never be great, that she had no potential, that she wasn't worth the money.

And what the hell, right? Novels had sold for a hundred thousand dollar advance. Dave Eggers' first book had sold for that much. If she was good enough, if she was talented enough…This was, of course, how all bad decisions were made.

As she entered the vast marble hall assigned to the arts graduates that morning, she looked around at her classmates—at her competitors, at her cohorts, all about to enter the same unpromising field—and she still had a tiny glimmer of hope that she was going to do it, that she would make good on that promise she had made to herself when she sent in her acceptance letter to a fancy school in New York—that she was going to become a great writer.

Which made her, more or less, still an idiot.

A few blocks from Lillian, a young man pulled up his small grey-green van to the gates of Fortuna University and stepped out of the driver's door. Though the sign on his van showed that he had no official affiliation with the day's events, his youthful energy echoed the optimism of the green-donned graduates who were beginning to emerge nearby.

"Let's get the table out first," he said aloud, as if instructing a small army of cheerful young men. From the back of his van, he pulled a long folding table that he assembled on the broad Manhattan sidewalk, encouraging himself as he worked. "Gorgeous day. Let's get those legs up. Nice work."

He cheered on his invisible team of assistants as he assembled a collapsible tent above the table. The tent was marked with the logo on the side of his van—the single word "BOLT"—and a drawing of a nut and bolt in cartoon-large proportions.

"Okay. Good. Nice." On top of the table, he arranged assorted items: grey-green mugs, grey-green signs, and a stack of forms, weighted down against the light spring breeze. Under his own command, he began circling the table, rearranging, dividing the stack into two stacks, then three, one at either end of the table and one in the center.

"Excellent," he concluded, and having gained the approval of his inner boss, he took a seat, picked up one of his business cards, and read it to himself with satisfaction.

"Clyde Upson, Account Executive." He had not gotten as far as the 6th Avenue address before a passerby drew his attention.

"Are these mugs free?"

Clyde looked up to see two green-robed young women standing at his table. The shorter of them was embarrassed, her red hair pinned back in a ponytail. She was wearing the hood of some illustrious graduate degree. Her taller, darker friend now held a mug in her hand, turning it over while she waved a cigarette in her other hand. The graduation ceremony must be over at last, which meant it was time for Clyde to get to work.

"Free?" Clyde hesitated. The sign in front of his table included the word "free," but free was a complex issue, and he parsed it with care. "Well, let me start by saying this..."

"Do I have to sign up to get a mug?"

"Nadya," chided the friend.

10

But Clyde wasn't concerned. "It's a great program. The interest rates—the starting APR could save you hundreds of dollars, if you're carrying a high-interest balance on another card. I mean, can I ask you—do you mind if I ask you how many credit cards you have?"

The girl replaced the mug on the table. "Too many."

"No, wait. You don't have to sign up. It's free. Really." The girl turned back, and he pressed the mug into her hand, adding, "But I tell you what. Why don't you take one of those application forms? Take one for yourself, one for your friend. Look at our interest rates. And if you don't think it's a great deal, a really great deal, you don't have to do anything. In fact, you can sign up now, try out the card for a couple of months, cancel it anytime. There's no monthly fee…"

The girl took the forms from his hand and rolled them up into the mug. "Thanks," she said, and turned to continue up the street as her friend threw Clyde an apologetic smile. He watched them go. Within half a block, the girl had pulled out the rolled up applications and tossed them in a trashcan.

"It's a start," he told himself.

After all, now she had something with the corporate logo on it, something she would look at every day. She might sign up for a card, sometime. True, he would not get the commission, but it would help his company.

"It's called branding, people," he said aloud.

"Bolt owes me a mug," said Nadya as they turned the corner toward their apartment a few blocks away. "My brain is officially the property of Bolt Bank for the next thirty years."

"Did you go to that financial aid exit thing?" asked Lillian.

"No. I'm going to pretend I don't have student loans until I get a job."

"I wish I could do that. I'm completely freaking out."

"At least you're interviewing for that tutoring job. That's better than me. I'm totally unemployed," Nadya said. "Even a free mug helps. But oh, speaking of free stuff, my friend Chris said he'd take me out to lunch at L'Arnaque today. You should come."

"I can't afford that."

"He'd pay for you, too, I'm almost sure of it. I'll tell him you're an orphan."

"No, don't, Nadya. Please."

"He works at a hedge fund. You're doing him a favor—he doesn't know what to do with all that money."

"I promised myself I'd write. Today."

"But you have to come. Otherwise, it's too much like a date, and I don't want him to think I'm on a date with him," Nadya said. "Come on, celebrate! You just completed a master's degree."

Lillian smiled, cheered up in spite of herself by the word "master." She glanced up and down Broadway, looking at the green trees, the green overflowing onto the middle of Broadway from the vast manicured lawns of Fortuna. She thought of the book that awaited her on her laptop, the daunting mass of verbiage upon which her future happiness hinged. She ought to face it, today. She ought to sit down to work, because this was the moment of truth, here, the moment when she must face her own talent and find out if it was all worth it. This was the moment when she must face herself.

"Sure, why not?"

L'Arnaque had maintained itself with decorum just across the street from Fortuna University for over sixty years, even during the decades when that section of Broadway was too rundown to be worthy of such a fine dining establishment. While not as old as Fortuna itself, L'Arnaque viewed itself as an important part of college life: here had many a star professor been asked about his plans to write a book; here had many a visiting dignitary been asked about his plans to teach; here had many a student been asked about his plans to do anything besides vacationing in Amsterdam over summer break. Decorated outside with a pale pink awning, decorated within with pale pink seats, it maintained the

dignified awareness that it was the only place in the neighborhood for decent people to dine, ignoring the falafel joints and
Subway shops that might crop up next door.

Lillian's first view of this great institution was the tiled floor,
as she entered a few feet behind Nadya. Nadya had traded her
robes in favor of a slim black dress and sandals. Lillian wore a
cheery yellow sundress that was three years out of fashion, decorated with faded white daisies that had lost their clarity after too
many turns in the dorm dryers.

"Are you sure I should be here?"

"We're meeting someone. We'll wait at the bar," Nadya informed the young hostess who greeted them. "Don't be boring,"
Nadya added to Lillian.

"I feel bad. If it's a date…"

Nadya slid onto a mahogany barstool and flagged a young
bartender in a pale pink dress shirt. "Two martinis," she commanded. "We're celebrating."

"Graduation?" the bartender asked, but Nadya didn't dignify
this with a reply.

The main dining room was full, and Lillian had no trouble
recognizing the new graduates, as they relaxed behind large
leather menus, surrounded by multigenerational groups. She reflected on the calm that came to children when they were being
taken care of by their parents, even if the children were thirty-five
and getting their Ph.D.s. She felt adrift, looking at the well-to-do
clans that made up the clientele: little boys in white polo shirts,
gray-haired fathers in silver-framed glasses, mothers with spheres
of blonde bobbed hair.

Her sense of displacement was confirmed by the arrival of
Nadya's friend, in a whirl of kissed cheeks and a good-quality
sports jacket. Chris glowed with the aesthetics of prosperity:
tanned skin, tailored clothes, the relaxed smile of someone who'd
never had to worry about money. He was beautiful, even if you
had a reflexive class hatred, and Lillian didn't. She was too busy
feeling awkward about the cheap white sneakers she had worn
with her dress.

13

"This is my friend Lillian," said Nadya. "You're buying her lunch, too."

"Of course I am."

"She's an orphan, you know."

Lillian more or less knew what to expect from the moment she saw Chris. Smart, charming, Harvard grad—he made witty and literate references, but not so many as to seem pretentious, and he spoke, of course, with incredible supportiveness about their arts degrees. Financial types were always overflowing with kind words for people who worked in the arts, social work, or education.

"Congratulations to you both," Chris said. "It's awesome. It really is."

"What's awesome?" Nadya said. "We're pretty much in debt until we die."

"But that's good," Chris said. "Debt is good. Take your credit score. I know a girl who has no credit at all because everything was paid for her. Trust-fund baby. Never rented an apartment, never had a job. Now she can't get a loan for a car, buy a home. She basically can't function as an adult."

"Except because of our debt, we'll never be able to afford those things," Lillian said.

"You don't know that. That's the thing about investing. I mean, a Master's in Fine Arts. That's a risk, right? You're betting that you'll make it as a writer. But statistics are against you, right?"

Lillian gave a bleak smile.

"No, it's great," Chris hurried on, realizing they were not reassured. "See, that's—that's the kind of risk half the guys I work with would never take. You two would be great venture capitalists. You're staking your whole livelihood on your faith in yourselves."

"And are most venture capital projects successful?" asked Lillian.

Chris hedged.

Lillian's keen awareness of her post-graduate poverty made her want to despise Chris, but she couldn't make herself, and not only because he was charming. It was because of the brief moment, as they surveyed the menus, when he did a double take upon learning that Lillian was actually—actually—an orphan.

"I guess that's the one positive about not having to deal with parents," Nadya said to Lillian. "No one to criticize you for making a bad financial decision."

"You mean—you don't have parents? Not really?" Chris asked.

His eyes showed real concern, like maybe there was something he could do about it, and Lillian's heart softened toward him. There was something endearing about someone who had reached the age of thirty and still didn't know that such things actually *happened* to people.

"Lillian wrote an amazing short story about it," said Nadya.

"Probably the only good thing I've written."

"You can't listen to the professors, Lill."

"That's right," said Chris. "They don't know the value of anything. You won't know if it's any good until you put it out there and see what someone is willing to pay for it."

"So that's the value of something? What someone will pay?" Lillian asked.

"How else would you define value?"

"By how much something helps people."

"If it helps people, they pay for it," Chris said. "Don't they?"

"So which is more valuable to you, a kiss from a girl you like, or a kiss from a girl you paid for?" Lillian asked.

Chris smiled, stumbled in answering, laughed at himself.

"You win," he said.

Lillian reminded herself that liking him was unwise. Nadya's beauty created a romantic vortex from which most men couldn't withdraw their attention long enough to notice anyone in her orbit. Lillian told herself that Chris was probably going to marry Nadya. She could see their whole future together: buying an apartment in the West Village, getting some kind of tiny dog.

15

He caught her look and said, "Are you okay?" and Lillian nodded her head, embarrassed.

She turned her focus to the twenty-five dollar lunch entrees on the menu, looking for something that was twenty-two, or nineteen. Though she wasn't paying, she couldn't bring herself to order something that cost more. Tears came to her eyes in a rush.

What had she done? She'd clawed her way up from a public high school, gone to college mostly on scholarship, and now had thrown it all away, put herself in debt for a useless master's degree from a fancy school, like a gambler betting on a long shot.

"I'll have the risotto," she said to the waiter when he arrived. It was eighteen dollars. The restaurant could charge that much for a bowl of rice, as Chris would have said, because somebody was willing to pay for it.

At that very moment, Clyde Upson was surveying the small stack of completed credit card applications in front of him, the depleted stock of Bolt-green mugs. He smiled to himself, feeling good, feeling that things were heading the right way for him.

He had reason to be hopeful about his future. He had exceeded his sign-up goals for the day by one hundred and fifty percent. He had more reason to be hopeful, maybe, than the two recent graduates of the prestigious Fortuna writing program, who owed over two hundred thousand dollars between them.

2

There's two ways to get money from a guy. One is to put a
gun to his head. But if he doesn't have the money, then
what do you do? You shoot him, you still got no money. You
let him go, there's no gun to his head anymore. So the other
way, the better way, is you put the idea of a gun in his
head. Then it's like he's carrying it around for you, pressing it against his own head for you, everywhere he goes.

IVAN BULOWSKI'S *Autobiography of a Gangster*

"IS THERE ANYTHING YOU WON'T DO?"

Always a dangerous question in a job interview.

The pleasant woman in the gray business suit offered Lillian a
polite smile and waited for a long moment.

"Anything I won't tutor, you mean?"

"You say here that you can do math as well as science, and
you know some history, you know Latin, your specialty is
writing…"

"Oh, well, I'd prefer not to do the SAT, if that's all right with
you."

"You mean, not at all?" The woman seemed stunned.

"I really don't mind helping kids with their academic work,
but I just wouldn't feel comfortable helping these wealthy kids
to do better on that test when, you know, poor kids won't have
access to the same service."

"You do realize that's a big part of what we do here."

"I know, but I was hoping maybe I could skip that part."

"I see."

"I just don't want to help rich kids cheat the system."

17

"How is it cheating the system to help somebody reach their potential?"

Lillian sighed. Perhaps it wasn't, any more than helping rich kids with their English homework or their math homework was. But SAT tests were different to her because they were supposed to be a great equalizer, a way of creating a level playing field for applicants from different backgrounds. Lillian's mother had run an antipoverty center in Baltimore, and Lillian knew that poor kids got no preparation for these tests. SAT tutoring, to Lillian, had always been the symbol of a rigged system.

"I'm sorry," Lillian said. "If you don't want to hire me, that's okay."

"You actually said that?" Nadya demanded four hours later. "Jesus, what a Girl Scout you are. I totally respect it, actually. Fuck the wealthy. They make it impossible to afford to live anywhere in this city anymore. I just don't know what we'll be doing for rent, that's all."

It was their last official week in campus housing, and Lillian and Nadya were in the middle of packing. It didn't put Nadya in a good mood.

"No, no, they actually said they'd hire me anyway," Lillian went on. "They have a job—just one—that's just tutoring in writing, right now, but it's fifteen hours a week. So if I can do that, then it'd pay me enough to survive and still write."

"And pay your student loans."

"I hope so. It'd be sixty-five dollars an hour."

"That awesome," Nadya said. "See, I could never do that. I'd probably stab the kid." As an artist, Nadya considered it her duty to claim for herself as many bad traits as possible.

"Well, what are you going to do?"

"I don't know. Something will come up." Nadya lit a cigarette and walked to the window. "Here's the thing, I'm just—I'm not going to work at some job I hate, you know? I'm not going to do it." Nadya sat on the sill and tapped her cigarette out the window.

"That's fine. I wasn't pressuring you."

"No, but some people are."

The fact that Nadya's parents were probably helping her financially always remained unspoken between them, even though they had been roommates for over a year. Lillian wondered if it was part of Nadya's cool that such things were never acknowledged.

"Let's go out," Nadya said. "Last time, you and me, Uptown Bar?"

"I'll come later," Lillian said. "I have to write tonight."

"No, you can't. It's our last week in this neighborhood. You can't do this to me."

"I'm not. I'll be there later. I have to stop putting this off, though."

"In an hour I could be on my way home with some guy."

"Well, take that as a challenge, then. If you manage that, then you won't need me there, will you?"

"You're terrible. Leaving me alone. This could be the last time we ever go there, and it's an institution for us, and you won't go?"

"I need to get some writing done. I promise I won't have any fun."

Nadya was mollified enough to spend the next twenty minutes digging among half-packed boxes for a pair of high-heeled boots before she headed out the door, reminding Lillian that Lillian had better be writing the next fucking Pen Prize masterpiece.

When Nadya was gone, Lillian went to the kitchen and poured herself a bowl of Cheerios. It took fifteen more minutes before she sat down to work on rewriting her novel. And she immediately felt like jumping out the third floor window.

She hadn't always felt this way about writing. As an undergrad, she'd fallen in love with writing after producing a single, successful short story about her parents' death that had been accepted into *The Antioch Review*. She'd spent the following two years happily producing historical fiction at the rate of fifty

19

pages a week—chaste, polite books that read like milquetoast Jane Austen, marbled with just a hint of anger at the poverty of her Irish forbearers. Lacking as they did in sex scenes, they were hard to categorize and unlikely to be published. So she had applied to writing school.

Her choice of Fortuna had proved fateful. A more cynical teacher at a lesser college might have told her to add some steamy stuff, and Lillian might have made a decent career of bringing Lord So-and-so and the spunky pastor's daughter into the hay together and then into the marriage bed.

But Lillian—wanting to be a good writer and not just a successful one—had accepted the offer from Fortuna's prestigious program. Fortuna was intent on turning her into a great novelist who dealt honestly with the Human Experience.

So after reading the work she submitted meekly for approval, the faculty posed the following questions:

"Why did her heroines always find love in the end? Was that a realistic portrayal of the Human Experience? A novelist's job was to dig deep into life as it really was, to explore the things that weren't easy, even the things that seemed unspeakable. Were Lillian's stories Honest? Was this as deep as she could dig?"

Lillian had to confess that her stories probably weren't honest. Not yet. But she knew she could do better. And over the course of her two years at Fortuna, she tried.

During her first year, she wrote the following short stories: A teenage boy commits incest with his sister, a religious fanatic commits suicide, a priest molests his best friend's son, a baby is starved to death by her traumatized teen mother.

These stories pleased the faculty somewhat. "They're better," Lillian was told. "But do you think you can delve deeper?"

During her second year, she wrote the following short stories: A Hiroshima victim slices off her own ear; a Kansas farmer arranges to have his gay lover killed by his gay-bashing son; a child enjoys his being sexual molested by his mother because he's so hungry for her attention.

"Interesting," said the faculty. "But are these as honest as you can get?"

Her thesis novel was about a religious fanatic who cuts herself and has an affair with a young priest who eventually kills himself because of incest with a sister who has murdered the baby she had with an abusive meth addict boyfriend who died in the Iraq War.

For some reason, Lillian grew very depressed whenever she sat down to work on her book. She told herself this was probably because she was a bad writer. This suspicion was confirmed when she submitted her book to the faculty for their approval.

Early in April of the year she was supposed to graduate, her favorite teacher, a woman with graying blonde hair, had looked earnestly at Lillian when she came in for her final review and then said: "I feel like it's missing something. It's missing your experience. Where are *you* in this book?"

Lillian said, "Um."

The portly man who was chairman of the program said, "Do you really feel like this is your best statement on the human experience?"

"It feels like…" offered the kind woman, "it feels to me like you went a little far. It's very dark, but it doesn't quite ring true for me."

"It's not honest," said the man. "Do you want to try a rewrite?"

Lillian started to cry.

"Don't worry," the man said. "We're still going to graduate you."

Lillian left their office with a red nose and a packet of tissues from the chair's assistant, mulling over the fact that the one person in her program who had immediately gotten a book deal had written a mystery novel with a plucky, overweight Southern heroine who was also a Cajun cook.

Now, sitting down to "fix" her book, Lillian felt a powerful urge to throw her laptop out the window. But that was probably just a sign that she was undisciplined about her craft. So instead, she made herself sit there for four hours, refusing to go out, her head throbbing, cereal half-eaten, trying to think about how she could dig deeper into the human experience.

21

3

So here's a question. Say your husband buys you a tas-
sel necklace at Barneys that's a little last season, and
you like it, don't love it. If you return it and spend the
four thousand dollars of store credit on a Martin Grant
trench you've had your eye on and a pair of Balenciaga
sandals, does that mean you've fallen off the shopaholic
wagon? And—second question—will your husband be insulted, even if his assistant picked out the necklace in
the first place? I'm hoping some of my fellow shopaholics
will weigh in. How does everybody else handle a situation
like this?

CANELLA MCBRIDE, www.shopacovery.com, April 29, 2008

AT EXACTLY 7:45 A.M., THE SELF-MADE MAN WALKED OUT
of his building on Park Avenue, got into a waiting town car, and
opened his laptop. At 7:46, he was reviewing a draft of the
speech he would make at his company's quarterly party. At 7:49,
he was reading an email about possible interest rate fluctuations
in light of instability in the housing markets. At 7:53, he was calling his office to request a phone connection with a junior senator
in Washington, D.C.

As a self-made man, he didn't look out the windows of his
car. He had seen the view from home to work exactly once,
when he had forgotten his laptop at the residence four years
ago. It would be a waste of time to indulge in the same view that
he could see every day.

As a self-made man, he didn't look at the driver who was taking him to work. It didn't interest him who drove, unless his car
was late, and it was never late. A car service was ordered precisely twenty minutes before he needed to leave every day, and

his assistant called the driver exactly fifteen minutes early, to make sure the car was in its place.

At exactly 8:01, the Self-Made Man stepped out of his town car, crossed the plaza to the Bolt Corporation Building, and informed the junior senator that he was about to get in an elevator and their conversation might be cut off. At 8:04, he walked into his twenty-fourth floor office, followed by his executive assistant, by name Bella Pointer, who hoped to get his signature on some documents before his meeting with the marketing committee. She saw that he was on the phone, stepped politely into the hallway, and waited until 8:09, when he had finished the conversation, pretending she wasn't listening at the door, before she entered and placed a pile of four documents in front of him, with "Sign Here" stickers in the appropriate places.

"Documents extending our loans from Lehman Brothers," she said. "Marcie from Legal and Jonathan Reese are standing by on two if you have any questions."

At 8:10, he signed documents one, two, and three, and then pushed the blinking button on his phone.

"The fourth loan agreement," he said to the waiting silence, "did we renegotiate this rate, or did we just automatically renew what we had last time?"

"That's been renegotiated," responded a male voice. "That's actually a quarter point lower than last year. We couldn't do better until we see what the Fed's going to do."

"Fine. I want to make sure we check these things, and people aren't automatically renewing things. We should always try to get a better deal."

"Of course," said the voice on the end of the line, and the Self-Made Man hung up the phone and signed in large letters, "Henry Bolt."

Bella picked up the documents as her boss turned his attention to his office computer, which had already been synched to the documents that he'd had open on his laptop.

"Are you ready for the meeting with the marketing committee?"

"Not yet. I'll call you when I'm ready."

The Self-Made Man knew that the marketing committee would wait. Nobody ever started a meeting without him. He began reviewing his speech again.

"Get Carver on the phone," he said to Bella just before she closed his office door. "I have a question about some of these ethics guidelines."

"Right away."

Carver Braydon was a Senior VP of Legal, and Bella knew that he might be in a meeting. He might be in the car or about to board a plane. But it didn't matter. Carver would take his call. Everyone took his calls. That was what it meant to be a self-made man.

"You're the tutor?"

Lillian found herself facing down a tiny dark-haired woman who was approaching her in a zigzag, dodging three dachshunds, a round table with a vase of delphiniums, and the bright-cheeked young woman who had opened the door of the apartment.

"I'm Bronnie," the tiny woman went on. "This is Julie, our nanny for our daughter, Amy. My son Cal's the one you'll be working with."

Lillian shook Bronnie's hand, and managed a faint smile at the sweet-faced Julie before Bronnie led her down the hallway and took a sharp right turn into the formal dining room. Bronnie was small and slender, high cheekboned and well made up, and wore slim jeans and thin silver bracelets. She moved with an air of constant frustration at the obstacles in her way, yet she seemed to steer herself ever onward toward the next hurdle: a dog toy, a vacuum left against the wall ("Rosa! Why is this still here?"), a large mahogany chair pulled out from the table. The zigzag effect was echoed in her conversation.

"He's not home from school yet. I wanted to talk to you alone first. You don't want anything to drink, do you?"

"No, I'm fine."

24

"Now tell me about yourself. You went to graduate school at Fortuna, is that right, and undergrad at—Brown?" Bronnie was seated, now, and gestured for Lillian to take a seat as well. She flipped through a printout of Lillian's resume, which sat on top of a copy of *Yoga* magazine.

"That's right," said Lillian, sitting in an upholstered seat. "I'm finishing a book. But I really love kids, so..."

"We should talk about Cal. My husband is a business-man. He's very successful. You should know that. We have high expectations for Cal. We expect him to go to an Ivy League school, or a small Ivy like Amherst."

"Okay...."

"Do you write fiction?"

"Yes, I'm finishing a novel..."

"I've been thinking of taking a fiction class. Did you have any professors who were good?"

"Oh! Well..."

"Here's the thing about Cal. He needs someone to keep him on task. These kids today, they're so easily distracted. The texting— they stay up texting until two in the morning. But he knows how important this is. He wants to go to Fortuna. You tutor for the SAT, right?"

Lillian hesitated. "I haven't done that very often," she began.

"Because that's the main thing we wanted you to work on, along with the writing. Do you have a blog? My friend Canella has a blog. She's getting a book deal out of it. Oh, and he has ADHD, that's another thing, we're getting him diagnosed, so what we want is for him to try the SAT, timed, in June, which is really just three weeks away, and then maybe he can take it un-timed in the fall of his senior year, if we can get the paperwork in. Cal," she called out in a loud voice, at the sound of the front door, and then went on.

"He'll show you the writing stuff he's been working on. But I also want you to start SAT. Today if you can. But he'll show you his English homework. Cal? Come in here."

An attractive young man with dark hair and blue eyes appeared in the doorway. He was dressed in white shorts and carried a tennis racket, and he moved with the awkward forward energy and free-floating shame of a boy who was not living up to expectations.

"Yeah?" He glanced between them with the ghost of a nervous smile.

"This is Lillian. She's going to be your new writing tutor."

"Oh. Hi." He spoke as if the concept of a writing tutor had never been mentioned to him.

"Now, make sure you do SAT with her as well, okay? Your last scores weren't so good."

The boy flashed Lillian a glance to see how she took this information, then nodded. "Yeah, okay. Um, I'm doing this now? Can I shower first?"

"Do you have to?"

"Kind of."

"As soon as you shower, then." Bronnie looked at Lillian as her son ducked out of sight. "I guess on Thursdays, you should come at five, so he has time to shower after his tennis lesson." She thrust her hand toward Lillian to shake. "And you're going to get me that name of a professor who teaches fiction-writing. Maybe I can do a one-on-one tutorial; that's all I have time for."

"I'll look into it," Lillian said.

Bronnie headed into the kitchen to speak with the nanny, and Lillian rose to look out the windows onto 68th Street. Teaching SAT. This job had seemed so perfect: sixty-five dollars an hour, fifteen hours a week. She could pretty much live on that and still work on her book. And how much did it matter, after all? Someone was going to end up tutoring him in SATs. Why not her?

No. It was a question of principle. She had to draw a line somewhere.

She rose, followed Bronnie into the kitchen, listened to the incipient argument Bronnie had begun with the nanny. "But she needs the haircut now. Can't they see her earlier?"

"They're booked until two," said Julie.

"They can't be booked until two. You need to ask them to squeeze us in. We have to get to Long Island by four, otherwise the traffic is impossible."

Julie bowed her head in apology. She had the rosy cheeks and long oval face of saint in a medieval painting.

"You have to tell them we've been coming there for nine years, and we can't just—did you need something?" Bronnie swung her attention to Lillian.

Lillian hesitated, twisting her hands.

"The thing is, I'm not very experienced at SAT. I thought I should tell you, because—maybe you can find someone else for the SAT tutoring, and just use me for the writing..."

"Oh, that's fine. I trust you. You did well on the SATs, right?"

"Yes...." Lillian watched as Bronnie turned back to Julie.

"Tell them it's an emergency," Bronnie said to the nanny.

There. Lillian had tried to do the right thing. That counted for something, didn't it? And Bronnie had just placed trust in her. How could you let down someone's trust? The eight hundred dollars a month she owed in student loan payments didn't even factor in.

She reminded herself that she was just doing this, in the first place, so she could have the time to write her novel. She could have gotten a full time job in publishing, or as an agent's assistant, but she wanted time to write. She thought of her interview: *Is there anything you won't do?* She was an artist, right? She ought to be willing to do anything for her art. Okay, maybe not kidnapping or murder. But if she was serious about her novel, then she needed the time to finish it, right?

"Anyway," Bronnie added over her shoulder to Lillian, "he already did some SAT tutoring last fall. He just needs some brushing up."

At exactly seven o'clock in the evening, the Self-Made Man placed his laptop in his briefcase and walked past his assistant's office to the elevator bank. By 7:02, Bella was on the phone with the residence, saying that he would be home at the usual time so the cook could finish her final preparations for the family's 7:30 dinner. At 7:07, he stepped into the town car that had been waiting since exactly 6:40. As his car door shut, a hand caught the handle.

The Self-Made Man looked up to see a man wearing a leather overcoat and two large gold rings on each hand. He was perhaps seventy, with a single shock of hair that rose from the center of his forehead and a long delicate scar that trickled from his temple to his ear. He stood holding the heavy door, stooped just enough to see the man inside.

"Hey, Harry," the stranger said.

"Ivan. I'm heading home. Can this wait?"

"No, it can't wait."

Before Henry could reply, a large figure emerged from the lobby of the building in a gray-green Bolt security uniform.

"Mr. Bolt, is everything okay?"

Henry looked at the guard, nodded curtly.

"Everything's fine, Paolo."

Ivan, though an elderly man, still had the musculature of his powerful youth, and he threw the guard an amused smile as the guard stood, arms folded, unwilling to return to the doorway.

"Let's go for a walk," Ivan said to Henry Bolt.

And the Self-Made Man stepped from the car and followed his companion down the street and around the corner, into the dark doorway of an Irish pub, and up a set of stairs to the back corner of the second floor.

4

She. Waited watched. Until the man was on one knee then two then. Slam went the whip. Slam Open Your Mouth. You pathetic little thing. It was a boring routine almost dull sometimes she was thinking about her grocery list slam.

Selection from *Cut It. Out* by NADYA RAHLIN

THERE ARE THREE STAGES OF HIPNESS THAT COME TO A New York City neighborhood. At the first stage—the outpost stage—a small group of struggling hipsters move into a poor, ethnic neighborhood in the city. These first arrivals are typically scholarship students from local art colleges, driven by economic necessity into a dangerous neighborhood with little to recommend it except proximity to the nearest subway line. They get along well enough with the locals, at first. They are few in number, they lug around heavy canvases or musical instruments, and they are viewed with some pity by the locals in the neighborhood where they've set up outposts. There is even relative safety for the newcomers, who are seldom mugged because they are accurately judged to have no money anyway.

At the second stage—the settler stage—the hipsters are followed by more of their friends, some with money, some of whom begin to open small businesses to serve the needs of the increasing hipster population: boutique clothing shops, record stores, organic grocery shops. Now more tension develops between the locals and the hipsters, as the locals start to recognize that they are being forced out of their usual haunts. What was once a dive bar becomes a hipster dive bar, and the old drunks find their favorite beers have gone up by two dollars a bottle. Where it was once possible to get a cheap apartment, hipsters now give the landlords bigger down payments and provide

29

parental cosigners to buffer their credentials. Bitter verbal disputes emerge between the new settlers and the original population about the volume of street music on the one hand and the hipsters' dogs and cigarette butts on the other.

At the third stage—the status stage—the rents begin to spiral upward, and neither the ethnic locals nor the poorest hipsters can afford to live there anymore. A new set of hipsters arrives, typically supported by their parents' money and part-time jobs at snarky magazines. The older businesses are forced out by rising rent, and the first Starbucks appears. The remaining locals despair and may lash out in physical violence, mugging the new arrivals—but this is just the last gasp before they begin their migration to more affordable corners of the city where they will struggle to create the sense of community they had in their former neighborhood. The peak of the "status stage" signals the beginning of the "buyout," in which wealthy investors pick up properties in order to turn them into sleek new high rises with running tracks on the roofs and pools in the basements.

Thus do young hipsters do a great service to the city, not unlike the brave settlers of the American West. They move into an area and drive out the indigenous (and typically browner) population, not so much by conscious intention as by force of numbers and a cheerful, can-do attitude.

The neighborhood of Williamsburg, Brooklyn, was at the peak of the status stage in June 2008, and two of its newest settlers had only managed to find an apartment of near-affordability by its distant location from the nearest L station. The vanishing ethnicity of the local neighborhood was Italian, and these two young pioneers now sat on the floor of their new apartment, surrounded by unopened moving boxes, partaking in a box of local cannoli and a lit joint.

"Never again," Nadya was saying to Lillian. "I will never again move myself. I'm way too old for this."

"At least we got exercise."

"Hot yoga is exercise. Moving a sofa up a flight of stairs is a sign that you need a boyfriend."

"You could have called Chris."

"Chris, God, what am I going to do about him? He keeps calling me."

"Don't you like him?"

"Yeah, but he's not my type. And we've been friends forever, so I can't just sleep with him, you know?"

Lillian didn't know, and Nadya rolled onto her side, took another drag, and looked up at the cracked ceiling.

"I'm too adventurous for him. He's the type who's going to want to get married, and I don't believe in marriage."

"Not ever?"

"People get married, and they get boring. I've seen it. Perfectly cool friends, and all of a sudden they're having kids, and talking about their kids, and they just stop trying, you know? Speaking of, I ran into Bryan at a reading last week and he was asking about you."

"Oh, okay," Lillian said, sounding bored. Bryan had graduated a year ahead of them and was a dark poetic soul who cited Dashiell Hammett and Borges as his chief influences. He was smart and sometimes funny, but Lillian had always felt a little afraid of him, perhaps because he produced precisely the kind of fiction that the faculty adored.

"What? He'd be perfect for you. I never understood why you didn't get together."

"I should focus on my work right now."

"Oh, speaking of, I got a job, did I tell you?"

They had rented the apartment on the strength of a cosigning agreement from Nadya's father, who ran a construction company in Orange County, California.

"Yay! What job?"

"Writing for a real estate blog. I have to write about different neighborhoods in the city, different properties, tell how great they are. Basically I'll spend all day visiting apartments I can never afford to live in."

"But that's great."

"It's a job. Anyway, I'm not really inspired to do any writing right now, so maybe it'll give me material. So do you want to go out and celebrate? My treat."

"No, I promised myself I'd work on my book tonight."

"Again? No. Start in the morning. Come on. You don't actually want to start tonight, do you?"

"I swore to myself. I'm being disciplined."

"Be disciplined tomorrow. We're celebrating. We have a new apartment, we deserve a night off."

"I just don't want to spend a lot of money."

"But we won't. I promise. One drink. I can't spend much money either, not until my first paycheck."

The money Nadya and Lillian spent that night was as follows:

$0.22 to Con Edison. Hot water for showers.

$0.43 to Con Edison. Electricity for Nadya's hair dryer.

$12.00 to Union Pool Hall. Two Pabst Blue Ribbons and tip, before Nadya met the bartender, by name Mark Gugino, who also grew up near Laguna Beach. "That's crazy—seriously?"

$4 to Union Pool Hall. Coke, plus tip, which Lillian, feeling guilty, insisted on paying for after Mark comped them the next two beers. Lillian had to stop drinking. It was already close to one, and she was getting up early to write in the morning.

$3.50 to Centipede arcade machine at Barcade bar, where Nadya tried to beat an attractive young man by name Colin, who hailed from England.

$18 to Barcade bar, which Nadya spent on buying the next round for herself, Colin, and Lillian, while Colin was busy playing Ms. PacMan. It was Nadya's turn to pay, and after all, she had a new job.

$10.75 to All-nite Deli. Cheerios and a half-gallon of milk, which Lillian purchased while walking home alone at 2:24 a.m.

$6.75 to All-nite Deli. One pack Camel Light cigarettes. Lillian had officially quit, but just in case writing went really badly.

32

$225 to Nadya's pot dealer, who agreed to come to Colin's house at 3:41 a.m., after Colin said he'd buy some, too, if the guy was serious about delivering.

$4 on ATM fees ($2 that Lucky Deli located on Colin's street charged Nadya to withdraw money, $2 charged by Nadya's bank for using another company's ATM).

$2.97 to iTunes. Three songs Nadya downloaded at 5:17 a.m. in a debate with Colin about the relative merits of Cat Power and Barbara Manning.

Total expenses to Nadya and Lillian for the evening (not including the cost to the young men): $281.17*

Nadya's weekly income from her blogging job, after taxes: $334.21

*This does not include the $16.24 that Lillian spent on platform sandals ($14.99 at Daffy's plus 8.25 percent New York State sales tax), which Lillian wore that one night only.

ᑫ

The following day, Lillian woke at noon and wandered around her apartment for half an hour, coming to terms with the fact that Nadya wasn't there to distract her from what she ought to be doing. Finally, after two cups of coffee, a shower, and a few minutes of checking email, she was ready to start working on her book. This was going to go well. It was going to go great. She felt rested, ready, focused, creative.

The first paragraph she encountered was: "The funeral home reached out toward the driveway like a gloved hand, taking hold of each somnambulant visitor in a secretive grip of oppressive silence, stamping out breath, bringing coughs, mysterious aches to the liver and kidneys. Mourners forgot the dead and thought only of the hissing sound of their own unsteady feet shuffling apologetically across the heavy brown rug."

"Jesus," she said aloud.

She had a terrible suspicion that her book should be thrown away in its entirety. She needed to talk to somebody disciplined, somebody who knew about art and books and being serious.

She picked up her cell phone and dialed.

"You've reached Bryan Ruggiero. I don't always check these messages." *Beep.*

"Hey, it's Lillian. Just calling to say hi. I haven't talked to you in a while. I was hoping you could give me some advice about life after graduation, or something, or trying to be a writer, since you seem to be one of the other people I know who isn't on a trust fund, so...I'm rambling now. Anyway. Um, call me if you want."

Lillian hung up the phone and sat staring out the window, trying to pretend she was thinking about her book. She could picture Bryan listening to her message late that evening while he poured himself a glass of Grenache and listened to a symphony by Mahler. He would know how to help her. He seemed to get this whole artist business.

Cal Bolt cared deeply, obsessively, about his SAT scores, but his concern didn't happen to translate into a desire to study for the SAT. What he really wanted to do, what he was really passionate about, was strategic speculation. It was an addictive habit, something he worked over in his head the way an anxious child works over a soft blanket.

Lillian and Cal would start off each tutoring session well enough, with Lillian reviewing a few practice test questions, and Cal making attempts at responses. But after five minutes of working, Cal would suddenly stop Lillian mid-sentence, while she was explaining the meaning of "jeremiad" or how to apply the Pythagorean formula to a triangle within a circle.

"So really. Be honest," he'd say. "What score do you think I need to get to get into Fortuna? Because my friend Peter says 2300. Do you think that's right? Or could I get, like, 2250? Because right now I have a 2040, and I think I might be able to get that to a 2200, but I think breaking 2300's going to be hard."

Lillian would hedge and encourage him, and finally she'd point out that his score wasn't going to rise at all unless they got back to work. A few moments would pass, and then he'd say, "2040 isn't that bad, right? Like, if I was going to a state school, that'd be pretty good, wouldn't it?"

And before Lillian could answer...

"What if you got a 2200, but your grades were really good? Would Fortuna take you? I bet you'd have to be really good at something. There's a girl in my class who's played violin at Carnegie Hall."

He speculated on whether Fortuna was easier or harder to get into than the University of Pennsylvania or Amherst. Were small liberal arts colleges easier or harder? Did it matter if he applied early? Would the fact that he took AP classes matter more than the fact that he'd only gotten a three on one of his AP exams? A three was pretty decent, though, right? Did recommendations matter? Did it matter if you got a recommendation from someone famous, or was it better to get one from someone who knew you well? Because his father knew a lot of famous people. Famous in the business world, anyway. Had she heard of Sumner Redstone?

Every time Lillian tried to get him to buckle down, Cal worked as hard as he could to spin the conversation back to soothing his anxieties. Yet the more they discussed these questions, the less reassured he felt. Never was there a guarantee. Never could she tell him that he was definitely getting in.

Finally, one day, he said, "What if my dad gave a million dollars to Fortuna?"

"Wouldn't hurt," Lillian said, trying to be droll.

"A hundred million? They'd have to take me, right?"

"I don't know, Cal."

"Seriously? A hundred million dollars?"

"I honestly don't know."

"It doesn't matter. He isn't giving anything. He said he wants me to get in on my own."

"That's good."

"But what if I can't?"

"But you can. You're smart, Cal."

Cal sighed, frustrated with the whole conversation. "I don't see why he sets these goals for me. He went to a state school. I mean, I want to go to Fortuna and all, but if I can't get in, what's the point in applying?"

"What does your father do for a living?"

Cal was stunned. "Really? You seriously don't know?"

"I seriously don't know."

Cal savored the moment before proceeding. "Well, you know Bolt Bank, right?"

"Oh! Okay." She looked at Cal Bolt with a polite smile.

"He founded it when he was like, twenty-six."

"Uh-huh."

"I thought everybody knew that."

"Nope."

"Anyway, he could probably give Fortuna a hundred million dollars, if he wanted to."

"Mm-hmm."

Cal thought about it for a while. "I can't believe Fortuna wouldn't take me for a hundred million dollars. I bet they would. They'd have to, right?"

"Cal. You can do this. Let's get back to work."

Cal slid down in his chair and said nothing.

"Come on," said Lillian. "Trust me."

She felt sorry for him. She knew all his strategizing covered a bubbling river of self-doubt. He was so afraid that he would fail that he couldn't bring himself to concentrate on trying anything. It was a feeling she had come to know well whenever she sat down to write. But, at the same time, she caught something in his look that worried her. As he flipped back to the practice test, she saw him throw her a secretive glance, as if he thought he was the older and wiser one, and she was being naïve.

"A hundred million dollars," he said, almost to himself.

"Come here a second."

Lillian stopped midstride, as she was crossing through the Bolts' front hallway and turned back to see Bronnie, who was perched at a desk just outside the kitchen. That desk was like the family hearth: children, nanny, everyone crowded around it from time to time to check the drop-off schedule, to read email. "Oh," said Lillian, "I've been looking for writing teachers for you…"

"Don't worry," Bronnie said. "Canella's going to help me start a blog. If it's good enough, she said she'd show it to her agent. So how's Cal doing?"

"Okay. He has trouble focusing."

"Right, well that's very—come here and look at this blog entry."

"Sure."

Lillian approached the computer, while Bronnie clicked onto a web page, adding, "My friend Canella's blog is good because she's got something to write about. She's got a shopping addiction. She used to buy so much that she had four storage units filled with shopping bags she never even opened. So her blog is about how she's getting rid of all of it, now that she's found this therapist. Anyway, I've been trying to think of what I have that's like that."

"You mean a problem? "

"Exactly. I need a problem."

Lillian forced a smile.

"I mean, I have problems, but none seem good enough to support a blog, you know? Or they're problems everybody has, like dealing with the kids. But I was thinking I could write about having a husband who's a workaholic, and how you deal with that."

"Okay."

"Tell me if this is good."

Bronnie read from the page: "It is two a.m., and I hear the sound of typing. Oh, no. It's a familiar sound. I roll over and try to go back to sleep, but my brain keeps whirring. Should I have married someone who has another love of his life?"

"That's…great."

"I'm going to show it to Henry. See what he thinks." Lillian would have loved to be there for that. "You have to tell Cal to stay focused. He only has one more chance to take the SAT before he sends in his early application."

"I know. I've reminded him."

"And did I tell you the evaluation was a no-go? On the ADHD? We're going to try someone else, though. Anyway, I'm keeping you late. We're up to date on payments, right?"

"I'll check my…"

"He needs to focus. 'Cause if he doesn't, there's no point, you know?"

Waiting in the elevator lobby outside the Bolt apartment (the only apartment on the floor), Lillian began thinking about the figure of one hundred million dollars. She made a mental list of all the things that could be done with that amount of money, aside from getting a boy into college.

Immunizing one million children, for example, assuming approximately one hundred dollars a head.

Protecting ten million people from catching malaria, if mosquito nets cost about ten dollars each.

Sending a thousand students to Fortuna's MFA program, to create a thousand great novelists, just like her.

All the same…

Ten million children could get malaria protection. Or Cal could get into Fortuna, and Fortuna could get a new gym—or, more likely, a new biotech lab. It fascinated her, an amount of money like that. Where did such money come from? Where did it go?

A portion of her student loans—the private portion, above and beyond her federal loans—was serviced by Bolt Bank. She was, in effect, paying her own salary.

As this cheerful thought entered her mind, the elevator doors opened, and she almost ran into a young man about Cal's age as he stepped out.

He smiled at her, let her pass, looked her up and down. She returned the look as the elevator doors lingered and seemed to close in slow motion. Necktie and vest over a button-down shirt. Sideburns. He was smoking some kind of hand-rolled cigarette, which he stamped out in the lobby before turning to knock on the Bolt's front door, like some extra out of *Gossip Girl*.

The elevator doors shut, and she smiled. Rich kids in the pupa phase were kind of touching. When they were in their twenties, they might actually be that arrogant, but now they were just trying to appear arrogant, and the cracks still showed in the façade. The smile stayed on her face all the way to the 68th Street subway stop, when she remembered that she had to go home and work on her book. It had better be good, her novel. Really good. It had better be worth ten thousand kids getting malaria.

5

"How has the housing downturn affected the luxury market? Not much, answers John Shapiro of Corcoran Realty. "We've seen a slowdown on some of our newer condos, but the most desirable, established properties on Park Avenue and Central Park West have not seen a big drop in demand." Shapiro pointed out that his top-end properties currently sell for about $3,400 per square foot, down only about five percent from this time last year. "This may be a good time to buy," he added. "It's only going to go back up again."

"Real Estatements" by Nadya Rahlin: June 2, 2008
www.realestatements.net

AT $3400 PER SQUARE FOOT, YOUNG PETER WICKA WAS taking up $61,200 in property value lying on his friend Cal's bed. Like most Park Avenue children's bedrooms, Cal's room was an architectural afterthought, a ten-by-twelve-foot box overlooking a glorified airshaft, where, if Cal pressed his forehead against the glass, he could see an off-duty doorman having a smoke in the center courtyard.

"So I've been looking up snuff films on the Internet," Peter was saying, pressing Cal's stuffed Mets mascot between his fists.

"Oh yeah?" Cal glanced up from IMing on his computer.

"Yeah, I mean, if we're going to put it in our movie, we ought to know what it would look like, authentically."

"Are there any real ones?"

"Oh, who knows? It's so hard to tell."

There was a brief silence while Cal typed a message to a girl in school. Peter filled it by taking his own photo on his iPhone and then changing his Facebook profile picture. Peter was one year older than Cal and had already been accepted to Fortuna for the coming fall. He was busy riding out his high school career with the bare minimum of effort, while Cal was still busy racking up SAT IIs and Advanced Placement credit. Peter's sole purpose at school, these days, was to arrange for Cal to be able to join Fortuna with him. Peter had a long-term plan in which he and Cal were going to be filmmakers with the aid of Mr. Bolt's financing, and he didn't want Cal ending up outside the confines of Manhattan.

Cal looked up at last. "Bennie changed the date of her graduation party. When is our start date for shooting our film? Because my parents want to take me to France this summer."

"Where in France?"

"I don't know. I think maybe just Paris."

"I was thinking sometime in August we could shoot."

"You said your friend's dad is a Hollywood producer?" Cal asked.

"Agent. Did you ask your dad about financing us?"

"Not yet. I have to see how I do on my SATs."

"Did you think about my idea for that?"

Cal shrugged, looking nervous. There was a gentle knock on the door.

"Come in," Peter said from the bed.

Julie entered. "Cal, your mom asked me to check how studying is going."

Peter cast an appraising eye at the rosy-cheeked girl. "Julie, you speak French, right?"

"Oui, un peu."

"Can you help us with the take-home part of Cal's French exam?"

"No," Julie shook her head. "I can't. I'm sorry."

"Why not?"

"It wouldn't be right."

Peter sat up straight. "Julie, let me tell you something about ethics."

"I've got to get back."

"Just let me say something, okay?"

Julie stood watching him with patient eyes.

"The French test is due in twelve hours. All we're asking is for you to look it over. We just want a second opinion, that's all. In the real world, as adults, wouldn't we be able to get a second opinion? Wouldn't we show our work to someone else, just to check it, before we turned it in to the boss?"

Julie bowed her head.

"Julie?" said Peter. "Come on. Help Cal pass for the year. You don't want Cal not to get into college, right?"

"I'm sorry, guys."

"What, are you really Christian or something?"

"Yes."

Peter was intrigued. "Really? Where are you from?"

"Albany, near Albany. I'm just—I think you should learn the material on your own." Julie roused herself for one final sally: "Get back to work, okay, guys?"

"Oh, yeah. Definitely." Peter watched as she closed the door behind her. "Did you know she's religious?"

"Yeah, I guess. Her dad is a minister. He has a big church upstate."

"Really? That's interesting."

Peter tossed the Mets mascot up and down again, considering. "So my mom said she'd buy me a signed Warhol print for my graduation present. I'm thinking about this one of Ingrid Bergman dressed as a nun."

A few hours later, Julie, the Bolts' nanny, tiptoed into her small bedroom through the bathroom door and eased it shut. Julie's bedroom was even tinier than Cal's—an eight by six foot converted linen closet off her young charge's bathroom, with a second doorway that led to the hall. She glanced at a digital clock, which read 9:48 p.m., then jotted down the time in a journal labeled "Amy's sleep schedule," which sat open on her desk, ready for a parental inspection that never came. She turned and flicked on a small television monitor next to her bed that glowed to life, revealing the image of a sleeping seven-year-old girl. Julie set the audio level just loud enough to hear the child's breathing.

The child video monitor was a well-established part of the Bolt household, predating Julie by a full six years. When Julie was hired one year ago, Bronnie Bolt had explained that they were getting rid of three rotating night and day nannies, "for consistency," and replacing them with a single, twenty-four-hour nanny. Julie could expect exactly one day every week off duty, but only between ten a.m. and eight p.m., for the next two years.

Julie had loved her charge at first sight. Young Amy's chin still quivered like a newborn's while she slept, and her bed was lined with a thick set of sheet covers—plastic on one side, cloth on the other—that were the accoutrements of a habitual bed-wetter. Amy's hair, recently carved into a chic layered cut, always ended up tucked in her mouth, and her bed was lined with objects of comfort: seven bears, two dolls, and a Hannah Montana pillow, which her mother considered tacky and which Julie had to bring out of its hiding place every night at 8:30, at the start of their bedtime routine. On the floor was a life-sized stuffed Alaskan malamute dog—the kind every kid wants at the toy store until the parents check the price tag and see costs seven hundred dollars.

In short, Amy was the kind of child you fall in love with if you need to be needed. Amy's new sleeping habit—which everyone agreed was bad, but which no one had committed to breaking—was to fall asleep with Julie as a pillow. At 8:45 p.m., Amy would complete her bath, change into her pajamas, get her hair brushed, and then head into the kitchen to say good-night to her mother (at her computer there) and into her father's study to say good-night to her father (at his computer there) and then she and Julie would retreat to her room, where Julie would be instructed to lie lengthwise across the bed so that the soft part of her belly formed a cushion for Amy's head. Julie would stroke Amy's hair while telling her stories about her uncle's farm until Amy's two fingers drifted into her mouth, taking a lock of hair with them,

43

and she started breathing soft slow breaths. Everyone agreed—everyone of course but Amy—that this was a bad and unsustainable habit, but everyone allowed it to go on. Julie had even begun to look forward to it. It was Julie's only physical contact all day, unless Amy sat on her lap while they read a book. Julie did not have a boyfriend—and, in any case, had committed to wait until marriage for the kind of physical contact that some young women might have preferred at the end of the day.

Julie changed into her nightgown as if expecting, at any moment, a cry from the next room or a knock from the hallway. She then flipped open her laptop so she could jump onto the apartment Internet and check her email. There was nothing in her inbox except her father's biweekly letter to his followers, so she sat back for a moment, opened another window in her web browser, closed it, struggling with a temptation. She looked at the topic of her father's letter to his followers for the day: "Planning for Retirement: How Jesus Can Help."

Julie was not exactly sure why she had taken this job. She had graduated from college with honors a year ago, burdened not by student loans but by her father's frequent references to how hard he had worked to pay for her schooling, how expensive her SUNY program was. It was worse, in some ways, than having debt. She was never sure exactly what she'd cost her father—only that it had not been easy, that he had made a thousand small sacrifices "every day since she was born" to put aside the money that would allow her to attend college. During school, she had lived at home, had eaten dinner every night with her father, who liked to extemporize about the value of a dollar.

Like any dutiful child, she had learned her father's script, had internalized the fine web of his logic to such a degree that she could talk like him, and at dinner each night she had analyzed the behavior of friends and classmates, anticipating her father's wording, applying to their juvenile antics and spendthrift habits his particular mix of wisdom and scorn. But her father was never satisfied with these displays. He seemed always to be waiting for the inevitable disaster, expecting that at any moment she would

44

reveal the same reckless, oversexed habits he attributed to her whole generation.

So when she graduated from college in only three years, armed with an education degree and a high GPA, she found herself withdrawing from the prearranged plan of living at home, saving her money while she worked at a local elementary school, waiting, perhaps, for a nice young man to make an offer. Instead, she had sought out a well-paying nanny job in New York—her father's "least favorite place on earth"—with the kind of people her father most despised. The Bolts bled money, and Julie knew it. She had watched them drop ten thousand dollars on a weekend in the country. She had watched Bronnie buy a four thousand dollar dress for a thousand-dollar-a-plate dinner and then decide not to go because she felt stiff from an overzealous workout at the gym.

But Julie secretly enjoyed their spending habits. She saw something healthy in their willingness to let their financial vigilance slide. She wondered if her father's stubborn penny pinching was the very thing that had doomed him to the struggling middle class, in spite of his pride at his substantial retirement savings. Did people who didn't know how to spend really know how to live? She suspected that she was probably being paid more than her father. There was a delicious decadence to that, even though she knew it was morally abhorrent, a sweetness to the financial freedom she was gaining by working for the Bolts. She felt ready to fulfill her father's prophecy and spend her money with abandon. But she didn't. She had started an IRA.

With this thought in her head, she typed in a keyword search: "Peter Wicka."

"Peter Wicka is on Facebook." She clicked on the tiny image of the handsome face that she found, and looked at it for a long time. He was beautiful, and he was four years younger than she was, and Cal's best friend, and morally corrupt. And she admitted to herself in the secret silence of her closet bedroom that he was the sexiest thing she'd ever seen.

6

THE EARLY 1970S WERE THE LAST GASP OF THE DREAM OF
New York as a sleek, modern metropolis before the city settled
into the drug-addled depression that would last the next twenty
years. The World Trade Center was completed then, and all
along upper 6th Avenue—or "Avenue of the Americas," as only
the tourists called it—a row of skyscrapers rose, dominated by
brutal vertical lines and walls of black glass. The Bolt Building,
completed in 1973, was forty-two stories high, and by the early
summer of 2008, a total of 4,418 people entered and departed
that building every day, not including food deliverers and FedEx
people. A total of 2,445 of those who entered worked for the
Bolt Corporation, while the rest were employees at two Internet
startups, a small hedge fund, and a real estate company that had
just purchased twenty miles of former conservation land on the
Jersey Shore.

One of the earliest arrivals today was Paolo Cincotti, who
walked into the loading dock at 6:02 a.m. to start his shift. Paolo
carried his heavy frame like a boxer, shoulders leaning forward,
eyes flitting to potential opponents, who appeared to be everyone he saw. He stopped at the back doorway to greet Larry Hill-
ock, an elderly black guard who sized up Paolo for a long moment before offering any recognition.

"Good morning," Larry finally said.

"Good morning?" Paolo replied. "Not for me, man, I was up
'til four a.m."

"No, no, that ain't good," Larry said.

"I earned four hundred bucks, though."

Larry declined to pursue this interesting fact, so Paolo muscled his large frame through the back door of the main lobby, holding it open for a janitor who was rolling out a trash bin.

Paolo took his place at the front security desk and then tried again on Ronelle, the night guard. "I can't believe this shit," he said. "I was up 'til four, and I don't want to be here."

"That's your own damn fault," Ronelle said.

"I earned four hundred dollars, though."

"Oh, yeah?"

"Not bad for one night."

"Security work?"

"Not exactly."

"Well, I gotta get home and get my kid up," she said, putting on her jacket.

"How's he doing?"

"He's fine. He's a boy, that's all. I shoulda just had girls."

Paolo watched her go. It wasn't until his co-worker Marcus arrived, about thirty minutes later, that he finally got a bite. Marcus was a good ten years younger than Paolo, and looked up to Paolo as a model of badass, ready and willing to do the rough part of security work, should a fight be required. It never had been.

"Four hundred dollars. Yo how'd you do that?"

"Underground wrestling."

"Wh-a-at?" Marcus turned the question into three full syllables.

"I just started. I had three fights now."

"Where's this?"

"All over. We keep moving it. You want to see my cut from last night?"

Paolo pulled up his shirt to reveal a nasty slash across his belly, covered in bloody tape. "That's from barbed wire."

"Yo man that's disgusting," Marcus said, impressed. "You got to go to the hospital for that."

"Only if you want it to heal clean. It helps your reputation you let it heal all fucked up. Scares your opponents."

47

"Man." Marcus looked disgusted, and Paolo was pleased.

Paolo moved to the seat closest to the magnetic turnstiles, which had been installed as additional security after the building's downtown cousins were destroyed on 9/11. Now the turnstiles made up a good part of Paolo's morning activity, as various people approached him each day with stories of where they'd left their card key: their girlfriend's apartment, their other pair of pants, their parents' place in Connecticut. Paolo would listen to these stories with the right blend of skepticism and sympathy before having each petitioner sign in and buzzing the person through the gate.

The first of these sad cases arrived earlier than usual, at close to 6:45: an attractive young woman whom Paolo had watched with interest for over two years. Bella Pointer was in the latter end of her twenties, part Inuit and part Dutch, and would have been beautiful if she ever stopped trying to get things done. Today she lacked some of her usual briskness, her eyes red-rimmed.

"I am so sorry, but I forgot my card today."

"I know you. You work for Mr. Bolt."

"Yes. I'm sorry. I was up 'til four, and I just totally spaced. Can you just—"

"So was I. Up until four."

"Can I just go through…"

Paolo flashed a benevolent smile.

"Go ahead."

He pressed the buzzer for the gate without even making her sign in, and she hurried past him toward the elevator bank. Paolo watched her, his face softening, until Marcus spoke.

"Man, that chick is never going to go for you."

"Why not?"

Marcus just shook her head. "She's way over your head, man."

Bella Pointer was, in fact, approaching four hundred feet above their heads as Marcus spoke. Her morning routine started with a quick stop in her boss's office to make sure everything was in order after the cleaning people's work there the night before. She set the UV protection blinds low in the windows, checked that Henry's three silver pens had ink, watered the plants, and made sure his printer was on and had paper in it.

Then she sat at her desk, called the car company, and confirmed Henry's car service reservation for 7:40 a.m. She opened any mail that had been dropped off by the mailroom late last night, including anything labeled "Top Secret: For Henry Bolt's Eyes Only," which was almost guaranteed to be a cold solicitation from a total stranger. She flipped through her email inbox to see if her boss had sent her a message during the early hours of the morning, then pulled a yogurt out of the mini-fridge and checked the clock. It was close to seven.

She opened a document on her Desktop, selected the "Track Changes" option in Microsoft Word, and modified the document as follows:

> It is two a.m., and I hear the sound of typing. Oh, no. It's a familiar sound. I roll over and try to go back to sleep, but my brain keeps whirring. Should I have married someone who has another love of his life? [bpointer: perhaps clarify that the other love of his life is his business, to avoid possible tabloid allegations of infidelity.] He has been working on this deal for several weeks now. [bpointer: Citibank deal was not publicly revealed until May 15th. Change to: "for two weeks now."] However, it feels like an eternity to me. I haven't had sex since the real estate market lost half its value. [bpointer: Half its value is an exaggeration. Current RE markets down about ten percent. Change to ten percent to avoid perception we know something others don't.]

Bella's phone rang, and by reflex she opened her contacts file while picking up the receiver, in case she'd have to look up the caller by name.

49

"Henry Bolt's office. This is Bella."

She listened, never speaking, for a long time.

"No, I'm not mad. I'm not. I'm not. It's not that important to me, honey. No. Don't, Greg. Don't. Don't." She burst into tears. "Please. I'll take off work today, okay? Okay? Please? Don't get on a bus. I'm exhausted—Greg, I haven't seen you in two years, I don't want you to—"

A long silence. "Okay, goodbye. Be safe. Don't get into trouble."

She hung up the phone, cried for exactly four minutes, then dabbed her eyes with a tissue and returned to her work.

By 7:35, exactly ten minutes before her boss was scheduled to get in his car and open his laptop, she wrote the following: "Per your request, attached please find my suggestions for modifying Bronnie's blog to address shareholder concerns and family privacy. Pending your approval, I will send to Bronnie's web assistant for posting today."

At 7:40, exactly two minutes before Henry Bolt disconnected his laptop from his household Internet and headed downstairs to his car, Bella clicked "Send."

Five minutes later, a third person out of the 4,418 entered the building. Clyde Upson said hello to Paolo at the front desk. He said hello to Marcus, who was helping a woman at the wheelchair gate. He said hello to the four people he joined in the elevator, though only one seemed to know him.

"Gonna be a nice one," Clyde observed. "Gorgeous out there."

"Twenty-five?" asked his coworker, a tall blonde who stood nearest the elevator buttons.

"No, twenty-two. I'm getting breakfast. Have you seen the kitchen on twenty-two?"

"No, why?"

"They got—not just an espresso machine. They got, like, granola bars, and cereal, and all kinds of stuff. I get my lunch there everyday now."

The blonde woman curled her lip in a skeptical smile.

"You save ten dollars a day on lunch, that's three thousand dollars a year."

"I guess so."

"They got, like, oranges, and apples, and granola bars. Yogurt. Power bars. Cliff bars. Bags of nuts—almonds, pecans. Microwave popcorn."

"On twenty-two?"

"Customer service," Clyde said, stepping off the elevator. "You got to try it some time. It's awesome."

Clyde loved everything about his job at Bolt. He loved that his gym membership was fifty percent off because Bolt got a block rate with New York Sports Club. He loved that he got twenty-five percent off Broadway shows if he bought them through the girl at Employee Retention. He loved the free donuts they had in the lobby on Fridays, the yearly weekend retreat to the Jersey Shore, the Yankees tickets that were sometimes up for grabs when they weren't being used to entertain clients. It was an antidote to his childhood in the Bronx, when his mother had struggled to pay for his baseball uniform, and they had to wait four hours at a clinic to see a doctor. A kind of miniature socialist country existed within the confines of the Bolt Building walls—free drop-in childcare, paid health care, unlimited sick days, all provided to the hardworking employees who kept the credit card customers paying their bills and the homeowners paying their mortgages. All of which is to say Clyde had discovered that wonderful truism: *Everything is cheaper when you have money.*

Five minutes later, Clyde was on the twenty-fifth floor, laden with two yogurts, a cup of espresso, and a Luna Bar in key lime. He stopped to say hello to four more people on the way to his desk, and discussed (in sequence) the Yankees, with Eduardo, his search for a new apartment, with Angela, whether or not to

51

do online dating, with Yelena, and the Yankees, with Paul. He was efficient, and this sequence took him only an additional five minutes. He was at his desk by 8:04 for the best part of his day—calculating the number of new accounts he had made in the last twenty-four hours and emailing the figure to his manager, who emailed the summary to the VP, who emailed that to the Senior VP every other week. Quarterly, the figures were presented to Henry Bolt himself.

It was satisfying to Clyde to be part of a hierarchy that led all the way up to the man who owned the company. The company organizational chart, accessible for viewing on the Bolt company intranet, was not just a set of interconnected relationships. It was a road map. Here you are, it said, underneath Senior Account Executive Todd Walsh. And here is where you can go. Clyde would click on the intranet photo of Henry Bolt once a day, just to look at him. Every couple of weeks he'd read about Henry on Wikipedia to see if anything in his profile had changed.

To Clyde, there was order to the universe, and the guiding principles were as follows:

1. Love your mother, because she raised you.
2. If you show hustle, anything is possible.
3. Leadership qualities are finite and can be learned.
4. Henry Bolt is a great man.

So later that morning, when he received an email about how employees were invited to research some aspect of the company and present it at the quarterly party, Clyde was the first person out of 2,445 to respond.

"Henry Bolt is my hero," he typed as a subject heading.

7

Now I am just a simple man, a simple man. And I suppose there's a lot out there in the world that I don't know, or can't understand. I don't pretend to understand everything about the economy or the government here in Albany or in Washington, D.C. But here is what I can tell you, even if I am just a small-town man. I know that taking on a debt is a lie. It is a lie to yourself about what you can afford. And when we lie to ourselves, then we lie to the whole world.

PASTOR PRESLEY WALSH'S sermon, Sunday, June 28, 2008

WRITERS ARE ALWAYS WORKING ON TWO STORIES AT once: the fictional story they are hoping to publish, and the fictional story of their own lives, which they are constantly revising in their heads. Unlike a reasonable person, who views life in terms of concrete accomplishments (marriage, family), writers are inclined to view their lives as epics, marked by tragic mistakes and startling revelations about the human condition. This can make them tiresome at parties.

But these two competing stories also create tension. If the writer is deeply invested in a self-image as the doomed hero of a tragedy, he or she may have trouble with the fairly conventional things necessary to succeed in a career. The drama of failure can be more compelling than the banal self-promotion of success.

Before grad school, Lillian had struggled for a compelling personal narrative. The death of her parents in a car accident had thrust upon her the role of Orphan, but she wanted to make sense of that, to use it to turn her life into something meaningful. But what? Was she talented? Or just another wannabe writer, with passion that outstripped her abilities? When she was accepted to

Fortuna, she felt a soul-deep satisfaction in knowing she'd at last found a narrative for herself—the hero's quest, the underdog up against impossible odds, ready to conquer that highest mountain: the publishing world. She even thought that her grad school debt would contribute to this adventure. The sheer vastness of her loans had been romantic, another hill for her to climb, an obstacle in her way. It was supposed to force her to keep working, not to give up, never to quit.

But when she graduated and her magnum opus was proclaimed a failure, she began to wonder if she should reconsider the narrative structure of Lillian Fitzgerald. Perhaps her story wasn't a hero's journey, after all, but a bewildering modernist fable of meaningless loss and despair. Living with Nadya increased her doubts. Nadya seemed completely assured about her identity as an artist. Every boy Nadya slept with, every drug she tried, was proof she was a creative soul. She met literary agents at bars and chatted with them about her work, and even though none had yet chosen to represent her, it was really only a matter of time. So the narrative of the roommates' relationship had become, in Lillian's head, that of protagonist and sidekick. Lillian was a footnote in Nadya's life. A cautionary tale about grad school debt. A dramatic foil.

This secondary status was in Lillian's mind when she picked up Nadya's cell phone while Nadya was struggling to zip up a pair of thigh-high boots.

"Can you get that?"

"Sure…This is Nadya's phone."

Lillian listened for a moment. "Um—just a second." She held out the phone to Nadya, fingers pressed over the receiver.

"Who was it?"

"Citibank. They say you owe some money on your credit card. I thought you had a Bolt card, didn't you?"

"Oh." Nadya took the cell phone and looked at it for a moment, then closed it. "Well, we're not going to take that call."

"They said they were going to start legal proceedings…"

"Oh, yeah, they say that. I've already paid it off. They just haven't received it yet in the system or something. You never get calls like that?"

"Not usually."

"That's what they do now. Strong-arm tactics. It's a racket. It's ridiculous. I should sue."

Nadya looked at Lillian for a moment. "Don't worry, Lill. It's already paid."

"Are you sure…"

"Lillian, please. It's a standard corporate bastard phone call, and it's their screw up, not mine. You're so easily worried. I feel sorry for you when you get like this."

Lillian was silent.

"You know, the best thing for you would be to go out and sleep with a couple of total strangers. Have fun. You can't let financial worries consume your life, okay? Money isn't real. Here, I want to show you something."

Nadya opened her pocketbook and took out a ten-dollar bill.

"Come here. Come here. This will be good for you."

She walked to their tiny kitchen, followed by Lillian, and turned on the gas stove, then held the bill in the flame.

"This is all money is, okay? You see? You see what I'm willing to do? You have to be able to—Ow, fuck!" Nadya dropped the bill. "That was stupid."

"Are you okay?"

"My fingers, fuck." Nadya, shaking her fingers, added, "You get my point, though, right?"

"Money isn't real," said Lillian. "Would you like a Band-Aid?"

Bryan Ruggiero called Lillian the next day. She picked up the phone and listened, embarrassed, to his weary but intelligent greeting.

"Sorry I didn't get back to you sooner. I was in a sort of self-imposed writer's exile."

"Oh, that's great."

"Mostly it was torture. So what's going on?"

"I just wanted to catch up and see if you—if you had any advice about surviving after grad school. And still being a writer."

"Wow." There was a long moment of silence.

"I just—I don't know quite how I'm going to do it, you know. Still be a writer and pay back my student loans."

"It's impossible," he said. "Once they suck you into taking those debts, you're doomed forever."

"That's kind of what I've been feeling, is that it's just—so is it just—hopeless?"

"Yes, pretty much."

She was silent until he said, "We could meet up for coffee or something, if you want."

"Sure. Sure. If that's okay with you. When?"

"Oh, anytime. I guess I can take a break. I've written twenty pages in the last thirty-six hours."

A couple of hours later they stood sipping espresso with milk on a stretch of the East River that was dwarfed by the rising towers of the Manhattan and Brooklyn Bridges. Bryan looked out across the water for a long moment at the Manhattan skyline.

"Fucking Manhattan," he said. "That place is the moral cesspool of humanity. If you want to find out what's driving everything wrong with our world—the wars, the terrorism, the destruction of natural resources, all of it starts there."

"Central Park is nice."

"That's because rich people are willing to pay to have a nice backyard. Have you seen Prospect Park lately? It's falling apart."

"So what are you doing these days?"

"I don't know," he said with a sigh. "Working for the man."

"But you're writing."

"Yeah. I actually got a publisher for my book last month. Just a small press based in England that's trying to restore some intelligence to the novel. It's like novels have basically become movies, these days. You have to hook them on the first page or they walk away and buy something else. How is it even possible to write something worthwhile? We live under the whim of the ten-second attention span."

"Congratulations! That's great. Is this the one you were working on during…"

"Yeah, my deconstruction of the detective novel."

"I heard some of that. I liked it."

"I was just getting so tired of books where everybody finds out who did the murder at the end, you know? I wanted to do—you know—something where even the detective doesn't know what happened, but he thinks he does, so he's in this fog of self-delusion."

Lillian nodded, and Bryan roused somewhat. "So how are you? I always liked you in school. You seemed intelligent. A lot of people there just seemed like rich kids, you know?"

"Well, I'm definitely not a rich kid."

"What are you doing with yourself?"

"Tutoring rich kids in their SATs."

"Jesus. They get us all, don't they?"

"Well, I'm sure all those people who worked for the Medicis in medieval Florence felt the same way."

"You should just—when you publish a book and make it big, you should tell them their kids are all shit."

"Yes, and make the children cry, hopefully. Nothing makes me happier than a child weeping."

"I'm not kidding. Those people don't have a conscience."

"Of course they do. It's just been slightly undermined by money."

"Slightly? They would have you destroyed in a minute if it was helpful to them. Their kid gets below a 600 and they'll plow you over with a car."

"I'll look out for that."

"We've been trapped. We were lured into going to grad school by the idea of becoming writers, and now they've got us as wage slaves for eternity. We sold out to the corporate industrial complex. If we'd been smart, we would never have gone."

57

"But you're getting published."

Bryan sighed. "Yeah," he said with a sigh. "But not for any money. Not that money matters."

Lillian nodded, and they looked out at the skyline for a moment.

"I don't think I'm ever going to sell my book for anything. It's just a mess. I'm starting to hate it," she said in a rush.

"Do you want me to take a look at it for you?"

Lillian was surprised. The offer was more personal than an offer of sex, in writers' circles.

"I mean, if you want…" he said.

"Yeah," she said. "That would be great."

She was terrified.

"I'm sure it's fantastic."

"Don't be too sure."

"You're a good writer."

Lillian smiled. "What stuff of mine have you read?"

"I don't remember, but I know there was something."

As they walked back to the subway, he added, "Oh, *Key Largo* is playing at the Quad if you want to see it. They're doing a whole Bogart noir retrospective, which as you probably know is kind of my thing. It's lesser Bogart, but still. I'll be going next Friday, so if you want to see it, I could meet you there."

This was how Bryan asked Lillian out on a date.

She said she loved Bogart films, even the lesser ones, and he kissed her on the cheek as they said goodbye. On the subway ride home, she sat wondering which short story of hers he had read and forgotten. She went home and with the aid of two of Nadya's cigarettes and three bowls of cereal, managed to pull the frayed strands of her book into a shape coherent enough to email it off to a Real Writer.

8

IF YOU HAD WALKED INTO AL'S GARAGE IN MOUNT
Vernon, New York, on a Friday night in mid-June, you would
have been handed (in exchange for your entrance fee) a bold,
handwritten sheet of paper with the following information:

TONIGHT'S FIGHTERS
D.M.V. (aka Frankie Tonko)
Age: 22
Height: 5'11"
Weight: 192
Signature Move: the Hub Cap

The Enforcer (aka Paolo Cincotti)
Age: 32
Height: 6'5"
Weight: 255
Signature Move: the Slice 'n' Dice

Loudmouth (aka Mark Freidman)
Age: 27
Height: 5'9"
Weight: 218
Signature Move: the Frog Hop

Leonardo da Badass (aka Leonard Potts)
Age: 24
Height: 6'1"
Weight: 179
Signature Move: the Bustamove

LET THE SLAUTER [SIC] BEGIN!

The Underground Wrestling Club of Yonkers considered it-self an up-and-coming, no-holds-barred version of the Under-ground Wrestling Club of New York. The New York club, in the view of many Yonkers members, had "gone soft," and it was the role of the Yonkers wrestlers to keep up the authentic, brutal, anything-can-happen experience that underground wrestling was supposed to be. "It's not the Money, it's the Mayhem" was their unofficial motto. Their club president had even considered trade-marking that phrase, but hadn't gotten around to it because he'd been too busy with his father's landscaping business.

Ten minutes before the fight, The Enforcer was sitting beside the makeshift ring talking to da Badass.

"I just feel like I can't get anywhere, you know. And I'm a gentleman. Holding doors, that kind of thing. I got girls in high school. It's just now, I don't know. I went out with a girl like five times, and now she won't return my calls."

"Did you do anything wrong? On the dates?"

"I don't think so." Paolo cast back his mind, thinking hard.

"Let me ask you this," da Badass replied. "How many girls you ask out in the last month?"

"I don't know," said Paolo.

"'Cause 'you don't know' sounds to me like you haven't asked out any. It's a numbers game. You ask out ten girls, you get one date."

"My friend Marcus says I got to be earning more money."

"How much you earning now?"

"At my day job? About forty."

"That's enough. For who is that not enough? You couldn't marry and raise a baby off of that, maybe, but you could take a girl out."

"But I work in a building with all these bankers, and the girls are just…"

"Who says you gotta date the girls there?"

At that moment, a small man entered the center of the ring clutching a mic attached to a large speaker with a hole chipped in the side.

"Ladies and gentleman, welcome welcome welcome!" began the tiny man. He was wearing a leather vest, vintage Ozzie Osbourne T-shirt, and jeans that were too long and hung crumpled on top of his brown leather boots. "Are you ready to get down and dirty? Are you ready to get vicious?"

The crowd gave a vigorous verbal assent, and Paolo began wrapping a bike chain around his forearms.

"I could hook you up with my cousin," da Badass told him. "Ask me afterward for her number." The theme from *Shaft* started to play on the sound system, and da Badass raised his arms and stepped into the ring.

"What are you here for?" the ringmaster said, waving the mic in da Badass's general direction.

Leo Potts grabbed the mic, thrust it against his lips, and replied in a voice two octaves below his normal register, "To fuck people up!" The crowd roared.

Marcus, of Bolt Security, entered the garage at that moment, just in time to see his coworker Paolo entering the ring to the familiar riff of Metallica's "Enter Sandman."

Marcus was escorting a young woman wearing a hot pink T-shirt that commanded those around her to "Stop Looking at My Chest!" She appeared unimpressed by her surroundings, and noted, "Twenty dollars. For that much I could stay home and watch a fight on HBO."

"Not if it's de la Hoya," Marcus replied.

Marcus pointed out his coworker, who was now wearing a bike chain strapped around his chest and a barbed wire tied to his upper arm. Paolo raised his fists above his head.

"The Enforcer," said the emcee. "Da Badass says he's going to send you to the hospital. What do you say to that?"

"I say I'll be sending him to the morgue."

More applause.

Paolo added, "If he's sending people, then that makes him a postman, and I'm the mad dog."

Applause, but somewhat less spirited. Extended metaphors didn't play to this crowd. The tiny man stepped back and signaled the fight to begin.

"Here are two men who know how to tear it down," the emcee shouted as Paolo held his barbed wire over his head and shouted a threat laced with the proper amount of obscenity. Paolo was already bleeding from his left arm, damaged by his own prop. He liked to say that he had a high pain threshold, but in fact he just didn't notice the pain until he was sitting down again.

Paolo clearly had the upper hand on da Badass this evening, beginning by grasping his opponent in what the emcee called "The Enforcer's signature headlock, the Drill bit." There was a struggle that involved some awkward grappling, a nasty incident with biting fingers, and eventually a bell signaling the end of the round and the beginning of more repartee.

"You folks came here for blood, and you are going to get blood!" cried the host for the evening, before tripping on his microphone cable and scrambling out of the ropes again.

For round two, da Badass grabbed an old air filter provided from the sidelines by Loudmouth, while The Enforcer was supplied with a tire iron by D.M.V.

Paolo was raising his tire iron for some jousting when he glanced into the crowd and saw an unexpected face in the back. An older man, rings on both hands, a single, familiar curl of white hair pressed to one side of his forehead...Paolo took an air filter to the eye.

"Oh! No! We're getting ugly. That's blood sport," the emcee said as Paolo tumbled to the ground. "What's going on? How about it, Enforcer—you need a break?"

But The Enforcer shook off his surprise, rose again, grabbed his bike chain, and started swinging it. The fight ended when Leo conceded a few moments later, minus two teeth and half a pint of blood. Paolo spent a good ten minutes nursing an eye ringside before he acknowledged his victory. He first needed to be convinced that he hadn't been blinded.

"Did you see that guy?" he asked strangers, but no one knew what he meant. He hailed Marcus to his side. "That guy, you see him? That guy with the pinky rings? Old guy, scar on his face? I saw that same dude talking to Mr. Bolt one time."

Marcus pretended to be impressed. "No shit."

"What's he doing here? He still here?" Paolo searched the room with his one good eye. Marcus shook his head, and Paolo kept looking around.

"Good fight, man," Marcus said.

"That was pretty good," Paolo agreed. "Small crowd, though. People don't like to come so much on Friday nights, Saturdays we do better."

"Damn, your eye is bad."

"I should get it cleaned up before work, huh?"

"Tell them your mom beats you."

Paolo smiled. "Who's this?"

"This is Teena. She wanted to see what the whole underground wrestling thing was all about."

"Sorry about your shirt, Teena," Paolo said.

"It's all right," Teena replied, blotting a blood splatter. "It's a cheap one. If I wore something nice I woulda been pissed."

"What'd you think?"

"It's all right. It's not really my thing."

"We do a different place every time. You should come next week, we'll be at an old movie theater."

Da Badass approached Paolo. "I wrote down my cousinth number. You should call her."

"Your teeth okay?"

"Oh yeah. Ith cool. I think you'll like her. Sheth a special education teacher."

Paolo examined the number. "I don't know. I've had such bad luck with women, man."

Marcus said, "So my man Paolo, here, he's been trying to get this girl at work to go out with him. It ain't going to happen."

"I'm going to do it," said Paolo. "I'm going to do it. You'll see. She'll go out with me sooner or later." He held up a fistful of cash. "That's three hundred dollars I made from winning tonight."

"Three hundred dollars?" Marcus reached over and took the wad, held it in front of Paolo's good eye. "You know what this is? This is poor people money. This is poor people money. You need to have rich people money. That's what you need."

9

WHEN DECORATING A HOME IN MANHATTAN, A SMART shopper could justify almost any expense by using the furniture store hierarchy:

Those who bought custom-made furniture were getting a great deal, because they were not paying for foreign imports.

Those who bought Pottery Barn and Crate&Barrel were getting a great deal, because they were not paying for custom-made furniture.

Those who bought Ikea were getting a great deal, because they were not paying for Pottery Barn or Crate&Barrel.

Those who bought off Craigslist were getting a great deal, because they were not paying for Ikea.

The only deal that wasn't great was to accept free furniture from one's parents. A young person's search for self-expression might be compromised if it involved anyone's tastes but her own—her own and those of the mod-loving European designers who worked for corporate conglomerates.

Using this logic, Nadya had gotten a great deal when redecorating her apartment. She and Lillian were one step above the Craigslist level—her real estate blog was now supplemented by a job writing promotional materials for various nightclubs—so she'd made a Sunday trip to the Elizabeth, New Jersey, Ikea, armed with a new Bolt credit card, a Zipcar, and a man she had no intention of dating, to spend two hundred dollars on a new sofa.

Two hundred dollars was, of course, a really great deal for a new sofa—marred slightly by the fact that she then spent two hundred dollars on pillows and wall hangings and a rug to match the sofa, plus one hundred and fifty dollars on some 1960s-style lamps. All the same, five hundred and fifty dollars was not bad for redecorating a living room—marred slightly by the thirteen hundred dollars Nadya had recently spent on a new Macintosh laptop—which was a really great deal, when you considered how much more it would have cost without the student discount. The laptop would be used exclusively for word-processing, music, and the Internet—all of which a laptop costing half as much could do, but style counted for something, didn't it?

When Lillian came home from tutoring one evening at close to nine p.m., it was as if she had entered the den of a London swinger circa 1967.

"New sofa," she said.

"Oh, yeah," Nadya agreed. "I was inspired by some of these apartments I've been seeing. You should see this place I visited in Soho yesterday. Philip Seymour Hoffman is thinking about buying it. The place is amazing."

"What happened to our old sofa?"

"Chris gave it to his nephew. It's downstairs. They may be coming by later to pick it up."

"Okay, but..."

"Don't worry if you can't chip in. I got a really good deal, especially when you know how much it could have cost. Anyway, I think I got a job writing for a fashion blog. Just a little extra to boost my income. As well as the nightclub thing."

"That's great!"

"Nothing definite yet. But it'll happen." Nadya's airy confidence was a continual source of bewilderment to Lillian.

"So I have news, too," Lillian offered, sitting down on the foam cushion. "Nothing quite as good as your writing job. But Cal took his SATs on Saturday, and I was worried about how much they'd need me for the summer after that, but now they've also asked me to tutor his sister in writing while we wait to hear about how Cal did."

"How old is the sister?"

"Seven."

"And you're teaching her what exactly?"

"They want to get her started on essays. Just to get a jump-start. Her mom said we can do creative writing too."

"Jesus Christ."

"I know, it's a little..."

"Rich people are so fucking crazy."

"Well, maybe she'll be the next big thing," Lillian said. "I'm sure she'll get a book published before I will."

"So how do you think Cal did on his SAT?"

Lillian thought back to Cal's proud, nervous look as he told her it had gone really well, that he'd been at the top of his game, that she had done a great job tutoring him. It must have been a disaster.

"Okay."

Right before their doorbell rang, Lillian added, "I guess I should get working on my book."

At the door were Chris and a young man Chris presented as his nephew, Wes, a sophomore in college who had inherited the long, horsey face of Chris's family but none of Chris's effortless good looks.

"Thanks for the sofa. It rocks," Wes said.

Nadya looked at him with faint pity for his lack of discernment.

Chris said, "You guys want to come get something to eat? Wes and I were thinking about sushi."

During the meal, Lillian entertained herself by coming up with new descriptors for Chris. He was no longer JFK, now that he was tired and a bit rumpled from helping his nephew move all day. He was a tennis-playing WASP from a 1970s Woody Allen film, the one Allen had to compete with to get the girl. That wealthy English guy from *Chariots of Fire*, practicing the hundred-yard dash with champagne provided by his butler.

Wes sat across from her, looking up from his dragon roll to Nadya with hopeless longing. Lillian felt sympathy for him. She'd seen people look like that at Nadya before.

"So you're getting a new place?" Lillian asked Wes.

"Sort of. My roommate kicked us out."

Chris smiled. "His roommate poses a mystery."

"Yeah, seriously," Wes agreed. "Four of us lived together all freshman year. But Frank's name was on the lease, and now he suddenly wants the place to himself."

Lillian raised her eyebrows. "How can he afford that?"

"I know, right? I mean, he's a bright guy, but he doesn't come from a lot of money. He went to Bronx Science, you know?"

"Tell them about the outfits," Chris prompted.

"Oh, yeah. He comes and goes in different outfits. One day he'll have, like, a goatee, and the next day he has his hair dyed blond."

"Drug dealing," Nadya offered.

Wes nodded. "Yeah, pot dealing is the obvious thing. That's what we thought. But he didn't store anything at the apartment. And we found lifts in his shoes once."

"An actor?" Lillian offered.

Wes snorted. "Not likely."

"It's intriguing," Chris said. "I want to figure it out. Have you ever tried to follow him?"

"No. Why?"

"To find out where he goes?"

"Who cares," Wes said. "I just needed a new place. We spent the last month staying in this apartment owned by my roommate Nate's parents, but they're kicking us out in July. His dad's retired and they come live there every few months, when they're not in Italy."

"I want that life," Nadya said with a smile.

Chris smiled. "Me, too."

"But you could have it now," Nadya said. And there followed a ten minute debate about what it really cost to retire in Lake

Como and never have to work again, and why Nadya was over-estimating Chris's wealth, and underestimating the cost of living in Europe. Chris admitted he'd had a friend who'd recently retired from working at the age of forty-two, but that took a lot of preparation. Realistically Chris estimated you'd need at least twenty million set aside, just to feel "safe." And that wasn't even to live well. Lillian sat there amused, and Chris noticed her private amusement.

"I guess I sounded kind of crazy right then, if you're still paying off your student loans."

"No, it's just...come on," said Lillian.

Chris laughed. "I hear you, I hear you," he said. "You just don't know how the guys I work with think. For them, twenty million wouldn't even be enough."

"For what?"

Chris smiled. "Most people I know just like expensive stuff, I guess."

After dinner, Lillian found herself walking down the street next to Chris. She half expected him to ask, "Is Nadya interested?" Lillian had spent most of high school walking next to boys who wanted to know if some friend of hers was interested. But he said nothing for a while.

Then he said, "I want to follow him."

"Who?"

"Wes's roommate, Frank."

"You really want to know what's going on?"

"I've always wanted to be a private detective," Chris said. "It was kind of like a childhood dream. I once helped a friend get back a stolen bike. We caught the guy who took it and everything."

"That's great."

"Don't you want to know what's going on with that guy?"

"Sure."

"Well, let's look at the facts," Chris said.

"Changes outfits."

"Prostitution?"

"He's not a prostitute," Wes called from a few feet behind them, where he was showing Nadya a new app for his iPhone.

"How do you know?"

"He's not that attractive."

"It takes all kinds," Chris said.

"No woman would pay to sleep with him. Or man." And Wes turned back to Nadya, talking and shaking his phone up and down.

"Do you want to come follow him sometime?"

Lillian looked at Chris, distracted. "What?"

"I want to track him. You want to come?"

"Oh…Sure, that'd be fun."

"Maybe in a couple of weeks, when I get back from a trip to London. Just see what he's up to. If he's turning tricks or what. It would be fun to drive around and follow him, wouldn't it?"

"Yeah, of course." For a brief moment, Lillian felt herself blushing in confusion.

"I also kind of wanted to talk to you about Nadya, to tell you the truth."

And there it is, thought Lillian. "Sure," she said. He didn't realize she was an expert at conversations like that.

10

What defines an addict? Lem and I were talking about it in session this week. What we decided was that it's not necessarily when your problem interferes with the rest of your life. Mitch and I were doing well financially when my little habit spiraled out of control. He had just gotten a raise at Citigroup and he barely even looked at the credit card bills. No, kids, you're an addict when the lies begin. The lies you tell yourself.

I was thinking about that when I met a young lady in Barneys this Wednesday. Tall, attractive, and clearly no money, yet there she was. (And there I was, but I didn't buy anything, I promise.) She was looking at these Christian Louboutin platform sandals and I stopped her and said, "Couldn't you just die?"

She nodded and put them back. "I'm not here to buy anything."

"Oh, yes you are, honey," I said. "I know you. I was you."

I took her out to lunch.

"If you're buying stuff you can't afford..." I started. We were doing the prix fixe at Tao. A holdover from my last days at Bergdorf's, before I began therapy.

"But I'm going to have the money eventually. After I sell my book."

"You're a writer?"

"I've been talking to agents. I could have a book deal next week."

"How over your head are you?"

"You know what drives me crazy? I go into rich people's apartments all day, for my job, and they have the ugliest stuff. They have all the money in the world, and they buy crap. See, if I had money, I'd buy beautiful stuff. Only stuff made by artists. Christian Louboutin is an Artist."

"But you don't have the money."

"I just feel like I'm one of the people who actually appreciates it. So I just go to the store and look at stuff. It's like going to a museum. Except sometimes something's on sale."

"Honey, look at me," I said. "Look at me, okay? If you don't need this stuff, why are you buying it?" It was a question I had asked myself a hundred times. And she gave the answer I always had.

"But I do need it."

"Honey," I said. "You are an addict."

This week, I've decided to get rid of a Hermès bag. My very own Birkin that I was on a six-month waiting list for back in 2005 when Jean Paul Gaultier took over the line. It's orange, fits over the shoulder, will last forever, and is just divine. I'm posting it on eBay, and I hope you'll all have a look, but first I have to make my goodbyes to it and take it out to lunch on Saturday. I'll miss you, baby Birkin. Kiss kiss.

Canella

Shopacovery by Canella McBride, June 28, 2008

www.shopacovery.com

THE LINE FOR THE ATLANTIC CITY BUS IS ALWAYS long. If you proceed down two escalators in the Port Authority bus station at 42nd Street and 8th, you will always find them waiting there, at eight p.m. on a Tuesday or at six a.m. on a Friday morning: the hopeless, the drug addled, taking the cheapest way down the Turnpike to the most dilapidated segment of the Jersey Shore. Twitchy veterans, chain-smoking old ladies, men with unkempt hair clutching worn-out duffel bags.

This particular Saturday morning, two men found themselves sitting next to each other in the last row of seats on the bus, closer than they would have wished to the bathroom door. Neither was the typical passenger to Atlantic City—both had an air of optimism that separated them from the rest of the morning crowd.

"This sucks," said the larger man without malice as he squeezed his heavy frame into the seat. "I can't believe I'm here, man. My goddamn truck is in the shop."

"I know," agreed the young man next to him. "I used to own a Jag. This is a pretty big step down."

"You own a Jag?"

"I used to. They took it as collateral."

"Damn. That's a tragedy."

"I'll get another one, though. That's what this trip is about. Getting back in the game. I'm a professional poker player." The smaller man assessed his traveling companion, and then thrust out his hand. "I'm Greg Miller, by the way."

"Paolo Cincotti."

"Can I ask you a question, Paolo?"

"Sure." Greg had the demeanor of a salesman, but Paolo didn't mind. Paolo was feeling social, he liked stories, and he might get the opportunity to show his wrestling scar.

"Do you play poker?" Greg asked.

"No, man. I don't gamble."

"Poker isn't gambling. It's a game of skill. Can I tell you something? I once paid off a two hundred thousand dollar debt playing poker."

"Two hundred G."

"Two hundred," Greg agreed. "What I've been trying to do now is teach it. I've been giving people lessons. I got a guy—he's training to play in the World Series of Poker. I'm his coach."

"You serious?"

"I can give you a free tip right now, if you want."

"But I don't play poker."

"A tip for life, then."

"Okay."

"This is free, but I give lessons."

"Okay."

Greg fixed Paolo with a serious look. "I'm going to tell you two things, and one is a lie, and one is true, and I want you to tell me which is which."

"Shoot."

"The goal is to spot my tell. Are you ready? My poker tell?"

"Ready."

"One. I went to Harvard University. Okay? And two. I am the owner of a Mercedes Benz."

"Huh." Paolo gave it a moment. "I'm going to say you went to Harvard."

"But you're not sure."

"No, I'm pretty sure."

"Not positive, though." Now Greg leaned forward. "You know how you can tell? By the amount that I tilt my chin. People always tilt their chin more when they're lying. That's a poker tell."

"Really."

"You should take my class," Greg said.

"Say it again. I want to see this."

"I went to Harvard University. And I am the owner of a Mercedes Benz." Greg smiled. "Did you see my chin?"

"I saw it," Paolo said. He hadn't.

"That tip alone is worth a lot of money. Spotting someone's tell."

"I don't doubt you, man," Paolo said, trying to sound amicable. He reached into his bag and pulled out a tiny DVD player. "You don't mind if I –"

"No, go ahead."

Paolo put in a DVD of the Rock's greatest hits, from back in his wrestling days. The Rock had the kind of impressive chin that would have made an excellent test case for Greg's theory. Paolo stared at the screen. When the Rock went up against Hogan, when he said he could take him, was he tilting his chin?

A long moment passed. Paolo looked at his seating companion, the shirt cuffs just a little worn, the jacket just a little out of fashion. Greg was pulling on his arms, shaking himself, showing

74

a little of the eagerness that buzzed around several other people on the bus.

"Harvard?" he asked.

Greg nodded.

Paolo shook his head and said nothing. He was reminded, inexplicably, of Bella Pointer, Mr. Bolt's beautiful assistant. She'd probably gone to a school like Harvard. And where had he gone? He'd gone nowhere. To community college, and he hadn't even finished that.

He was a loser. He knew it. But that could change. It could change today.

Some places just made you feel poor, Lillian decided, as she stood waiting for Nadya, an iced latte in her hands from the Starbucks in Trump Tower, looking at the people passing by on Fifth Avenue. Fifth Avenue between the stretches of 42nd Street and 60th Street was one of the major shopping destinations of the city, though it had always struck Lillian as odd that tourists would be attracted to a street where most of them could afford nothing. It wasn't as if people even went into most of the stores. Your average out-of-towner didn't wander into Prada or Fendi— they were smart enough to know better. Instead, they packed the Avenue itself, hitting the occasional affordable flagship store like Abercrombie and Fitch and leaving the debutantes and trophy wives to wade through the throngs to get inside their personal open waters—the exclusive retail shops full of European luxury goods.

Or maybe Lillian was just feeling cranky. The truth was she'd been hoping to get some work done on her novel and had brought her laptop with her to Starbucks—the lone affordable coffee stop on the Avenue—but the inner monologue she was trying to write, from the perspective of a dying priest wrestling with the nature of faith, had been drowned out by the conversation a woman was having with her teen daughter about whether buying something from Armani was the same thing as buying something from Armani Exchange.

"Mom. Mom, listen to me. It's not the same. It's just—everybody wears Armani Exchange."

"Everybody does not wear Armani Exchange."

"But what I mean is, nobody wears anything that's actually Armani, so why can't I? Just this once? Please?" The girl was perhaps sixteen, with long sleek black hair and tiny terrycloth shorts with a pink logo on the back. Her mother was matronly and wore her sunglasses around her neck on a green and white beaded lanyard.

"Why can't you what?" the mother interrupted. "What do you want me to do? I'd like you to tell me what you expect me to do, because that T-shirt was a hundred and seventy-five dollars and it was the cheapest thing in the store."

"That's the same amount you'd pay for a pocketbook if we got it at Macy's or something."

"Which you would use every day. If you wear that T-shirt every day for a year, then I'll get it for you."

They were silent for a moment, and Lillian began typing, but before she could correct a dangling modifier, the mother began again: "And I guarantee you something else, which is that nobody from Mentor's going to know the difference between Armani and Armani Exchange."

This caught Lillian's attention. Through an odd coincidence, Mentor, Ohio, was one of the locations of Lillian's novel, and she had characterized the town in her book (though she'd never actually visited it) as a locus of American purity and Christian faith—the one place to which the characters longed to return but never could. She regarded the two actual, real-life Mentor residents as the girl said, "This sucks," and her mother replied, "Well, life sucks."

Lillian shut her laptop and walked outside.

Nadya was supposed to be finishing surveying a new apartment for her real estate blog in a pre-war wedding cake of a building just south of Trump Tower. The plan was for Nadya to meet Lillian at the corner and together they would grab a burger in the Parker Meridian Hotel and eat it in Central Park and visit museums to "talk about art or something." Being an artist—or at least calling yourself one—was a silly but real antidote to Lillian's feelings about Fifth Avenue. Being an artist was possibly the only way of making it feel cool to be poor. She wondered if the social category of artist had been invented for no other purpose.

Nadya was late, of course. No surprise there. What was surprising was that she had a tiny bag with her from Fendi.

"Nadya," said Lillian, startled. "You didn't buy anything, did you?"

"No, not really," said Nadya. "But it was on sale and it's just a scarf and I'm telling you, it's going to be a mainstay of my wardrobe. This scarf is going to change my life."

At Lillian's insistence, Nadya opened the tiny box that held her tissue-wrapped treasure. Lillian surmised after careful examination that it was a red scarf.

"It's pretty..." she said, then stopped herself from saying more.

"Oh, I can't stay and get lunch today. I have to go to an open house. Again. I'm getting sick of this job already, but whatever, I have to go or they'll fire me. They're already threatening to fire me already, can you believe that?" Nadya kissed Lillian's cheek. "Go be deep without me, okay? Go look at something fabulous and inspiring in the Met or something and come back tonight and tell me all about it."

"You promised me."

"I'm sorry, okay? I'm trying to keep my job."

"It's not that, it's just...you have all this credit card debt and you're buying all this stuff."

"I'm going to be okay, Lillian, I promise. Now don't be grumpy."

Nadya half-hugged her, and then she was gone, and Lillian was left to walk up Fifth Avenue in the general direction of some of the world's greatest art masterpieces. Instead of entering the Met, Lillian bought a hot dog from a cart and sat alone on a bench just inside the entrance of Central Park, glaring at the wealthy Manhattan women jogging past her, tiny whippets of female form in skintight running shorts pushing thousand dollar strollers.

Why was she so angry? Was it Nadya's shopping expedition, or was it that she herself couldn't afford to shop because she was making just enough to live on while she wrote a novel barely coherent enough to read? Was it that she was doing it all by SAT tutoring, which Bryan Ruggiero had been so disturbed by, which had reminded her that she ought to be more disturbed herself? What would her mother have said if she knew what Lillian did for a living—that she had sold out, that she was maintaining the economic injustice status quo?

Peering into the windows of the super-rich was enough to make anyone cranky, even a nice lady from Mentor.

The approach to Atlantic City crossed an open expanse of flat wetlands where the wise traveler would keep his eyes on the glittering towers in the distance and not the empty lots and pawn shops that surrounded them. Paolo took in both with equanimity as the bus pulled into the station. His traveling companion's hands were yanking on his shirt cuffs as they pulled up, and Greg shot Paolo a look of stark terror, the way someone would before jumping out of a plane.

"Here we are," he said.

Paolo shook his hand. "Hey, man. Good luck. If I ever need lessons…"

Greg thrust a business card into his hand: Greg Miller, Poker Professional. Cell phone number, no address. "You call me," Greg said. He launched himself forward.

Ten minutes later, Paolo was walking up to the driveway of a broad two-story beach home, the kind known as an "upside-down" because the living room is on the second floor for a better view of the water. The house bore the marks of two separate building periods. It had the large windows and vinyl siding of the late 1960s, but sometime in the 1980s someone had added four vast white Grecian columns to the front and a new outer staircase with small white statues of Aphrodite, which in the ensuing two decades had developed a faint crust of sand. Through the open door to the garage, Paolo could see a large burgundy Lincoln Town Car with gold detailing and a small dent in the back bumper.

The door opened to his knock, and a husky blond man exactly his size pointed him into a small office off the front hallway.

There, seated behind a cluttered desk, surrounded by bookcases cluttered with photographs, sat the pinky-ringed man Paolo had seen twice before, his shock of white hair plastered down to one side of his forehead, his long uneven scar flushed pink.

"Close the door, Kevin," said the stranger to the burly blond doorman, and Paolo found himself alone with the elderly man, who thrust a small bowl of mints in his direction. "Butter mint? Have a seat."

Paolo grabbed a small handful of mints and took a seat in a faded leather armchair opposite the stranger.

"Since my wife died, I keep my office here. I used to have a place downtown, but you get to a certain age, you don't have to impress anybody anymore."

"Look, I gotta say," Paolo said, "I'm happy with my job. Your message said you were just looking for someone on weekends, right? I mean, I could use the extra money, but I don't want to do anything that could get me in trouble, you know."

"You're getting ahead of yourself," said the man. "That's the first thing you have to learn not to do. Now, I want to know if you've heard of me. If you know who you're dealing with."

"Ivan Bulowski? No, sorry."

Ivan sat back and nodded. "Now, let me tell you what I know about you. I know that you are a man who is skilled at intimidation. Not violence. Intimidation. That's what I've been looking for. I'm not interested in violence. I'm interested in psychology.

There's strong people and weak people. The strong control the weak by means of the mind."

"I gotcha."

"When I saw you fight, I thought, he is using his mind. You do the thing with the barbed wire, that's psychological."

Paolo nodded. "Yeah, that's what I was trying to…"

"Psychological," Ivan went on. "I am not a violent man. Never have been. I have survived in Atlantic City sixteen years. I was in Vegas twenty-five years before that."

Paolo ate his butter mints while he considered this information. "What kind of work are we talking about here?"

"Go with Kevin today. See if you like it. It's debt collection, that's all it is. We buy debts from some of the bigger agencies, bring them in. That's all. That's not my only line of work, but that's where I need help right now. With the drop in the real estate market, we are seeing a lot of problems. A lot of problems. People aren't making payments."

"Are you connected?" Paolo asked. "I have total respect, I'm not saying I don't, but I just want to know."

"Only socially. I'm not a made man, is that what you're asking?"

"Just curious."

"A lot of good friends," Ivan said. "A lot of good friends. I myself am not."

Ivan's phone rang, but he ignored it. He and Paolo looked at each other for a long moment.

Then he shouted, "Kevin, get the goddamn phone!"

The ringing stopped.

Paolo was a fan of mobster movies. *The Godfather. Goodfellas.* His father was Italian, and Paolo's wrestling nickname, "The Enforcer," was pulled from one of Al Capone's henchmen, Frank Nitti, who had been played in the movies by such luminaries as Sylvester Stallone, Billy Drago, and Stanley Tucci. Paolo was flattered that people assumed he could pull off the real thing, even if he wasn't sure that he agreed.

"Okay, can I ask you a question, though?" he said at last. "How do you know Henry Bolt?"

"Who says I know Henry Bolt?"

"I saw you talking to him one time. Outside the Bolt Building. I work security there."

"You work in the Bolt Building?" Ivan considered this.

"Yeah."

"Okay. I see. Well, now." Ivan smiled, sat back, considered. "Let's just say that I have lived a varied and interesting life. It would not even—they should make a book of my life. But if they did, no one would believe it. No one would believe a goddamn word."

Kevin Muise, Ivan's chief debt collector, was a man of few words. He drove in silence, his large hands hanging relaxed above the dashboard as he manned the leather wheel of the Lincoln with his wrists.

"You like the work?" Paolo asked.

Kevin shrugged. Five minutes passed before he spoke.

"I'll give you one piece of advice."

"Okay."

"You got to decide before you enter a room whether you're going to hit the guy. You got to already have your mind made up before you go in there."

"All right."

"Because if you decide when you're in there, you lose control of the situation. I always pick exactly how many times I'm going to hit a guy. Between zero and fifty. Sometimes it's zero. But I got to know ahead of time."

"So what's it going to be today?"

Kevin let another long moment pass. "The point is," he said as he pulled into the parking lot of the Trump Taj Mahal, "that I've already made up my mind."

Kevin led the way into the freight entrance, walking in dead silence up the platform, shoulders swaying from side to side. He thrust a wadded-up bill into the hands of the back entrance guard.

"Poker room four, right?" he asked.

The guard pointed the way.

Kevin and Paolo walked down two long corridors, past a large, busy kitchen, and up a half-flight of stairs. Without breaking stride, Kevin pushed open one of the side doors, entered a dark space upholstered in red, and grabbed a man from one of the tables, shoving him against a wall.

"Back in town, and you don't come see us?" Kevin shouted. His voice had only two volumes: low and ear-splitting, and he'd chosen the latter. Paolo recognized the victim, with surprise, as his traveling companion from the morning. He wondered if Greg was "teaching" these men poker, but from the unsurprised faces of the other four at the table, it didn't seem likely. One of them, a skinny young blond man in expensive sunglasses, snapped up his chips with an instinct for self-preservation, and then edged towards the door.

Greg veered to look at the departing poker player. "Frank. Frank. Wait. Help me. Help me, man."

"Right…" said the young blond man in a drawl, and walked out the door.

Greg turned back at Kevin, giving him his most sincere, earnest look. "I was here getting your money. I'm trying to pay you back."

"Do—you—have—the—money?" Kevin said, enunciating every syllable as if talking to an idiot rather than a man with a Harvard degree.

"I'll get it. By the end of the day," Greg said. "I swear, I –"

Paolo looked at Greg's chin. It was tilted. Greg's eyes darted toward him in confused recognition, and Paolo looked away.

"No wait, listen! Wait! Oh, God. Don't do this, please."

Then Paolo counted ten hits, exactly.

11

DID YOU KNOW THAT A GIFT TO FORTUNA UNIVERSITY
can help you support your heirs?

Were you aware that, through the use of a life income gift,
you could make a charitable donation to Fortuna that will give
your loved ones an annuity for the duration of their lives, and
then transfer your gift to support Fortuna in perpetuity? Just ask
the planned giving department to help you find a tax-deductible
way to secure the financial future you want for your family.

Penny Danner, a woman of middle years who sat in an office
overlooking the green central courtyard of Fortuna, was an expert on "life income" gifts. If you asked her the tax implications
of an IRA donation for the four hundred and fifty thousand dollar bracket, she could tell you without reaching for a calculator.
If you asked her the pros and cons of donating your vacation
home in Florida, she could check them off on her ten slender
fingers.

"I have a head for figures," she would say with a smile. Her
favorite list of figures was the "*Forbes* 400 List," which stated
the four hundred wealthiest people in America. She could tell
you, without checking the magazine, that Henry Bolt was somewhere around one hundred and seventy-five. She could also tell
you (though this was not public knowledge), the age of each of
Henry's children, the name and age of his wife and where she
went to college, and the name of his own alma mater, along with
where he had begun (and dropped out of) an MBA program.

But Penny had another gift of even more use than her head
for figures. She had a kind voice, which registered in low, vi-
brant tones a deep sympathy for those who were about to give
her money. It was a voice that would have made her a wonderful

kindergarten teacher or a hospital nurse, the one who could draw blood without hurting. She could discuss the handoff of millions of dollars to Fortuna's overstuffed coffers as if she were discussing the handoff of an orphan child.

"I know it's hard," she would say to the hesitant donor. "It's so hard to find the right place. You just want to give to the right place. The place where your contribution will grow as a part of what you believe in, the things you hold dear. You want your gift to build upon your values."

Some donors cried on the phone with her, discussing the heartbreaking behavior of their grandchildren, who were already angling for a piece of the postmortem pie.

"They love you," Penny would say. "They're going to realize how much when you're gone. And when they do, they're going to be so glad you gave to a good place, a good cause. Something you believed in. They're going to respect that."

The key, as Penny would explain to her young trainees, was not to multitask. "Don't check your email while someone is crying. I keep a notepad on my desk where I have all the important names. Before I get on the phone, I know his wife is Ruth. His daughter is Morgan. That way if he refers to someone, I don't have to say, 'Now, who is that again?'"

At the bottom of her notepad, she would write down a figure, an estimate. Then at the end of each conversation she would ask, "And how much would you feel comfortable giving?" Her guess was always within ten percent.

Mid-June was a busy season, following up on the reunions scheduled earlier in the month. She had six alumni lunches this week (she ate light, in case she had to double-book), as well as two dinners. But she had made time for one more task, laying the groundwork for one more target.

"Janine," she chirped into her phone. "Thank you so much for getting back to me. How are your summer plans shaping up? Going to the Cape again?"

After a few minutes of empathizing about the traffic on Route 6 and sighing over Hillary Clinton's recent concession

84

in the Democratic primaries (though Penny had no real political affiliation, she agreed it would have been nice to see a woman president), Penny continued, "Now let me explain what I need, and you tell me if you're comfortable sharing it with me. Just feel absolutely free to say you're not comfortable. As I mentioned, Mr. Bolt's son was born at your hospital seventeen years ago, in August of '91, and his daughter is seven, so that's June of '01. All I'm looking for is the pattern of giving. It would help me a lot to know whether he tends to donate prior to big events, or afterwards." Penny nodded, listening for a long moment. "Just a rough idea is completely fine, I don't need amounts."

Penny nodded, jotting something on her little notepad. "You know you have such a great hospital," she said. "You do such a wonderful job there." Then she stopped writing. "What's interesting?"

She listened for a long moment. "Janine, I'm getting a taxi to meet you. Will you not tell anybody else about that? Please?"

Near Bathgate Ave and 187th Street, not far from St. Barnabas Hospital in the Bronx, Celia Upson and her son Clyde stood at a corner deli buying lottery tickets.

"'Set for Life' is ten dollars," Celia was saying. "That's a lot of money. That is a lot of money for one ticket."

"Well, why don't you get five of the 'Fortune Cookie' and get five of the 'Loose Change'?"

"I don't like the 'Loose Change.' I don't like that one."

"Well, Ma, what do you want, then?"

The woman looked up at the array of scratch tickets, lined up behind the glass of the tiny deli counter. "I'll get five of the 'Shop 'Til You Drop.' And I'll get a couple of the 'Win $1000 a Week for Life.'"

The man behind the counter unrolled the tickets and asked, "Any for you, Clyde?"

Clyde Upson shook his head and took out a twenty to pay for his mother's scratch tickets and milk. He picked up her black deli bag and followed her out of the store. She hadn't gotten more than twenty feet before she stopped to pull out one of the tickets, pressing it against her small purple pocketbook.

"Just one," she said. "I'll do the rest at home. I just have to find out if I'm going to own that big house in Westchester someday."

"Ma, I told you. I'll buy you whatever house you want."

"I know, honey," she agreed, studying the numbers. "But I can dream, can't I?"

Clyde tried again to make his point. "But you won't need to dream when I start doing better."

"But if I win the lottery, then you wouldn't have to work. Wouldn't that be nice?"

Clyde frowned as his mother started to walk again. She'd spent half his childhood buying scratch tickets, especially after his stepfather had died. It was her "stress reliever," she always said, although she didn't seem calm when she did it, she seemed to be in a kind of dreamland while rubbing out the metal foil that separated her from her fate. Once a month, she visited a casino, and he'd sometimes gone with her. She brought a hundred dollars each time, and she placed it in the slot machines quarter by quarter, her eyes sad and dull, waiting for something to happen. Twice, she'd come home with more money than she'd left with. Twice in Clyde's whole twenty-seven years. But that had been enough to keep her going.

Clyde was irritated by his inability, no matter how well he did in school or at his job, to convince his mother that something other than luck was going to determine their fate. The day after he graduated high school, in the top twenty percent of his class, she had gone to a psychic for news about his future.

"Ma. I'm gonna be fine."

"I know," she'd replied. "But I just want to make sure."

It was as if she was expecting a tidal wave to rise up from Long Island Sound and wipe them out or sweep them to some new shore of bliss. There was no possibility of incremental improvement, in Celia Upson's view of the world. You were either chosen or doomed.

"I think I'm going to get a bonus this year," Clyde added as they started walking again. "I was talking to Joanne, in my office, and she said we usually get at least fifteen percent. And they're letting me make a speech at the quarterly party, did I tell you?"

"Yes, you told me."

"I'm doing research for it now. I've been going in depth, you know. Finding out stuff that even the corporate relations department doesn't know. Like for example, did you know that before Bolt Bank, Mr. Bolt owned a Wally's Donuts?"

"A Wally's Donuts?"

"Yeah. In New Jersey. Mr. Bolt bought the company. And Wally's did really well that year. They did incredible."

"I don't think you should be digging around for all that old stuff, honey. Nobody cares about that kind of stuff. People want to know about right now, don't they?"

"No, it's interesting. I'm going out to New Jersey tomorrow to talk to some of the people there. Find out how he made it happen for them so I can include it in my speech. I mean, I'm not saying I'm going to be made vice president any time soon, but it's possible, you know? At least I could get a raise or something."

"New Jersey? Don't waste your time in New Jersey. Just write something flattering about Mr. Bolt. He'll like that."

"What? Why do you always do this? You assume I don't know what I'm doing."

"When did I say that?"

"You just did."

"I'm just trying to help you, that's all. It's just that you were not born lucky."

"Ma, forget it. You start talking like that, and you can just forget it. I'm going out, okay?" He stepped a few feet ahead to

87

his parked car and started to open the driver's side door. "I'll be back later. I'm going to do more research."

"Researching a donut shop?" She made it sound ridiculous.

"You know, I'm not unlucky. Just because my father and stepfather died... maybe my bad luck ended there. You ever thought of that?" Clyde pulled open the door and stepped inside, slamming it behind him. His mother tapped on the window, and it took a long moment before he rolled it down.

"I'm sorry, Ma," he said. "But I'm moving out. I'm getting a place in Manhattan."

"In Manhattan? You can't afford that."

"I can afford it, Ma. I can afford it. I can."

"So that's it? You're leaving?"

He hesitated.

"But it's so expensive."

He started up the car.

"Clyde, wait. Wait! You're going to do great. I know that, sweetie. I know it. I trust you." Then she slid through the window a single scratch ticket. "But just for luck," she said.

12

NADYA AND LILLIAN STOOD IN LINE AT **11:00** A.M. ON A
Tuesday morning in a coffee shop tucked into a clothing store
between Prince Street and Spring. The walls were exposed brick,
the ceilings fifteen feet high, the latte cups made of brown recy-
cled paper to give the buyer the sense that she was doing something environmentally friendly by paying four dollars for a cup
of coffee.

"This was the old red light district, back in the 1850s," Nadya
was saying. "There was a famous bordello on this stretch of Mercer
Street. Oh, and you know what else I found out? See that graffiti
across the street? They leave it up on purpose. It ups the property
value."

"No, it doesn't."

"Everyone wants to think this part of New York is still cool, I
guess. I met this guy, works at a hedge fund...if you ask what he
does, he says he's a photographer. Because, you know, he owns a
Leica. Anyway, that's why I can't become a real estate agent,
even though I practically am one. If I get my real estate license,
then when I tell people I'm a writer, I'm just full of shit like everybody else."

Nadya tossed her scarf around her neck as she led Lillian
across the street to a large, spray-painted doorway. She pulled
out a labeled set of keys and unlocked the entrance.

"I stole these keys from Robert after the open house. I wanted
to come back here."

"You stole them? Nadya."

"Too late now."

Lillian looked at the graffiti. "I wonder if that's where the monthly maintenance fees go. They hire some guy to do the graffiti."

Nadya shook her head as they entered the lobby. "No, the fees go to someone in an office who has to listen to rich people bitch all day. That's what the residents here pay twelve hundred a month in maintenance fees for. The right to bitch at somebody." Nadya unlocked the fourth floor elevator lock, pressed the button, removed the key.

"Twelve hundred just in maintenance fees? Not even the mortgage?"

"If you need a mortgage you can't afford to live here, honey."

Nadya unlocked another large, metal door and they stepped into what had once been a factory floor where young women of their exact age and ethnicities (Irish and Russian Jew) had slaved over sewing machines. Now the space was almost empty, the large wooden floor painted white, with small prints by Ed Ruscha arranged on the scattered brick columns. A single white sofa floated in the middle of the room like a cloud in an empty sky.

Nadya went to the kitchen and poured herself and Lillian two glasses of red wine left over from the open house. "So this is where I'm going to live when I sell my novel and it becomes a huge hit."

"Can I visit?"

"If I let you. I don't know if I'll still see my old friends, I'll be so fabulous. But isn't this the most beautiful place you've ever been? Or do the Bolt's have a nicer one?"

"It's okay. Lots of prints of fox hunting."

"Oh, one of those."

"Cal's been driving me crazy. He refuses to do any studying for the October SAT until he finds out what he got on the June test."

"Little shit. But what about the little girl?"

"No meetings yet. They keep cancelling. They pay me for it sometimes, if they cancel it last minute."

Nadya sat on the sofa and slid forward until her head was almost level with her knees. "I'm never going to leave this place. They'll come to show it to clients tomorrow, and I'll be sleeping in the bed, like Goldilocks and the three bears."

Lillian looked at her friend for a long moment. "Nad, are you okay?"

"Sure."

"You seem down."

"Yeah, I was going to tell you something."

"Tell me what?"

"I was kind of—this is going to sound bad—but I was kind of depending on my dad to help me with our rent, you know? His business was doing really good. Had been. And then he calls me yesterday and says he bought up like fifteen houses last year he was going to flip, but the market dropped and he's lost fifty thousand dollars per house. Which adds up to three quarters of a million dollars, so…"

"Jesus."

"Yeah. He's underwater. And my parents are at risk of losing our home, too, so..."

"Oh, sweetie."

"It's fine, I didn't grow up there. But now I feel orphaned, financially." Nadya sat up after a moment. "I'm sorry, that was a stupid thing to say."

"It's okay."

"No, shit, I'm sorry."

"It's fine. My parents have been gone a long time."

Nadya stood up and walked to the kitchen to pour another glass of wine, removing her scarf as she did. "Maybe I should date Chris. He's rich."

"Can I ask you a question about him? Just in theory…if he asked me whether you'd want to go out with him, what would you say?"

"Did he?"

"No, but I think he will. Maybe."

91

"I don't know. What do you think I should do? If it were you, what would you do?"

Lillian hesitated for a long moment, then told the truth. "I'd say yes."

Later that evening, the Bolt's apartment door was opened by a strange humpbacked figure that turned out to be a petite young woman holding the slumped body of a seven-year-old girl.

"Hi, Amy," Lillian said to the small figure.

Julie smiled over Amy's unresponsive shoulder. "She's taking a break. Swim practice was stressful today."

"Oh, dear."

"I know you were supposed to start writing with her soon, but I think she's feeling a bit overwhelmed."

"Oh, yeah. Don't worry about it. I'll talk to Bronnie, we can put that off."

"Maybe in a week or two..." Julie trailed off, then added, "Henry wants to see you in his office."

Lillian stopped short. This was a new event. "Okay, I'll go tell Cal," she said.

"Cal isn't here. I think he went out or something. I'm sorry," Julie added.

And then Lillian understood. The SAT scores were in. She'd known they'd be available online sometime around now. They must not have been up to expectations. She was going to be fired. A moment's brief panic was followed by a sense of calm. At least she knew what was coming. She knocked on Henry's door.

"Come in."

Henry didn't look up from his computer.

"Have a seat."

Lillian sat in the small metal chair propped against a wall of his office. The only other chair in the room was Henry's large ergonomic office chair. Lillian wondered how many other people had been asked to take her position and await the firing squad: how many nannies who'd been let go or children who'd gone astray. He typed, unembarrassed, for another few minutes before he turned to face her.

"So how long were you working with Cal before he took the SAT?"

"Just about three weeks. It wasn't much time…"

"He did a lot better than last time. I'm not sure if you heard."

"No."

"…780 on the reading, 780 writing, 800 math."

"That's great. That's a big improvement for him." Her first reaction was relief. She wasn't going to be fired. Her second reaction was to realize that she was about to be fired anyway.

"So I think it means he won't be taking it again in October. So we won't be needing you to work on the SAT with him this summer."

"Okay. Well, I'm honestly just happy he did so well." Honestly.

"I think you must have done something to motivate him. A lot of his problem was motivation."

"I agree."

"But there are still things we might need you for. Cal will need help with his college essays this fall, and I understand you're doing a writing program with Amy…"

"Yes, we hadn't really gotten into it yet. She was feeling sick…"

"Close the door, please."

Lillian was puzzled. She got up and shut the door.

"I believe that every individual should do his own work. Take credit for his own failures as well as his successes."

"Of course."

"You've seen some of the writing my wife is doing for her blog?"

"Just one entry…"

"Now, I have some concerns about the quality of her writing. She isn't sure if she's found her voice yet. She's been very busy

93

with the kids, and writing is new to her, and I don't want her to get discouraged. I understand her friend Canella was very critical of the blog when she showed it to her."

"That's too bad."

"My assistant Bella has been working with Bronnie on doing some fact-checking for the blog, and I was thinking that perhaps you could sit down and read a few of Bronnie's blogs before they get posted and possibly do a little bit of polishing on them."

"Oh, sure! You mean, work with Bronnie…"

"I don't think Bronnie will have time to work with you. I mean work with Bella on fixing anything obvious that needs to be fixed. And of course keep this quiet. From Bronnie."

"But Bronnie will know that I'm doing this?"

"Bronnie just knows it's going through Bella. But Bella will pass it to you, since you're the writer. Anyway, I'll pay you the same rate we would have paid you for working with Cal. And you won't need to come here anymore, except when you're tutoring Amy. You can meet with Bella in my office about any issues that come up. But I want the writing to be Bronnie's, you understand. You should just be fixing sentence structure, things that will make it read more smoothly. The writing should be hers."

"Okay."

"You can close the door behind you on the way out."

He turned back to typing. Lillian rose and stood there for a moment, feeling foolish. She wanted to say something that would make it more like a normal conversation between two equals. But she saw that there was no point. Henry was making a display of power so habitual he didn't even notice he'd done it.

If she were smart, she'd just take the money.

"So to reach your assistant—"

"You can get the number from Julie." Without looking up.

"Right. Thanks."

No reply, so she turned and left, closing the door behind her.

Robert Blodnieks was the advertiser's version of the New York success story. You met him and knew that anything was possible in this city, that this is where people could rise from humble origins to late nights of drinking Remy in cool clubs and driving fast cars. He was square-jawed handsome, tall, and wore a tight blue shirt that shaded into purple, detailed with embroidery that hinted at cowboy. His hair was brown but crested in a wave of blond highlights, and his thick Brooklyn accent masked that his first language had been Russian, and he had (though born in New York) not heard a word of English until he started school in Brighton Beach at five years old.

When he and Clyde met, they clicked right away. The first words out of Robert's mouth were, "We are going to get you into an apartment today."

Clyde told his story: his mother, a worrier by nature, had made it very hard for him to leave home, at least while he was in college. But now...now. He worked at Bolt Bank in their new accounts department.

"Ah, Bolt Bank. I had a client there." Robert snapped at the air. "What was her name? A woman...Shit." He snapped again three times, searching his memory, before he waved it off. "Henry Bolt, I bet he has a nice apartment."

"I bet. You know, I've been researching Henry Bolt's life story. Writing up some stuff about the early days. I'm going to sort of present it to him at the quarterly party."

"That's incredible. Henry Bolt! I would like to have as much money as Henry Bolt."

"Me, too."

"Someday you will! So what are you looking for? What's your objective here?"

Clyde explained that he wanted a place near work but not too near work, modern but not too modern, big but not too big.

"I know exactly what you're looking for," said Robert. "I have exactly the place for you. This is a little on the expensive side, but you know, maybe you can afford it."

Robert apologized for taking the subway ("Parking there is a bitch, you know what I'm saying?") and the two of them took the N train to Prince Street, where they disembarked next to a Dean & Deluca. Robert paused to buy them cappuccinos and a babka coffee cake. He was on a roll, chatting about the various advantages of the neighborhood.

"When people used to think New York, they thought Times Square, but now they think Soho. Tribeca. The Village. You know?" Robert noted with pride that the actor Heath Ledger had died of an overdose only a few blocks from that very spot. "Because this is where everyone wants to live, you know?"

"I don't know if I can afford this, man."

"But you gotta see this place. You gotta see this place."

But when they arrived at the building, things started to go awry. Robert couldn't find the keys—could swear he had had them on the ring—and Clyde had to stand outside the graffitied door while Robert yelled at a couple of people on his cell phone.

"Someone is coming with the keys," Robert said when he at last returned, and then he passed the time by releasing a musical string of curse words, mingled with pointing out where Clyde could park his car, if he had a car, and where he could work out at a nearby gym and buy nice Italian clothes, if he wanted them. An art supply store was passed over without comment.

At last, a harried young blonde pulled up in a taxi and handed Robert a set of keys, and the two men made their way inside and upstairs to the apartment.

When Robert opened the door, no one was inside the vast space, but there was a skinny red scarf on one of the kitchen bar stools, and Robert held it up for inspection.

"Somebody is going to get fired," Robert commented, then turned to Clyde. "So the mortgage on this one, we could probably do, we could probably do five thousand a month, plus maintenance of about twelve hundred. So what do we think?"

Clyde looked around. "I love it, man. Maybe in about ten years."

Robert nodded. "I hear you," he said. "Just a little out of your range, here?"

"For now."

"For now."

13

THE CLOCK IN BELLA POINTER'S OFFICE WAS THE ONLY evidence of whimsy in her surroundings, and Lillian had been staring at it, on and off, for seven minutes.

"Great clock," she finally said. It was an Elvis clock, and the bottom half was Elvis's hips, swaying back and forth to tick off the seconds.

"Oh, yeah," said Bella. "My brother Greg got it for me. He spent a lot of time in Vegas." And she smiled for a second. "Now, I guess I'm still not sure exactly where your confusion comes from."

"Well, he told me to edit Bronnie's words, but not to change her words."

"So that's what you should do."

"But doesn't editing, by definition, mean changing?"

"Not necessarily."

"I guess my question is, how far am I supposed to go? I mean, is it supposed to be my writing or Bronnie's? Because on the last blog entry, Bronnie only wrote about four sentences, so am I supposed to expand on that or leave it as is?"

"I think," said Bella, "that you are supposed to go as far as Mr. Bolt told you to go and no farther."

"Well, my interpretation is that Mr. Bolt wants plausible deniability. I'm supposed to write the blog, but he doesn't want to have told me to write it."

"I'm not sure where you're getting that from."

"From Mr. Bolt."

"Mr. Bolt didn't mention plausible deniability, did he?"

"But," Lillian said, "the whole point of plausible deniability is you don't mention that you're doing it." There was a long pause. "Isn't it?"

Bella raised her eyebrows, and Elvis ticked on for a good ten seconds. Lillian was confused. It was clear that Bella was not stupid. So did she believe what she was saying? Was she a true believer in Mr. Bolt's infallibility? Or was she also aiming for plausible deniability?

Then Bella broke the silence by blurting out, "Can I ask you a personal question? Do you drink?"

Lillian hesitated, uncertain. "Um—I have, on occasion…"

"Because there's a bar with great mojitos on 9th Avenue. Maybe we can talk a bit more freely there."

"Thank Christ."

Downstairs, on their way out the door, a security guard with a cut on his eye stopped them.

"Hey, Bella," Paolo said. "I made two thousand dollars last weekend."

"Good for you," Bella said, without expression, and continued on her way.

Bella was the soul of discretion when under the influence of two mojitos, but that night she drank four.

Halfway through the third one, Bella was admitting to having a personal life.

"I guess I was always bound to end up at a job like this," she said, pulling a lime out of the top of her glass and contemplatively chewing on it. "I went to a good college, I went to Princeton, actually, but I didn't really know what I was doing there. I—for a while I was like you. I wanted to be a writer. But I don't know if I really have anything to write about, so—here I am. It pays for my house."

"You have a house?"

"Out in Hoboken. Just a little place, a condo. But it's nice. Nice street. Hoboken is nice, you know."

"I've heard that."

"And it's right on the PATH train. Twenty minutes to Thirty-fourth Street. I guess the idea is that if I ever met a guy, then we could start life together on the right foot, you know? If I keep at it, I'll pay off my mortgage by the time I'm thirty-five, and then I could stay home with the kids, if I had any. I don't know. I used to be married. Pointer is actually *his* last name. He was an artist. I supported him for a while. Then he left me for another artist."

Lillian said, "I have so much student loan debt that I'd feel bad getting married. How could I explain to some guy that I'd be putting eight hundred dollars a month toward my student loans?"

"That's not even that bad," Bella said. "There are people who could cover that for you."

"But how could I ask someone to cover it? What if I had kids or whatever? I'd be a burden."

"No. Don't think of it like that. It's just money. I mean, my brother owes me forty thousand dollars. And I don't even care, you know. I love him. But now every time he sees me, that's all we talk about."

The waiter came by. "Another round?"

"Oh, what the hell," said Bella. "I'm going to take a taxi home at this point, anyway."

"So what's your brother do?"

"He's got a teaching job down in Jersey. At least, that's what he said. I don't know. I don't trust him anymore. He's got a gambling addiction. Anyway, it's just—I don't really get along with my parents, so he's my whole family. And now there's this thing between us, and I hate it. I should never have given him the money."

"What if you said you'd forget about it?"

"I tried. That's the thing about forty thousand dollars, though. You can't forget it. He thinks it makes him a failure. And then he's obsessed with being some kind of huge overnight success. It's the overnight part that's the problem. You know—I mean I look at Henry Bolt. At least he worked his way up. He didn't take any handouts."

"That we know of."

Bella shook her head. "Trust me. He's a workaholic. He wouldn't have had time. It's funny. People are always complimenting CEOs, you know. They say, 'He deserves all the money he gets. He works so hard.' But I don't think Henry could not work hard, you know? I think he secretly hates being with his family. He loves them, I mean he loves them as people, but he hates being with them. Even when he schedules a day with them, he can't do it. He literally can't do it for more than an hour or two before he's back to answering emails."

"It's probably the one part of his life where he feels like he's not a success."

"Or doesn't have complete control."

The waiter arrived with the next round, and now it was Lillian's turn to level with her new friend.

"So you have to tell me how to write this thing. My income for the summer depends on it."

"Just do what Mr. Bolt told you. Make it read better," Bella said.

"But why does he even want me to write it? I mean, for God's sake. It's his wife. And she's talking about what a shitty husband he is. Doesn't that bother him?"

"You don't know much about rich people," Bella said. "Henry doesn't care what's in the blog, as long as it doesn't hurt his business. She could be writing about what a small dick he has. He doesn't care. It keeps her entertained. The important thing to rich people is not what their wives and kids are doing—it's that their wives and kids do it better than anybody else. That's what annoys Henry. Not that she blogs, but that she's bad at it. That's the embarrassment."

"I guess I'm feeling it's a little unethical, too. Not telling her, and writing under her name."

"Ethical. Right. The Bolts? You should see some of the stuff Henry's written to Fortuna."

101

"Fortuna? I thought he wasn't in contact with Fortuna."

"What do you think?" said Bella. "Do you really think he wasn't going to grease the wheels a little for Cal?"

"But he told Cal he wouldn't help him get in."

"Oh, he says that. Just to keep Cal from slacking off."

"Oh." Lillian stared into her Stella Artois. "So how much is he offering them?"

Bella pulled up her BlackBerry. "This is strictly confidential."

"Don't worry. What am I going to do? It's not like I'm going to tell the media. I'd get fired."

"And sued," Bella added. Then Bella glanced around the bar and slid the BlackBerry to Lillian, who read the following words:

Dear Penny,

Thank you for your letter. I can confirm a commitment of one hundred and fifty million dollars, given anonymously in three separate donations of fifty million dollars each over the next three years, with the first one on January 1, 2009 and the others following subsequently in January of 2010 and 2011.

You asked if there was anything you can do for me. In response, I would like to say that there may be some time, at some point in the future, when I ask you to do something for me. I may or may not make this request, but I hope you will be open to assisting me if I do so. I say this without having anything particular in mind.

Regards,
Henry Bolt

Lillian looked up at Bella. "There may be a time, sometime in the future... That's like the opening to *The Godfather*."

Bella smiled. "So don't be too worried about Cal's SAT scores."

"Oh, he did great," said Lillian.

"Well, cheers."

Paolo had watched *Goodfellas* fourteen and a half times since he first saw it at age eleven at his cousin Ricky's house. It was his favorite movie, and he had taken a number of valuable lessons from it, including the way to woo a woman. If you wanted a woman to like you, then you had to show her that you had cash and influence to burn, that you were in charge, that you could open doors.

Knowing this, Paolo had come up with a plan for attracting Bella's affections, and he had been waiting for the perfect time to put it into action. He had a friend named Alfie who worked as a dishwasher at the famous Mario Batali restaurant, Babbo, in the Village. Babbo was located in a small townhouse, so Paolo had gone with Alfie one night to scope out the back entrance, and if everything worked to plan, he was going to be able to lead Bella there, walk her through the back entrance, and seat her at a perfect little table in the corner that Alfie had promised would materialize out of nowhere.

Knowing that Alfie was at work on this particular evening, Paolo had obtained his coworker Marcus's permission to leave early and then followed Bella out the door, so that when she was done with the redheaded girl, he would be there to greet her, to hail her a taxi, offer to take her to dinner, and sweep her off her feet. After ascertaining her location at a nearby bar, he returned to work, changed out of his uniform into something more classy—black leather jacket, good shoes—and then returned to find (to his great relief) that she was still there.

Paolo took a seat by the door where he spent the next two hours consuming four beers and considering whether he should interrupt her conversation, but he didn't. At last, both young women got up, and Paolo followed them out onto the curb, where the redhead waved goodbye and turned a corner towards the subway as Bella attempted to hail a taxi. Paolo smiled at Bella, but she looked at him without recognition and then started to walk in the other direction.

He followed her. It did not escape Paolo's notice that Bella was something less than sober, but this might work in his favor. At least she hadn't eaten yet.

"Hey, Bella!"

She turned.

"It's me, Paolo. I work security at Bolt."

"Oh! Hi!"

"Hey, listen, I never got to talk to you much, but—"

Bella nodded, waving a hand at a passing taxi.

"You want me to get a taxi? I could do that for you…"

Paolo raised his arm and a black Lincoln Town Car stopped. Paolo held the door open for her.

"Let me see you home."

"Oh, no…" she began.

"It's fine. We'll split it. My treat."

"But I'm going to Hoboken."

"Well, he can drop me off in the Village first. Come on."

"Oh, no, that's okay."

"Come on. I'll be insulted. Come on, please. I had a question for you, if you don't mind." He held open the door until she wobbled in.

Directing the car to the Village had been a bit of a ruse. Paolo lived in Flushing, but he gave the driver the address of Babbo's back door.

"So how you been? How's work been?" he asked Bella, who now had a hand pressed against her forehead and her eyes fixed on the handle of her door.

"Oh, okay…"

"Mr. Bolt been keeping you busy?"

"Yes. You know. He works hard."

So far so good. Paolo explained that he knew exactly how hard she worked. He could tell her, to the exact minute, what time she had entered and left the building for the previous week, which seemed to impress her less than he had hoped.

"Maybe I should get out here…" she began.

104

"No, we're almost there. Are you hungry? You look hungry. You didn't eat anything at the bar, I saw you."

"You saw me?"

The cab pulled up to the alley and Bella edged her way out. Paolo followed her out the door.

"Come here," he said. "I want to show you something behind this building."

"What?"

"Right back here. Come on. It's great. I got it all set up for you."

Bella viewed the back alley with suspicion.

"Look, you're hungry? There's something to eat back there."

"Back there?"

"Yeah! There's a restaurant back there, okay? A really nice one. I want to take you out to eat."

"Oh, no, that's okay. Thank you."

"Can I just show you? Why can't I show you? Come on!"

Bella flashed a weak smile and stepped to the corner to hail another cab.

"Just look at this, okay! Right here! Look! Come with me! Come on!"

"What?" she asked, backing away.

Frustrated, Paolo took her arm and tried to steer her toward the alley. But now she was struggling in his arms, her eyes growing wider.

"What? What do you want to show me?"

What, indeed? He let go of her arm and stood there, hesitating, then figured that if nothing else would work...

"You want to see something cool first?"

He pulled up his shirt to show her his scar. But before he could finish untucking his dress shirt, Bella screamed, pulled away, and was running as fast as she could toward Washington Square Park.

"Hey, wait! Bella! What? What happened, what's wrong?" He started to run after her, then stopped, confused.

"Bella!"

It took Paolo a full block of walking to work out what had gone wrong with his plan, and why he was now unlikely to woo Bella into his arms.

"Oh, shit."

14

JULIE WAS SUPPOSED TO HAVE EVERY OTHER SUNDAY OFF between ten a.m. and eight p.m., but she never got out the door before 11:45 at the earliest. Bronnie always had plenty of detailed questions about Amy's day that she never remembered to ask until Julie had her pocketbook on her shoulder. Those questions somehow always transformed into the weekly meeting between Bronnie and Julie, covering topics ranging from Amy's diet to Cal's college plans to Amy's possible need for anxiety medication. Usually Julie didn't mind and would sit with Bronnie for a cup of tea, lingering until one or two p.m., talking about the family, about Bronnie's writing goals, about Amy's sleeping habits. But today Julie felt more restless than usual. Her nodding grew more reflexive, and her sympathetic look grew blank.

"But I'm keeping you," Bronnie finally said, with just a hint of venom. "That much is obvious."

Julie dropped her head. "I'm sorry, I just—I had plans. I had a date."

She was lying, but the intrigue of a date was enough to get Bronnie excited. "Oh, please! Go! You have to tell me all about it!"

"I will, I promise," Julie said, cursing herself for lying, unsure why she had done so. She swung open the front door and stepped into the elevator lobby. Maybe she hadn't lied. Maybe she had a date, or would have, by the time she returned.

It was only eleven blocks to Peter Wicka's apartment building, but it caused her an eternity of embarrassment, as did the ten minutes when she stood outside his lobby, in plain view of the doorman, deciding whether to go in. If Peter wasn't home, if his parents opened the door to her, if they told the Bolts about her visit…but she had a simple idea, at last, and walked up to the doorman who had just finished helping unpack an SUV.

"Do you know, do you happen to, if Peter Wicka is around today?"

The doorman smiled. "I think so. Would you like to have someone check at the desk?"

"I just—well, let me just…" Julie trailed inside to the second doorman who was manning a vast buzzer system with glittering brass hardware from the 1930s. "Hi," she said. "I wanted to see if Peter Wicka is around. But he's not expecting me. And can you—not tell his parents? Just tell Peter that Julie is here?"

The doorman smiled as he dialed up to the ninth floor. Peter came down a few minutes later, his ensemble making it clear that he had thrown on the first available T-shirt and slicked down his hair with water.

"Julie," he said. "Hi. What can I do for you?"

"Can I talk to you?" she asked. "Just for a minute."

Peter smiled, relishing the moment. "Of course," he said, trying to lower the pitch of his voice to a manly growl, as if women came to him all the time with that request. A few minutes later, they were sitting together behind Cleopatra's Needle in Central Park, a few feet from an earnest busker singing John Mayer songs on a guitar.

"A business proposition?"

"Sort of. I mean, I know you and Cal wanted to go into film together. Into filmmaking. Into the film industry."

"Yes, that's our current raison d'être."

"Excellent. Because my dad runs a big church upstate, I don't know if you knew that. He has his own cable access show."

"I would like to have the pleasure of viewing that sometime."

Julie was delighted. "Right. But the thing is, they have a really big budget, because they have like four thousand members, and even more people watching on television, and my dad has been saying that they'd like to start making videos. Christian-themed films. And I just thought, you know, maybe you guys would want to do that. Just for money and—and practice

108

and all. And maybe, I mean, I don't know what the movie you're planning to make is about, but maybe my dad would pay for it, if it—if you could make it have a Christian angle."

"Intriguing." Peter stood up and pulled a hand-rolled cigarette out of a tiny silver case. "I don't know if you know what our film is about…"

"No."

"Because it doesn't exactly qualify as Christian."

"But could it? With some changes?"

"Julie, let me tell you…" He sighed and lit the cigarette. "We're hoping to get our financing from Mr. Bolt, but I don't know if he'll go for it. I don't know if he has the vision."

"What is it about?"

"How Christian are you?" He smiled. "All right, I'm going to give you my elevator pitch." And he proceeded to do so.

To aspiring filmmakers, an "elevator pitch" is the version of the story that you would tell someone in an elevator. Peter's elevator pitch ran for eighteen and a half minutes. It began with the words, "Say you were an artist…" and ended with the words, "like *Bonnie and Clyde*, with a little of *The Matrix* thrown in."

In between, he told Julie the following story…

A young filmmaker has decided that the ultimate work of art would be to make a real snuff film—a film where someone is killed on screen—because audiences are so jaded that nothing else will have an impact anymore. However, he has enough of a conscience that he decides to find someone who already wants to die, so he kidnaps a young woman from the suicide ward of a hospital, where she has attempted to kill herself after her modeling career was derailed because of drug use. While he is holding her captive, they fall in love, and the young woman agrees to be his victim, but by that point he can't bring himself to do it. So the lovers agree instead to find someone who really "deserves" to die and kill that person. They kidnap her former drug dealer, torture, and kill him on camera, but meanwhile a jaded police officer is on their trail (himself with a drug habit). As they flee him and try to finish their movie, their footage gets destroyed when their car explodes. So in the ultimate artistic statement, they decide to arrange to film themselves being shot down by the police and filmed by the eager TV news crews.

Peter peppered this scenario with useful imagery drawn from other films *(Butch Cassidy and the Sundance Kid,* two Jean-Luc Godard films, and Luc Besson's *The Professional)* along with telling Julie exactly which actors he saw in the roles. Anna Paquin should play the addict, unless her unavailability necessitated the use of Olivia Thirlby from *Juno.* The young filmmaker role (which Peter seemed quite attached to) was still up in the air. Maybe a young Vincent Gallo could have done it, but now he didn't know. Maybe James McAvoy. You really needed classical British training to get the depth that the role required.

The police officer was, of course, Steve Buscemi.

Julie struggled during the pitch to figure out exactly what she was supposed to say. Was he looking for feedback? She opted to nod her head, looking fascinated and waiting for it to end.

"Well, that's the short version, anyway," he concluded.

She said, "It's Christian, in a way. I mean, it depends how it's done. It could be about what happens to—you could see it as the punishment of people who put themselves before God."

"Maybe, I guess," said Peter. "But I don't want to compromise it. It's a story about not compromising. I don't know if you got that."

"But you don't think they should actually do that, do you? Kill somebody? Wouldn't that make it—wouldn't we stop sympathizing with them?"

"I don't know. What I do know is that you can't judge art on moral grounds."

"I disagree with that," said Julie. "I really do."

"So you're going to stop liking Herman Melville because he beat his wife? Or Robert Frost? You'll never read Robert Frost again?"

"Well, but—I do believe that God judges us on our kindness to each other."

"I don't believe in God."

"Really? Not at all? But doesn't that make you feel lonely?" At last, Peter saw where his advantage lay.

"Of course it does," he told her. "Terribly lonely." Then he took her fingers in his free hand, feeling the slender bones of her knuckles, and rubbed it for a while, while she drew unsteady breaths, her hope rising and falling with her chest. A thread of his film pitch tugged at him, and he looked away. "I don't know," he said. "Maybe Buscemi is too obvious."

That night, Lillian went to see *Key Largo* with Bryan, who mentioned right before they entered the theater that he had finished her book, rendering her incapable of focusing on *Key Largo*, or anything at all except watching Bryan's face for the next two hours, looking for some hint of what he thought of the book. After the film, they grabbed a cup of coffee on 13th Street and Bryan spent thirty minutes holding a one-sided debate on whether the film was a flawed masterpiece or just flawed before she roused her courage to ask about her novel.

"Oh, yeah," he said, and then drew back. "I think it's good. Really good."

For some reason, this terrified Lillian even more.

"It's just…" He leaned forward. "Here's what I like. You didn't fall for any of that commercial bullshit. There's no plucky, likeable heroine, you know? Or career girls, or villains, or romance, or happy endings, or anything that would make the reader really like these people, you know? They're just—people, the way people really are."

"Which isn't likeable?"

"You get at how flawed people are, which is great."

"Great," said Lillian.

"The other thing I liked was that there was no suspense. There's not like, a kidnapping, or gangsters, or a ticking clock, or a big splashy ending, you know, where everyone shoots it out."

"So it's boring."

111

"But maybe readers need to be bored, you know? Maybe that's what's missing from our lives. I mean, are you telling me Melville was never boring? But that's what made him Melville, you know?"

"Melville was a failure in his own time."

"Which is what made him Melville."

"So…any specific suggestions?"

"Yeah, yeah," he said. "It just needs more of you. Your voice, you know? I wasn't sure what that was, from the book. Like, who you are."

"Okay."

Now it was Lillian's turn to be silent and thoughtful. Bryan broke the silence by saying, "I think you should quit that tutoring job."

"You think that's why I can't write anything good?"

"I didn't say that. Your novel's fine."

Lillian shrugged. "That's nice of you to say."

"Maybe you'll write something totally commercial, and it'll be a huge hit."

"Not that money matters," Lillian said, repeating him.

"Of course it doesn't. It doesn't matter at all. How many truly great artists were successes in their own time?"

"So where do you work again?"

"Oh, nowhere interesting. I just work for the Man."

"I know. You said that. Where is it, though?"

He sighed for a long moment and then said, "I do press releases at a hedge fund. Marketing materials. That kind of thing."

"Which one?"

"Xaverian."

Chris's firm. "Do you like it?"

"It represents everything I despise."

"Oh. Right on, then."

He shot her a look that said that they were probably not going to have a second date, and she was left wondering what the proper reply should have been. Perhaps, "Yes, I hate them, too. I hate them all. I hate them, too, while taking their money."

112

As they walked to the subway, Lillian added, "Thank you for reading my book."

"No problem. Can I be honest, and I don't want to hurt your feelings?"

"Sure."

"It left me a little depressed."

That night, Lillian decided to trash her entire novel (as she'd first written it, from the perspective of the young religious fanatic) and rewrite it from the perspective of the dead baby. The prospect was no less depressing than the original version, but it seemed to offer a new angle. She wrote:

"Last night my uncle prayed to me. He didn't know I was there. He thought he was praying to any angel in heaven for help. I watched him standing, knee deep between the pews like a desperate swimmer drowning in the waves of a wooden ocean, pressing his forehead against his hands, his fists clenched, his whole body shook like The Lovely Bones???????????????"

The last line referred to Lillian's sudden concern that she was co-opting the "dead narrator" approach of the 2002 New York Times bestseller, *The Lovely Bones*.

At this point, Lillian took a break, finished the entirety of a lemonade and gin and went online. She checked her "Sallie Mae" account and her Bolt Loans. Since graduating, she had paid a total of seventeen hundred and forty-two dollars to see her loan principal decrease by six hundred dollars, with the rest going toward interest.

Then she walked over to the computer and wrote the following:

"Henry has been working all night on the [get name of deal from Bella] deal. He claims he has to work harder these days, that the market will get worse before it gets better. So will our marriage, I want to tell him. I lie awake at night, thinking I'd get more loving if I were a stock index. I guess wives of doctors and lawyers have to deal with rejection sometimes—perhaps they worry about it when their husband loses a patient or a court case. But I know my status by listening to the NASDAQ. This just in—Stock

113

Market Widow's chances of getting laid tonight are down thirty points at the noon bell. Here's hoping they make a solid upswing in afternoon trading."

Lillian looked over her writing, made a few small changes here and there to amp up the effect, the humor, to make Bronnie seem witty and self aware with just a hint of melancholy hidden below the surface. Why was Bronnie's blog so much more fun to write than Lillian's book, even though it left her with a queasy sense of personal and ethical failure? It was so much more satisfying to pretend to be rich and miserable than poor and miserable. Then she emailed it to Bella under the subject heading, "Too much?"

15

CHRIS'S AND LILLIAN'S MISSION OF TRACKING WES'S former roommate had been put off twice before it finally took place on a Sunday afternoon in mid-July. First, Chris had flown from London to Miami for a series of meetings with the new office there about their real estate troubles. Then he had to work late two weekends in a row. When he at last showed up at one p.m. on a Sunday, Nadya was still asleep, her companion for the evening having already made his way home after eating the last of their leftover lasagna for breakfast.

"Is Nadya home?" Chris said in a low voice to Lillian as he glanced at the scarves and purse Nadya had left scattered on the sofa the night before.

"She's asleep. Do you want me to wake her?"

"No, let's just go."

For the occasion of his detective adventure, Chris had taken his convertible Mercedes out of the parking garage where the car spent ninety percent of its time for the rate of $485/month.

"It might have been more subtle to hire a town car," he said. "But I always wanted to track someone in a convertible."

"It's a beautiful car."

As they pulled onto North 8th Street, Chris smiled at her.

"All right," Chris said. "I have a theory about you. There are two kinds of people—the kind who love New York and the kind who tolerate it, and I'm guessing you tolerate it. Am I right?"

"You're right."

"Are you one of those Vermont farmhouse people?"

"No, not one of those."

"Well, give it to me. Let's hear it."

"What?"

"If you could live anywhere in the world."

"Paris. Is that too boring?"

"Paris is never boring."

Lillian wondered why he was bothering to talk to her, why they didn't get right onto the subject of Nadya. It was confusing—the feeling that she was being wooed so he could woo her roommate.

"For me, it's Italy," Chris said. "A beach somewhere. With a big pile of novels and a tennis court."

"That sounds nice."

"I'd go swimming, hang out with old Italian men, play bocce."

"Why don't you go?"

"Why don't *you* go?" he countered. "It's hard, right? I mean, I love to sail. I never sail. I'm looking for a place to keep my sailboat, but the only place that makes sense is the Hamptons. And the trouble is, it's the Hamptons, you know?"

"Oh, yeah. I run into the same problem."

Chris let out an easy laugh. "I'm sorry. You know what I mean, though."

"Not exactly."

"I don't want to just—a lot of guys, it's like they live on autopilot, you know? House in the Hamptons, ski trips, you know, it's like you stop living your life and you start just—I should take you sailing sometime. It's great. It's really great, have you been? I used to go all the time at my grandparents' place in Maine when I was a kid."

"Kennebunkport?"

He laughed. "All right, all right. I'm not that rich. Not like some people. I don't know," he said. "How do you talk about stuff like that?"

"I'm sorry."

"Are you really poor? You're not really poor."

"With student loans I'm worth less than nothing. Homeless people don't owe a hundred thousand dollars."

"But they don't have your brain."

116

"An overvalued commodity."

"I thought you made money tutoring."

"But that's not what I got my degree in. I'm supposed to be making my money writing novels about the human experience."

"You could write marketing materials. My firm pays, I don't know, probably seventy grand for someone to do that."

Lillian thought of Bryan, then shrugged. "I guess the point of going into all that debt was so I could make money doing something I liked."

"Yeah, but who does that? Nobody I know. Oprah talks about follow your bliss, or whatever," Chris said. "But I think she means in your spare time, right?"

"Which is why you aren't a detective."

"I'll tell you why I'm not a detective. Have you ever been to the Villa d'Este? It's this hotel in Italy. Twelve hundred a night. But it was like living in heaven. It was like living somewhere that wasn't real. I want to be able to live somewhere like that forever."

"And drop a month's rent per night on a hotel room."

"A really nice hotel room."

Neither of them said anything for a minute. Then they both began to talk at once: "The thing is…" "I'm sorry…"

"You go ahead," said Chris.

"I'm sorry," Lillian said. "I was being rude. I mean, it's your life. And you wanted to talk about Nadya?"

"Yeah, but wait a second. I'm not that bad, am I? I mean, I make, I earn my money by—by using my brain to make other people money. I'm not saying it's fair, but—if you can get paid really well for using your education, then you just…and I went to Harvard, I did really well, I could be doing other—and you end up with no life, you work eighty hours a week. Okay, I'm not saying feel sorry for me, but… it's not like it's a perfect life, that's why they pay so well."

"You don't have to justify yourself."

"Sure I do. It comes with the salary."

"I'm not judging you. I spent two years of grad school working on a book, and I hate it. I don't respect myself for my career choice."

"So do something else."

"I can't."

"Why not?"

"Because I want to finish that book."

"I respect that. Being a writer must be really exciting."

"You know what's exciting? Imagining being a writer. The best part of Fortuna was when I got in. And I thought, Wow. Fortuna. I must be talented. That was as good as it got."

"But you could still make it big. You never know."

As they crossed the bridge, she looked out the window at the harbor, the hazy green Statue of Liberty in the distance, dwarfed by the rising hulk of Wall Street.

"You never know," she repeated, but she was just being polite.

They finally got to their discussion about Nadya while they were parked outside Frank Wheeler's building with the top down and a pair of binoculars on each of their laps.

Chris's job was to look up at the window of the apartment to detect any signs of activity. Lillian's was to watch the front door and make sure Frank didn't sneak out on them. Chris's nephew Wes had provided them with some photos of Frank (though not in disguise) and what floor he was on. They made a promising beginning when Frank appeared for a few moments at the window talking on a cell phone. At least they knew he was in town. Then there was forty minutes of nothing, broken up by Chris's trip to a Starbucks across the street. Armed with an iced latte, Chris began…

"So Nadya."

"Yes."

"Do you know if, um, if she has a boyfriend?"

"No one seriously. I mean…no one she's really into."

118

"Right."

"She likes you."

"She likes me?"

"I think if you asked her out, she'd say yes."

"Oh." Chris nodded. "That's not exactly what I was thinking about. I mean, I was more, I'm a bit worried about her."

"Why?"

"Do you know how much her purse costs?"

"Her purse?"

"That red one. That's a two-thousand-dollar bag."

"How do you know?"

"Because my dad and I bought something like it for my mother once. I'm just wondering how she could afford that."

"Oh. She got it at a sample sale, she told me."

"Well, she also was wearing a coat worth about three thousand dollars. And shoes that are probably worth four hundred. Are these from her parents?"

"No. I don't think so. Her parents lost a lot of money in the real estate crash."

"Then do you know where she got them?"

"What's your point?"

"Just that if she was dating somebody wealthy, it would make sense."

"She's not dating anyone wealthy that I know of."

"I'm just saying that a girl her age, that attractive, suddenly having all this money…"

"She's not a hooker."

"I wouldn't put it that bluntly."

"You don't really think she'd do that."

"She's out late at night, though, right?"

"Yeah, but—if I've seen her hook up with anybody, it's always some slacker who does graphics for *Nylon* Magazine."

"But she's out in the city a lot. She spends the night there?"

"Chris. What an awful thing to say. You're taking this detective thing a little too far."

"I just wondered. I didn't mean to offend you, it's just these things happen."

"I mean, if I had to guess, I'd say she's getting a discount. Or she's putting it all on credit cards."

"Things like that don't get discounted."

"Well, I don't know. Maybe she has a friend who works for *Vogue*."

"I'm sorry I upset you."

"You didn't. Just…"

"What?"

Lillian was silent. She was afraid she had been wrong to stir up Nadya's hopes about Chris, and that made her angry, mostly with herself.

Just then, Frank exited the building. "There," she said. Chris started up the car, ready to follow him, and crawled forward half a block until Frank entered the same Starbucks where he'd just been.

"One of us should go in," Chris said.

"I'll do it." Lillian got out of the car and followed Frank in line.

As the young man ordered, she got a good look at him: slender, blond, sunglasses, with well-defined arms that seemed like the product of consistent effort. He was not, by nature, a muscular guy. More striking than his appearance, however, was his manner. It was something she had seen before in a philosophy major she once knew: a kind of reverse ingratiation, where he displayed such utter disdain for the common run of humanity that he managed to make everyone loathe him as he moved through his day.

When it came time to order, he picked up a CD from the pile on the counter and spoke to it in a long drawling voice.

"Caramel macchiato."

And when the perky cashier told him the price, he flipped over the CD to examine the other side while waving a ten-dollar bill at her with a flick of his wrist.

At the espresso bar, waiting for his drink, he tapped his hand against the counter as if astounded by how long it was taking, then grabbed the cup the moment it was set down and turned in a single bored, fluid motion to find a table.

Once he had seated himself and adjusted his chair, his drink, and his laptop, he heaved a long weary sigh. He shot Lillian a glance as she sat nearby, so she looked out the window.

A few moments later, Chris entered, ordered a drink, and took a seat on the other side of Frank. Frank opened his laptop, and Lillian shuffled a bit trying to see the screen. It appeared he was checking his bank account. Then he checked the Crunch Gym website about classes.

This went on for some time. Chris sat trying to ignore Lillian, and she sat trying to ignore him trying to ignore her. After twenty minutes, they started to get bored.

Chris walked up to her.

"Excuse me, I feel like I've seen you somewhere before," said Chris. Frank looked at the two of them and then back at his laptop.

"Oh, I don't think so," Lillian said. "Where'd you go to high school?"

"Exeter. You?"

"Public school in Maryland."

"Hmmm."

Lillian looked him up and down. "It wasn't—you didn't go to circus school for a summer, did you? Clown training camp?"

"Yeah. You went to clown school, too?"

"Yes, I did," Lillian replied.

"I remember now. You were a sad clown. You had the um— the giant hat with the flowers…"

"And the very small shoes. And you were a hipster clown."

"A hipster?" Chris said with a smile.

"The sort of ska look with the bowler hat?"

"That's right." Chris sat down. They were so involved in their fake conversation that they didn't notice Frank had company until a young man was already seated at Frank's table.

"Hi, you're James?" asked the eager new arrival.

"Yes," Frank replied.

The young man sat across from him swaying in his chair, not meeting Frank's eye. "Yeah, so I just—I know this sounds kind of, but I was just wondering, like, if I do get this job, how soon could I—like, how soon could I get paid?"

Chris and Lillian let their fake conversation taper off so they could listen.

"You need the money right away?" Frank asked, as if barely interested.

"Yeah, really—I mean if possible. I said in my email, and you said it might be…"

"May I ask why?"

"It's nothing bad or anything, it's just that I like, borrowed some money from my parents, without asking, just to cover this purchase, and it turns out they're coming back like tomorrow, so—"

"You can't just put it on credit card?"

"Credit cards take like three days to open the account and my other one is maxed out…"

This answer seemed to please Frank. "I might be able to help you," he said. "What were your SAT scores?"

"…770 reading, 770 writing, 800 math."

"Okay. Well, I'll need you to verify that by taking a test."

"Sure. When?"

"Now. If you have nothing …"—here Frank enjoyed a pause—"…more important to do."

"Sure, yeah… but I—I mean, what is this job again? It didn't say on Craigslist, just that it was for testing? Or something?"

Frank nodded. "Yeah. Something like that."

At that moment, Cal Bolt walked in the door and headed straight for Frank. Or rather, it took a moment for Lillian to realize that it wasn't Cal. Just a boy with the same coloring, the same haircut, almost the same height.

"How'd it go?" said Frank to the Cal lookalike.

The Cal lookalike handed him a sheet of paper, and Frank glanced at it. Frank nodded and handed him an envelope, which the Cal lookalike pocketed. "You want to do this again?" Frank asked the boy who was not Cal.

"Sure, why not?"

"I'll be in touch." And Frank dismissed the not-Cal by returning his gaze to the interviewee.

"I'll tell you what," said Frank. "I can advance you five hundred today. If you do well on the practice test."

"Five hundred?" The young man looked startled.

And then it dawned on Lillian why Cal had been so sure that he had done so well on his SATs. He had not been the one taking them.

Chris drove her back to Brooklyn. He was excited.

"We worked it out. We actually figured it out." Chris grinned.

"It explains the hair and the outfits," Lillian agreed.

"Frank had to pretend to be different students, take their tests for them."

"And he's subcontracting, now, because he doesn't look like everybody."

"We figured it out."

"We did."

"We make a good team."

"We got lucky," Lillian added, distracted, mulling the likelihood of Cal's treachery. She stared out the window as they drove across the Brooklyn Bridge. "People like that are amazing," she said.

"People like what?"

"Frank. People who walk around like everyone is beneath them."

"Half the guys I work with are like that," said Chris.

"Really? They think they're that special?"

"They must be. They went to Yale."

"But that doesn't make them, like, higher beings."

"To some people it does."

"Who?"

123

"The people who hired them."

"Who also went to Ivy League schools."

"But can I tell you something, honestly? We had one guy for a while who went to CUNY at my firm. Bright guy and all, but...You could tell the difference between him and the Ivy League guys. He wasn't as smart."

"So am I a good writer because I went to Fortuna, or did Fortuna accept me because I'm a good writer?"

"Touché. Anyway, you're a great writer."

"You haven't read anything I've written."

"I read your story in *The Antioch Review*."

"From undergrad? How did you find that?"

"It wasn't hard. It was good."

"It was about when my parents died. A lot of it was real."

"I figured."

Chris pulled up in front of Lillian's apartment building a few minutes later, cut the engine, and looked at her. "I didn't want to ask out Nadya."

"I realize that."

"I wanted to ask out you."

Lillian, stunned into silence, traced back in her memory any hints he might have given. It had seemed so remote a possibility that she'd never even considered what she'd say.

As the silence grew longer, Chris nodded.

"Okay."

Lillian said, "No, I'm sorry, I just..."

"You just..."

"I like you."

"But."

How would she tell Nadya?

"You read my story?"

"Yes, and I loved it."

"Okay. Yes. No. I'm worried about Nadya."

"You think she would be jealous? Because she and I never..."

"No, but I just don't know."

124

"That's fine. We'll wait, we'll just um—maybe we can go on a date or two and see what happens before we tell her, you know? Is that okay?"

"Yeah. Yes." Lillian smiled, at last.

"Do you want to go to Per Se or something for dinner? They have a great tasting menu. Or we could go to a show…"

"No."

"No?"

"I'm just so broke."

"My treat, of course."

"I know, but…"

She couldn't help it. She thought of Bryan Ruggiero's claim—that the rich could buy whoever they wanted. She didn't think of Chris like that, but something about going on a date she could never herself afford frightened her.

"What if we say that—that for a first date, we can't spend more than ten dollars."

"Ten dollars."

"Yes. If that's not too crazy."

"Sure. Done."

Lillian smiled.

"So next week, I'll be doing a little traveling for work," he said. "I have to fly to London for another meeting. But maybe in a couple of weeks, we can meet up."

"Yes. Okay."

"Ten dollars. I'll think about it." He leaned over and kissed her cheek, and she got out of the car and walked to the door in a daze.

Nadya had said she didn't like him. And yet never, for one second, had Lillian believed her.

☙

Chris's family had no relationship with the Kennedys. They were new money by New England standards (having arrived from Germany in the early 1890s) and Republican in the old fashioned, fiscally conservative sense. The Schott clan gathered each summer at the end of a long road in Maine, deliberately left unpaved to discourage trespassers, and discussed the progress of their children, the ills of the welfare state, and the folly of high taxes.

But, in one aspect, the Schotts were similar to the Kennedys—they had a family ethos of public service and philanthropy, which by the turn of the twenty-first century was growing less common among the wealthy. The Schotts had without fanfare built a library in their hometown in Maine. They also without fanfare ran a scholarship program that sent two deserving students to Exeter each year. The family had, within its immediate ranks, an Admiral in the Navy, a two-star General in the Army, a state senator in Connecticut, and a Yale philosophy professor who studied ethics. The family motto was: "Be of use."

Chris's attraction to Lillian would have been hard for him to explain, but it had originated the moment she confessed to her grad school debt, her worries about her novel, her fear of not getting published. Moving in the circles he did, drinking on weekends with successful, Type A female lawyers and doctors, it had been some time since he had met anyone to whom he could prove so useful.

16

IT WAS A SATURDAY MORNING, AND KEVIN SAT NEXT TO Paolo in the burgundy Lincoln and delivered his first five words of the day.

"Can you hit a woman?"

Paolo hesitated.

"Yes or no?" Kevin continued. "It's one way or the other. Some guys can, some guys can't."

"No."

"Okay, then. You got to figure out what you're going to take. You're going to take her television, refrigerator, what?"

Paolo looked at the dilapidated house they had pulled up in front of. It seemed remote that there'd be anything worth taking. He thought about it.

"TV?"

"TV. Fine. Let's go."

Kevin got out and started walking toward the house. Paolo understood, for the first time, why when you were acting as muscle, you always went in pairs. If you were by yourself, you'd never be able to go through with it. Most of being a heavy was about showing off for the other heavy. Paolo got out of the car and followed Kevin to the door.

"Knock," said Kevin.

Paolo pounded.

A small blonde woman opened the door. She was perhaps forty, tattooed, and tired. She looked back and forth between the two of them.

"Hi, Marie," said Kevin. "You got that money?"

"No," she said. "And I'm not ever going to have it. Where am I going to get forty thousand dollars?"

"Then we have to take your shit," Kevin said.

"Fine. Be my guest." She stood aside. "Fine. It's fine. Go a-fucking-head. Go ahead, you asshole. Fine. Take my fucking stuff. I don't have anything worth taking anyway."

Paolo stepped into the house with Kevin. Marie's assessment of her possessions was correct. A quick sweep of the room told Paolo that the most valuable object was probably her carton of cigarettes. Still, he had told Kevin he was going to take the TV, and he didn't want to back down.

He walked over and picked up an old Zenith twenty-inch television, and lifted it with effort.

"You fucking asshole. You're a fucking asshole. You know that? You're just taking my fucking TV to be a fucking prick."

"Yeah, I'm a prick," Kevin chirped as Paolo carried the TV out to the car and rested it on the bumper so he could pop the trunk.

"I'm a fucking asshole," Kevin called to her as he followed Paolo out to the car.

A gun was fired, and they whipped their heads around. She was firing a handgun in their general direction, not being very particular about aim.

"Go fast before she decides to shoot the windshield," Kevin said, and Paolo rushed to the front seat and started up the car as Kevin jumped in.

Ten minutes later, they stopped at a Wendy's for a snack. "It's good to know she's got a gun," Kevin said after sipping his milkshake. "Maybe we can get that next time. That's probably worth more than the TV."

"Can I ask you a question?" said Paolo. "What was the point of that? That TV isn't worth twenty-five dollars. She's never going to have the money."

"Yeah, but you never know. Sometimes somebody has family, and they'll call us and say, 'Stop bothering her,' and then we can get something out of them. It's about expanding the number of people involved, that's the trick. Marie's got a couple of teenagers. When they start working, we can go after them too."

"But they're not going to have forty thousand dollars."

"Here's how it works. Marie's husband gets sick. He goes to the hospital, in there for two months, but dies anyway. So she owes thirty thousand dollars and can't pay it. The hospital sends it to a debt collection agency, and by then it's worth forty thousand with late fees and interest and everything. This was maybe three years ago. Well, the collection agency realizes they're not going to get anything out of her because she's unemployed, so they sell the debt to us. But Ivan doesn't pay the forty thousand. He pays maybe five thousand for the right to collect it. So if we get five thousand out of her we break even, maybe ten to cover our time and costs. But we don't tell her that, we say she owes forty."

"And what if she pays it all off?"

"There's interest."

"And if she paid off that? Say she won the lottery…"

"I don't know, I guess we'd stop bothering her. I like Marie, though. Two of my last three girlfriends were girls I collected from."

So, to Kevin, this was romance.

"But the TV?"

"That's just to maintain the threat. Keep on the pressure. So when Marie's daughter gets her first job at Dunkin' Donuts, she'll give the first paycheck to me." Kevin took another sip and added, without looking at Paolo, "How the fuck do you think we get paid, man?"

Their next stop of the day was a strip club called Bare Necessities in Wildwood, New Jersey. Bare Necessities was located in a converted diner, and Paolo and Kevin entered through a front door with the chrome styling of a 1950s Chrysler. It was early in the afternoon and the lunch crowd consisted of four regulars eating wings under glittering disco balls while a single weary dancer in a shimmering purple bikini went through a mechanical grinding routine with her eyes fixed on the horizon.

The front door bouncer nodded at Kevin as they entered. Kevin glanced up at the dancer for a few seconds, as if expecting a nod of recognition that never came, before heading to a door behind the stage. Kevin stepped inside a tiny office and Paolo stood behind him at the door, letting the music of Ace of Bass drift inside the office.

"Shut the door," came a voice from the desk, and Paolo pushed his way in, standing six inches behind Kevin, and closed the door behind him. Half blocked by Kevin's shoulder, Paolo got a view of a man in his fifties with the mottled skin and sickly appearance of someone who was doomed to die of lung cancer.

"Carlene is pregnant," the man said to Kevin, as he started to count out some money from a drawer into an envelope.

"Again? Was she working?"

"Yeah, she says she was working. She's got a boyfriend, though, so who knows. I'm just telling you because Ivan said to tell you."

"Yeah. I'll let him know." Kevin took the money. "So who's on tonight?"

"Tammy. And Amber, maybe. It's been a slow summer," he said. "Economy's going to crash and burn."

"Oh yeah?" said Kevin.

"Oh, yeah. Oh, yeah. You got any money in the stock market?"

"Nope," said Kevin.

The man looked at Paolo. "How about you?" This was by way of introduction—the man had not spoken to Paolo before.

"No, not right now."

"Me either," he said. "I kept meaning to. Now I'm like, shit, I'm glad I didn't." Then to Kevin, "Tell Ivan it's been real slow, that's why we're short."

"How much you short?"

"Two hundred."

"I'll tell him, but he may send me back for the rest."

The man shrugged and lifted the envelope. "He wants me to take it from the girls, I'll take it from the girls."

Kevin took the money and walked back out into the club. This time he stood in front of the dancer and waved his hand from left to right at her approximate eye level until she looked down and nodded, raising the corners of her mouth in a facsimile of a smile.

"This is a good job to meet women," Kevin said. As they walked out to the car, Kevin noticed where a bullet had pinged a small hole in the trunk. He ran his finger over it.

"I want to go back and get that gun," he added.

Kevin dropped off Paolo at his truck, which was parked in front of Ivan's, and gave him instructions for how to complete the last task of the day. Kevin was going to sweep by Marie's to get her firearm and, he hoped, a date, so he wrote down an address for Paolo and then took off in the Lincoln, revving up his engine to full volume as he pulled up to a stoplight.

Paolo sat in his Ford considering Kevin's last words of advice before he departed: "If there's no TV, take some medical shit." He typed the address into his GPS.

Fifteen minutes later, he arrived in Absecon, New Jersey, one of the small, poor towns that ringed Atlantic City like the fallout from a bomb. He pulled into the driveway of a tiny bungalow notable only for the handicapped ramp that covered the front staircase. An attractive African-American woman in her mid-30s stood on the porch watching him approach.

"Can I help you?"

"I'm here from Ivan. Do you have the money?" Paolo felt embarrassed that he had no idea how much she actually owed. But it was standard operating procedure for it not to matter.

"What do you think?"

Paolo hesitated a half second before barreling onto her porch and through her front door. He felt like a jerk, which he knew was a problem. There was, in fact, a TV, and parked in front of it was a boy of about thirteen in a wheelchair, who bore the distinctive body contortions of muscular dystrophy. The boy was watching a minister on some local access TV channel, and he glanced up at Paolo with a look of terror.

131

Paolo realized he could not take the TV. He couldn't bring himself to do it, to shut off the cheerful drone of the minister ("and I tell you folks, it's family, family that's important...") and face the terror in the boy's eyes.

He spun around to face the woman at the door.

"What?"

"The money," he said in a near-whisper. "Give me what you got."

"I need to feed my child. I'm not giving you my money. I'll call the police if you bother me."

"I'll call the police and tell them you owe us money."

Her shoulder bag was in plain view on the table and Paolo walked over, picked it up, and opened her wallet. About fifteen dollars were inside. He glanced at the little boy who was still staring at him. He couldn't bring himself to take the fifteen dollars, either. Not even for show.

"Shit," Paolo said. He put down her bag.

The only obvious piece of medical equipment was the wheelchair.

"Just go," said the woman. Instead, Paolo sat on the sofa near the little boy and put his head in his hands.

"I'm not cut out for this shit," he said.

"Then why are you doing it?" said the woman.

"I am not cut out for this shit."

The boy looked at him. He looked at the boy.

Paolo said, rising, "Just don't tell Ivan that I didn't take anything from you."

"He ain't never going to get that money," said the woman. "I am not going back to stripping. I am done. That is a bad life." Paolo put out his hand.

"What's your name?" he asked.

"You don't know?"

"They didn't tell me."

"They didn't tell you?"

"Forget it." He turned to go.

"Wait a minute," she said. "I'm Vanessa. Who are you?"

132

"Paolo," he said. "I am not cut out for this." He walked to the door, pausing as a voice came from the boy behind him.

"God's going to bless you. God's going to bless you for this."

With the burden of that knowledge, Paolo got in his truck and drove away.

At 5:00 p.m. that night, while Paolo was heading onto the Garden State Parkway, Lillian stood on the corner of Metropolitan Ave and 7th Street in Williamsburg waiting for Chris to arrive by subway. He walked up the steps from behind her and kissed her on the cheek.

Then he held out a ten-dollar bill. "Do you have an unlimited ride subway card?"

"Yes."

"Perfect. Let's go."

The money Chris and Lillian spent that night was as follows:

Subway to downtown Manhattan: Free with Metrocard

Staten Island Ferry: Free

Two hot dogs and hot chocolates on the ferry: $9.50

Concert on Pier 54, New York City: Free

Donation to street musician: $0.50

A view of Manhattan from the river as the last reflection of sunset glazed the windows red and gold: Free*

* $54,321/year average shipping and handling costs.

After the concert, they stood looking out at the water and watching a tourist ferry make one of its endless circuits of Manhattan. Chris leaned forward and kissed her, and they were both happy and giddy. He took her back to her subway stop on the L train, and they stood together in the half-dark. He put his hands in his pockets.

"Do you want to do this again?"

"Sure. Maybe I can treat you. We could raise our limit to twenty dollars."

"You mean, just—never go to a nice restaurant?"

"Just for a while."

"What's really bothering you, Lillian? It's not like all I care about is money."

"I know."

"You know, anyone who goes into my field—you want me to say I'm overpaid, okay, it's true, I know that. I'm not curing cancer, here, okay? But I just—I want to be able to take care of my family. What's wrong with that? And we actually provide a valuable service. We invest in businesses. We help them grow. That's what Wall Street does."

"It didn't sound like what you did was invest in business. It sounds like you sell risk."

"Yeah, but –"

"I'm not judging you."

"Yes, you are."

"I don't mean to."

"You want to judge me, go ahead, judge me. At least tell me what you really think and give me a chance to defend myself."

"You're a brilliant guy."

"I hope I didn't give you that impression."

"You're smart. You're well read, you went to Harvard, and that's all great—it's wonderful. It's just you could be using your talent to—I know I'm selfish, too, writing novels is selfish, I'm not saying I'm a hero—and I work for rich people. I take their money to tutor their kids in SAT and stuff and I'm not saying I'm any better than you. I'm worse."

"But you're saying I should be out curing cancer."

"No. Maybe."

"But the money I make, I could give that away, I could support cancer research…."

"I know." She looked down. "Okay, so defend yourself. I've made my attack. You told me to say what I was thinking so you could defend yourself. So defend yourself, because I like you and I don't want you to—to not have a chance to defend yourself."

He said, "I don't care about money."

She looked skeptical.

134

"I don't. I care about family. I care about responsibility. I don't care about money. If there was—if it was ever a choice between a person, a human being, and a whole pile of money, I'd pick the person every time. Every time."

"And your company does what's good for people, not profits?"

"No, it's a company, that's different. I mean, what do you want me to say? There are some companies out there, they're inefficient, they're badly run, right? Are you saying no company should ever collapse? That no one should ever get fired again? The whole goal is to reward the efficient and punish the inefficient. That's capitalism. And eventually, as society gets more efficient, the wealth spreads to everyone –"

"It trickles down?"

"It does, though. And yeah, when we take over a company or whatever, people get upset. It's not about making people happy, it's about making our economy work. And that's a good thing."

"You say that you would always pick a person over money, if there was ever a choice. But you have that choice every day."

"You just think I'm a shallow materialistic asshole?"

"No, I think you're a really nice guy."

"Right. Okay, great." He nodded and said, "Goodbye, then."

"Goodbye," she said. He walked away, and she felt guilty. Maybe she was afraid to admit that she might just be afraid of money, of the way it would allow her (if she ever married Chris) to do nothing and be nothing of her own, to write nothing, to live off him, to turn into a fancy runner in Central Park, a Bronnie Bolt, who had somebody else to write her blogs. That would be death as an artist, even if she wasn't much of an artist.

Lillian spent the next hour working on her book while Chris sat on the subway going home. He'd had enough money for a cab, he'd always had more than those ten dollars with him, but he didn't want to take a cab. He was angry with Lillian, for a subway stop or two, and then as he entered Manhattan he just felt depressed.

How did all those companies cure cancer, anyway? Capitalism. Money. It had to come from somewhere. How did all those doctors get their medical schools built, their research paid for? Money from rich people, money from investors. Everything good that America had ever invented had required someone to invest in it at some point, right? And anyway, wasn't taking care of your family a good enough justification for your life? What was wrong with wanting to take care of your family—even if you didn't have a family to take care of, yet?

17

I call him a good provider. To my friends, I mean. I say he's hard-working and smart and he's a good provider. And they all know that means he's rich. That's the code all of us finance wives use when we're miserable. It's secret code for "he loves his work more than me." And we have to use code, because we know the rest of the world wouldn't pity us, not when our husbands bring home over a million dollars a year. Even to each other, we can't say the truth. But a friend smirks at me one day over lunch when I try to defend my husband yet again for another week of missed dinners, another forgotten anniversary.

"A good provider, yeah, so's mine," she says. "So who's providing you with Zoloft these days?"

The Stock Market Widow, July 21, 2008

www.stockmarketwidow.com

THE BOLT CORPORATION'S SUMMER PARTY WAS THE pinnacle of the year for the Employee Retention department. Every year in late July, 2,445 employees ate catered burgers and wings under big white tents and listened to remarks from the owner and founder of the company, his image projected on large screens.

This year, a special tent had been added for only the top executives, and it was from this location that Henry Bolt would give his speech. By 6:30 p.m., there was a tent, on the waterfront just south of the Brooklyn Bridge, where no occupant had cleared less than ten million dollars in 2008 (with the exception of Bella Pointer, who in a sundress was fussing over the microphone). The atmosphere was optimistic, the conversation loud, the barbecue shipped in from Kansas City.

Henry arrived at 6:48 p.m. He didn't eat barbecued meats and had spent the afternoon at home working on his speech, while he ate a tofu salad and then ran six miles on a treadmill. Bella met him at the curb and walked him to the appropriate tent, where he shook some hands and then stood behind the podium, hoping to avoid the demands of socializing.

At 7:01 p.m., he stepped to the podium and gave the following speech...

"Ladies and gentlemen,

"It is, as always, a pleasure to be here. This July, as many of you know, marks the twenty-fifth anniversary of the founding of Bolt Bank, and I can say with confidence that the success of this firm has been grounded firmly in our remarkable team of talented employees, so thank you. [Wait for applause.]

"On our twenty-fifth anniversary, it seems appropriate for me to remark upon the founding of Bolt. This is particularly apt given the current condition of the housing market. We have seen a difficult quarter, particularly in our real estate and mortgage department, and some people might be concerned that this is likely to hurt Bolt Corporation. I can assure you that we anticipate the growth of the firm in the coming months, as the stock market recovers from the minor downturn caused primarily by the subprime lending crisis. We have just renewed our relationship with Lehman Brothers, and I am confident that we will see continued growth in the coming year.

"I know this because I know what our company is built on. Bolt was founded on the highest ethical standards. We have never taken inappropriate risks. We educated ourselves in how to judge the market wisely and soberly, and it has been this sobriety that has allowed us to weather the upturns and downturns in the economy for the last quarter century.

"When we consider the origin of the current crisis, it becomes clear that the banking system is not to blame. The problem is with people who borrowed money, more money than they could afford.

"And now they find themselves in trouble. These individuals now find that, with the current interest rate adjustments, they have mortgages they can't afford to pay. But a debt is a promise.

We, the Bolt Corporation, make good on our promises to our clients. And we must expect our customers to do the same. We must continue to do what is right, ladies and gentlemen, because an economy cannot survive without men and women willing to stand by their promises.

"I ask you to maintain the high standards that have made this company great. Your success is deserved. Your success, our success, is the result of effort, not luck. I applaud that effort and thank you all for making this company everything it is today. Thank you all very much. And now, enjoy your barbecue." [Wait for applause.]

And sure enough, everyone applauded, and Bella led Henry towards his reserved seat at the closest table. But before Henry had taken ten steps, a young man approached him.

"Mr. Bolt, excuse me, I'm Clyde Upson, I'm going to make a presentation later and I was wondering if you could just answer a question for me to clarify, since I'm doing a presentation on the history of the Bolt Corporation?"

"I'm sorry?"

Bella looked at the young man, exasperated. "No one else can answer this?"

"No one, I tried. I asked everyone. They said nobody would know the answer but you, Mr. Bolt."

"Go ahead," said Henry.

"I'm supposed to give a presentation in a few minutes on the history of the Bolt Corporation."

"You said."

"And I was looking into some of the figures from your year with Wally's Donuts. I dug them out of storage. They were in a storage unit in New Jersey, but I didn't mind digging them out because I find this whole thing fascinating, I'm like a big fan of yours, and the company, I mean."

"I see."

"Can you just look at this document, because it looks to me, I mean, I don't like to put it like this, but it looks to me like some of the money…well, it's confusing."

Henry looked at Clyde, waiting. "I don't understand the question."

"It says on the documents that you borrowed money from Citibank, but no one there has a record of it. I know this because I was hoping to find out who—who gave you the money to get off the ground, right? And anyway my first thought was that it looks an awful lot like—I mean, I just thought it was funny how much it all looked like money laundering...To someone who didn't know..."

"Clyde, you said your name was?"

"Clyde Upson. I work in accounts, new accounts, I work in new accounts..."

"I would prefer that you not make that speech today."

"Of course, but..."

"Thank you."

Henry proceeded to his seat. Within five minutes, he was laughing with Carver Braydon and agreeing to try a pork rib. Clyde stood for a moment at the edge of the executive tent, dejected.

Bella walked over to him. "Will there be anything else?"

"Is he mad at me?"

Bella offered a polite smile. "He doesn't get mad."

"I shouldn't have said that. That was stupid."

"Do you need anything else?"

"No. Sorry. I just—he's my hero. I didn't mean to insult him."

"You can have a seat, now, Clyde."

Bella kept smiling until Clyde took the hint and walked back to his own tent.

"How did it go?" asked Eduardo. "Did you get that word you wanted with the big man?"

"Not really," said Clyde. And for the first time since he'd taken a job there, Clyde spent the next two hours in total silence.

18

LILLIAN HAD BEEN WAITING TO TALK TO CAL ABOUT HIS suspicious SAT scores until she saw him in person, when she came over to give Amy a writing lesson. But Amy's writing lessons were postponed for almost two weeks for the following reasons (in sequence): Amy was too tired, was too stressed-out from a French lesson, had a bad cold, had a playdate with a friend who was visiting from Florida...but Amy was really, really excited about writing....

At last, Lillian had a confirmed writing session at the Bolt residence, so she knocked on Nadya's door to strategize about talking to Cal.

"Is this going to get me fired?"

"Why would it get you fired?"

"They thought his SAT scores were so great. But they weren't his scores."

"You are kind of opening a can of worms. Do you mind if I smoke?"

Lillian had been living with Nadya long enough to know that this particular question meant marijuana, and she reflected on the idea of opening a can of worms as she watched Nadya opening her carved wooden stash box.

"Well, if I get fired, you can always cover our rent, right?" Lillian said in a lighthearted manner, watching for Nadya's reaction. "We can always rely on your job, right?"

"Right," said Nadya, as if she didn't care.

"To cover August rent?" Lillian pursued, continuing to joke. "We'll both just live off you."

"I have August rent, if that's what you're worried about." Nadya looked irritated as she inspected a pre-rolled joint.

"I just wanted to make sure. You said that your parents couldn't help, and…"

"It's fine. Everything's fine." Nadya lit up with care. "Don't worry about that."

"But are you sure you can afford all those handbags? And redecorating our place?"

"What handbags?"

"The new…"

"Jesus. I only have two. And I put them on a credit card. It's not like I have hundreds of bags."

"I know. It's me, not you," Lillian said. "It's just me worrying. You know me."

"That's why you can't finish your book. You get tripped up on the little bullshit stuff." Nadya took a drag of the joint. "It's not a big deal. Everybody has credit card debt. I'll just marry someone rich and then pay it all off."

"You don't believe in marriage."

"I'll pay it off when I sell my book, then."

"How much do you owe?"

"How much do we owe for student loans? It's all one big number. Who cares, what difference does it make at this point?"

"You could get a corporate job. Technical writing."

"God, what do you think I am? I couldn't handle that, and you know that. Anyway, I have to get ready, I'm going out." Nadya got up and started to put on makeup, but Lillian waited.

"How much?" Lillian asked.

"I don't know," Nadya said in a quiet voice. "Like fifteen thousand dollars."

"Like fifteen thousand dollars?"

"I don't know. My monthly payments are more than our rent. My rent. My half of the rent."

"Jesus. Nadya."

"It's fine, okay? I'll put August rent on my credit card."

"That's nuts."

"I've done it before. I just—I entered grad school with some debt. And I thought I'd be earning more than this, but I'm not, so I just have to add more debt, which sucks, but whatever."

"You have to get a better-paying job."

"I can't."

"Why not?"

"Because…because I would shoot myself. Okay? I would die. I would kill myself, okay?"

"Okay."

"I mean, I can't do that kind of job. I've tried. The whole point of going into all that debt in the first place was so I wouldn't have a job that I hate, right?"

"I know, but you have to…"

"I fucked up a little, okay, but it's going to be fine."

"Oh, honey."

"Don't feel sorry for me," Nadya said. "I'm going out. I'm going to drink a Manhattan and enjoy my evening."

Lillian got up. "Okay, well, have a good time."

"If I were you," Nadya called into the living room as Lillian put on her raincoat, "I'd let sleeping dogs lie about those SAT scores. It's not going to do anything but stir up trouble. For all you know, his parents paid for it."

Lillian wasn't sure why she cared. Maybe it was writing Bronnie's blog for her, and the queasy experience of writing something and having someone else get the credit, the queasy sense of helping a billionaire's son on his SATs in the first place. Somewhere along the line, her moral bearings had drifted in the direction of those of her employers. "Someday, at some point in the future, I may ask you for something," as Henry Bolt had said in his letter to Fortuna.

But she did care. She didn't like to see Cal get corrupted by money, even if he was content to get corrupted. He should believe in himself. He was smart. It was all so unnecessary. He would have done fine on the SATs. Very well, in fact. Even if he didn't break 2300.

To Lillian's surprise, Amy seemed excited about her creative writing lesson. She danced on one foot in the kitchen while Julie collected some thick lined sheets of paper to take into Amy's bedroom for their writing session.

"I've brought pictures that you can write a story about," Lillian said, holding up a Ziploc bag, and Amy said, "Yay! Pictures!" Amy's joy seemed out of scale with Lillian's small bag of photographs, and Lillian wondered if Amy had spent her childhood trying to please and flatter the various nannies and tutors who whirled in and out of her life. Then Amy hugged her arm, and hugged Julie, and asked if Julie could join them. Before Lillian could reply, Julie declined, saying she had to answer emails from Amy's teachers, and soon afterwards they were settled in Amy's room, where a flat-screen monitor hovered over her white painted desk. Lillian took out some pencils and paper, and they began to sort through the photos. This was an old trick—one of her professors had done it in grad school. Photos were supposed to help a writer loosen up, play around.

Amy selected a photo of a little boy sitting on a fence looking out at a horse, and handed it to Lillian.

"This one."

"Great. So tell me what you think this story is about."

"You go first," Amy said.

"No. It's your story."

"Just give me the first line."

"No. It's your story. What do you think is happening here? Is that the boy's horse? Or does he want the horse? Or is he afraid of the horse?"

"He's at a ranch in Argentina where he's getting horseback riding lessons."

"Argentina. Excellent."

"And that's going to be his horse because his daddy's going to buy it for him."

"Okay. Great. So how should we start the story?"

144

"I don't know. You start it. You write the first line," Amy said.

"But it's your story."

"You start it."

"But it's your story," Lillian persisted.

"Just give me the first line. Please? Please?"

"Once upon a time…" Lillian prompted, giving Amy the pencil.

Amy handed the pencil back to Lillian, leaning her little head against Lillian's arm. "Can you write it down? I'm tired. If I say what to write down, can you write it down for me? Please? I'm really tired."

"No, Amy. It's your story."

"Please? Please? I'm too tired to write."

Lillian's resolve to confront Cal suddenly grew stronger. She was not going to write this little girl's goddamn story for her. She handed the pencil back to Amy, forcing her little fingers around it.

"Amy," she said, a hint of menace in her eye, "nobody…is ever…*that* tired."

Amy looked back at her with an equal malice, and started to write.

When she knocked, Cal was in his room playing World of Warcraft on his computer. He looked up, nodded recognition, then turned back to the game. She took a deep breath, and then closed the door behind her.

"What's up?" he said at last, without moving his eyes from the screen.

"I need to talk to you."

"How come?"

"Cal. Shut it down."

He glanced at her. "Uh…" Then he turned back to the computer and continued what he was doing. "Why?"

"You took the SAT in June, right?"

"Yeah." His eyes flickered to her with just a hint of uncertainty.

"I'm a bit concerned. I'd like to know a little more about that."

Cal put the computer into sleep mode and turned. "What do you want to know?"

"What was the hardest question for you, Cal?"

"I don't know. Why?"

"How about the reading passages? Do you remember what any of them were about?"

"Uh…" Cal offered an awkward smile. He seemed amused by his own inability to answer.

"Let's say that I had evidence that you didn't take the SAT." She had his full attention at last.

"Wait, what?"

"Did you take the SAT?"

"Yeah I took the SAT."

"No, you didn't, Cal."

"I did."

"Look at me and say that right into my eyes."

Cal obliged, adding a little bit of insulted protest. Adding a few words about how wounded he was. He wasn't a good liar. He had the will to lie, but he lacked the spirit. A good liar believes what he is saying when he is saying it. Cal thought the words were enough.

"This is so ridiculous," he said, with just the ghost of an uncomfortable smile. "How can you even prove that, even if it was true? And anyway, I did well, so why should you be upset?"

"Because I want you to take the test yourself."

"What does it matter?" Then: "But I did take the test."

"No, I don't think you did."

"What? This is so…I'm going to tell my parents you accused me of this and they're going to be really mad. It's insulting. Seriously." The ghost of a smile, again. He was embarrassed at his own outrage.

"You're a bad liar."

146

"I'm not lying. What if I could prove to you that I took it myself? What if I could take a practice test, and I would score perfectly?"

"Sure. I'd agree to that, if you let me pick the practice test."

He shook his head. "This is so ridiculous. It's so unfair."

She said, "Cal, I'll tell you what. I'm not out to ruin your life. I just want you to take that test fairly, like everybody else. You're smart and I'm sure you'll do well. So here's what we're going to do. You and I are going to go tell your parents the truth. And you're going to cancel those scores. And you're going to take it again."

"You can't force me to."

"No, but I can alert the College Board. And Fortuna. And the police. Because I know who took it for you."

"Who?"

"And it's illegal."

"It is not."

"Let's go. Right now. To your mom."

"What if they don't care? What if my parents are like, whatever?"

"Well, I guess we'll cross that bridge when we come to it."

She stood up.

"Wait a second," Cal said. "I'm about to—my friend Peter and I are about to pitch our film to my dad. And that would—he's never going to give us the money if he thinks that—if he believes you about this, okay? So could you just wait, just a week or two, until we shoot our film?"

"I'm sorry, Cal. I can't."

"No, no, no, no, wait. Wait. Okay? Look, the whole thing was Peter's—Peter really wants to do this film, and we've been working on it a really long time, and my dad—I would never have done anything like that, but Peter—and does it matter? Really? What if I—I one hundred percent promise to tell my parents myself? On my own. Tomorrow night, after the movie pitch, And I tried really hard with the SAT prep, you know I did, it's not like I...I worked on that a lot, right? It's not like I didn't try."

"Then it should be no problem to take the test again."

"What if I paid you?"

She gave him a look. "Cal."

"Okay, sorry. Just give me twenty-four, just give me forty-eight hours, okay? Then I'll tell my dad everything. Please? I will work so hard on the SAT next time. I swear."

Lillian hesitated. She'd never had an instinct for the jugular.

"Forty-eight hours?"

"Just—let me think about how I'm going to tell him. Please? So he doesn't hate me. I'm scared he'll hate me. Please, Lillian. Please. Please. Please just give me a day or two."

"I'll give you forty-eight hours."

"Thank you. Thank you. I just need three days. Okay? Seventy-two hours. Until—maybe until next week, when you come back to meet with Amy, okay? When are you next meeting with her?"

"Tuesday."

"Tuesday. Perfect. I will tell them before Tuesday. I promise. How did you find out about this?"

"Cal, why did you do it? It was so unnecessary. You would have done fine on the SATs."

"I want to go to Fortuna."

"I went to Fortuna," Lillian said. "It doesn't change your life as much as you'd think."

Cal said nothing. She turned to go.

As she was leaving, Bronnie stopped her.

"How did the writing go, with Amy?" Bronnie asked.

"Okay. We started a story. She's going to work on it for next time."

"So do you think she has talent?"

Lillian hesitated. Bronnie never lost the ability to stun her.

"Oh, sure. I mean, all kids are creative, and Amy is—she's really…yeah."

"I think I'm going to have to hire a ghostwriter for my blog, did I tell you this?"

"No."

"It's just been so hard for me, keeping up, putting in the time…"

Lillian had been writing Bronnie's blogs, in their entirety, for two weeks now, so she found it fascinating to hear Bronnie's spin on the situation.

"It's satisfying being a writer, isn't it?" Bronnie said. "Have you read any of my blog?"

"Um—a little bit."

"W-w-w-dot-stock-market-widow-dot-com. I'd love to hear your opinion."

"I'll check it out. Thanks."

As Lillian left the apartment, she reflected that this was a difficult business, trying to be ethical after letting her ethics slip. It was like Nadya with debt. Once you got used to being in debt, then the amount of debt stopped mattering. It was abstract. Just a number. An idea. Like integrity, which also apparently had a dollar value.

19

HENRY BOLT, AMERICAN ENTREPRENEUR, 1955-
Henry Bolt (born 1955) is an American entrepreneur and
the CEO of Bolt Bank, a Fortune 500 Company. After studying economics at Rutgers University and dropping out of an
MBA program, Bolt spent time teaching surfing on Long
Beach Island [citation needed] and running a small donut
business before he came up with the idea for Bolt Bank in
1981 as an alternative credit card company. Bolt Bank started
offering traditional banking services in the late 1980s, and in
1994 Henry Bolt led the way in investing heavily in several
hedge funds, including...

www.wikipedia.org

"YOU SEE WHAT I MEAN?" PENNY DANNER ASKED HER
lunch companion in her friendliest tone. "Did something jump out
at you?"

"I suppose it did," came the mild-mannered reply.

"Doesn't that sound fascinating? A surfing instructor? I
mean, he's not your typical CEO, you know. He came from very
humble roots. Grew up near Newark."

"What struck me," her companion remarked, "was the 'cita-
tion needed.' I don't understand what passes for research these
days. Information on the Internet seems terribly unreliable."

Arthur Randolph was the director of admissions for Fortuna's
undergraduate program and a former professor of philosophy
who specialized in Immanuel Kant and the categorical impera-
tive. He and Penny had lunch once a month and engaged in
good-natured sparring about which applicants ought to be accepted. Dr. Randolph was determined that money should not enter into the decision-making process, so it was Penny's job to

150

sell him on each wealthy applicant for his or her own merits, a task at which she excelled. One applicant was not the child of a senator—she was a budding novelist with the wit of a young Dorothy Parker. Another applicant was not the offspring of two wealthy alumni—no, he was a disabled student who had struggled to overcome his attention deficit disorder and painful wheat allergies in order to succeed at a school named after his great-great grandfather.

Penny spoke about these children as if they were her own, although she had seldom met them. These were students who had needs, who had talents and dreams and goals. And if part of those dreams included going to Fortuna, then what was wrong with that? Wasn't that part of what Fortuna was all about?

Cal Bolt was a particular favorite of hers. She had been tracking his progress since sixth grade, although she'd never seen him in person. She liked the idea of bringing him into the fold of Fortuna. He was a New York City local, after all. He belonged there.

"Cal is such a great kid. I wish you could just meet him. I hope you'll take the time to interview him one-on-one."

"Just because his father is Henry Bolt…"

"It's not about that. If anything, that's a mark against him. I mean, he's struggled so hard to come out from his father's shadow. But that surfing thing. Isn't that just too much?"

"It's colorful."

Every time they met, Dr. Randolph tried in a polite manner to set clear boundaries about what he would and would not consider in his admissions decisions. All the same, he liked Penny, and she liked him, as she liked everybody, wielding her warmth and sincerity, her eyes welling up with passion at the causes she was advancing. It was a fact mentioned by neither of them that she had never lost a single one of her battles with him. Somehow, without quite meaning to, without quite noticing it, he had given in and accepted the students she recommended, every single time.

But something about Henry Bolt's Wikipedia entry seemed to have annoyed him.

"I don't know," he mused. "Things are changing. I don't like this getting all the information off the Internet."

"Well, that's not where I get all my information, Art."

"I don't like Wikipedia. I don't like truth by popular vote."

"I know a great deal about the Bolt family that I got through personal connections and research. Personal connections," she repeated. "That's very important to what I—to what we do. Don't you think?"

"Oh, yes," he said as if by rote.

"Can I tell you something?" she said. "I've actually found a little piece of information that I don't quite know what to do with." Penny hesitated. She mulled over whether this would advance or hurt her cause. It without doubt made Henry Bolt appear more colorful.

"I stumbled across a fact about Henry Bolt that I—well..."

Dr. Randolph wasn't going to prompt her, so she took a moment to twirl her pasta with a fork, then dished.

"It seems he had a son before Cal. A boy. Before he was married. I think the child may have died, but it's not in the record."

"How did you learn this?"

"The hospital. It was—we were talking about his giving pattern, Janine and I—not that he gave back then, this was about twenty-seven years ago, but it popped up."

"I think that may be an invasion of privacy."

"It was entirely accidental. But that would explain why Henry had such a big change of direction at that point in his life, wouldn't it? You lose a child, and everything must change for you."

This was going too far for Dr. Randolph. "I will look at Cal's application on its own merits," he told her.

"Henry Bolt has committed to one hundred and fifty million."

"I asked you never to give me figures."

"I know, and I'm sorry. It's just, it's part of the picture, here, isn't it?"

152

"Let's see how he did on his SATs, and we'll go from there."
Dr. Randolph placed a napkin next to his plate and folded his
fingers together, looking at her.

She smiled. "Absolutely."

According to Eduardo Castro Perez, all the troubles in Iraq
could be explained by a single thing—the lack of the New York
Yankees. In fact, most of the world's problems could be solved
by a wider expansion of baseball.

"It's tribalism," Eduardo explained to Clyde one Friday
morning, as they stood having "Friday donuts" together in the
twenty-fourth floor kitchen of the Bolt Building at 8:14 a.m.
"You got these two tribes in Iraq, the Sunnis and the Shi'ites,
and they're killing each other. Or Kenya. You got the Luos at-
tacking the—the other people. And you got to ask yourself, why
aren't we like that? We got Puerto Ricans, Jews, Christians,
Russians, Koreans, all living next to each other."

"You're saying it's the Yankees."

"It's pro sports, man. All pro sports. What do you think a
sports game is?"

Clyde shrugged. Eduardo was a master of the impossible-to-
answer Socratic question.

"A sports game is when two tribes get together, they put on
their war paint, and they fight a symbolic battle on a battlefield.
And what do they do? They yell, and they shout, and they get
out all of that tribalism. And that is why the United States is able
to survive without more ethnic conflict."

"There's racial tension."

"Not like there would be if we didn't have sports. Pro sports
leagues started in the North, you ever think about that? First big
sports teams were in New York, Boston…And as they spread to
the south, you see the number of lynchings drop. Houston Astros
started in 1962. Texas Rangers in 1961. And what do you get?
Civil Rights Act. 1964. Who passes it? LBJ. A Texan. Because
of baseball. So what we need to do in Iraq is build them more

stadiums, man. Give them their Yankees. The Baghdad Yankees. So they'll identify with their city, not their tribe."

"What if they like soccer better?"

"Shut the hell up. Come on."

Baseball suited Eduardo because he loved statistics. He referred to himself proudly as a "numbers cruncher" for Bolt Bank, and he could tell you the precise foreclosure and loan default rate in every major metropolitan area west of the Mississippi. He also enjoyed keeping track of the cost of the Iraq War.

"They told us it would cost two billion dollars," he'd say. "Wolfowitz goes on CNN. Two billion dollars. So they're off by like, two thousand three hundred percent. And it's the Chinese giving us the money. Yellow man loaning the white man money to bomb the brown man using the black man to fight. And Bolt Bank's the same way. You know we are leveraged in some departments four thousand percent? Four thousand percent."

"What I want to know is when are those Yankee tickets going to be available again?" Clyde replied. He fit, more or less, somewhere between the white man and brown man. His mother was Puerto Rican but she had always spoken to him in English, except when she was cooking or angry.

"Oh, no problem. I used to go out with Angela. She sometimes gets those tickets from her boss."

"If it's not going to bother her."

"No way. She doesn't mind. We're still friends."

Clyde walked to his desk, troubled by the thought of the national debt. It seemed to him that sooner or later it was going to have to be made up for in tax dollars, and that meant people might stop opening new credit card accounts. Or maybe it meant they would open more. He'd have to ask Eduardo about that. He tried to open his email, but it wouldn't open.

"Anyone else can't get on the intranet?"

His coworkers shook their heads.

"Oh, come on," Clyde said, leaning over to reboot his computer. It was his morning to calculate his new accounts, and he

154

wanted to get those figures to his manager right away. They were pretty good.

Senior Account Executive Todd Walsh stepped up behind Clyde's desk.

"Hey, Clyde," he said. "Can you come talk with me?"

It was in his tone. Clyde knew what was coming.

When Eduardo stopped by Clyde's desk at 9:30 a.m., Clyde was already packing up his stuff.

"What's going on, man?"

"I got fired."

"What? What for?"

"I don't know. They said the recession, economy, or something. I don't know. I was laid off."

"But you got the best numbers in your department."

"I know."

"Did you tell him?"

"Yeah."

"You were responsible for ten percent of the new accounts out of eighteen people. That means you're getting like ninety percent more accounts than average."

"Yeah, I know."

"That's messed up."

Clyde shook his head, and they were both silent.

"I don't understand it," Clyde said again, although a new idea was suddenly dawning in his head. A strange idea. Could it have something to do with that conversation with Henry Bolt? That nightmare moment at the quarterly party, when he was asked not to speak? It went against all of what Clyde believed about Bolt Bank, Henry, and the American business model. But ever since then, Clyde had had a strange feeling of impending doom, like a giant wave was about to overtake him.

Eduardo slid two Yankees tickets in front of him.

"Take these," Eduardo said in a quiet voice, and Clyde realized that the free stuff was coming to an end.

20

PETER WICKA WAS WEARING A PAUL SMITH LINEN SPORT
jacket, for the occasion, and a white linen shirt. Cal was wearing
a navy sport jacket, a Dolce & Gabbana shirt his mom had
picked out for him at Bergdorf's and a pair of seven for all man-
kind jeans. He and Peter had decided to meet his father at the office to make the whole affair more official. They arrived on
Henry's floor four minutes early, having waited outside the
building for seven minutes while Peter explained why four minutes early was perfect, that it was all about attitude, that you
needed to look eager but not too eager, that professionalism was
about respect, not just the respect you give them but the respect
they give you. Then Peter stamped out a cigarette and said,
"Okay, fuck it."

On the way up in the elevator, Cal asked, "Are you sleeping
with Julie?" Peter said, "Ask me later."

Their careers were about to begin.

As they got out of the elevator, Peter added, "Short answer.
Yes."

Cal was so impressed that he momentarily forgot what they
were going to ask his father. But that wasn't a problem. It turned
out they had time.

Henry Bolt kept them waiting for fifty-six minutes. He'd been
up at the CNN studios in the Time-Warner Building explaining
on television why the stock market was going to hit an upswing
in November, and when he returned, he was on a cell phone call
that he had Bella transfer to his office phone so he could finish a
discussion with a lobbyist who'd been tracking the Federal Reserve. At close to three o'clock, Bella at last ushered them into
his office with just the hint of a condescending smile.

Henry was at his desk, his computer on, reading an email. Cal (had he thought about it) would have realized that keeping people waiting while Henry read emails was a frequent ploy of his father, a way of establishing who was more important in the relationship. Henry did it to his children all the time. But Cal was too busy being nervous, and Henry's strategy made him more so. Even Peter was awed. After a while, he turned to the boys and smiled with a hint of pride and gestured for them to slide their business plan across the vast desk to him.

He flipped through it for a full minute or two, saying nothing. Then he said, "There's a missing comma on page three. Open your copies."

Cal and Peter opened their copies.

Henry said, "You see how some of your bullet points have a period after them and others don't? That looks unprofessional."

This was not how Peter had envisioned his first pitch. "Mr. Bolt," he said, "I think you're missing the bigger picture here…"

"The small picture is always the big picture," Henry said, looking for more mistakes. "If you're going to send this to Hollywood, you want to get these things right."

"I think people don't notice that kind of thing if they like the story—" Peter started, but Cal knew they were on the wrong track, and he interrupted.

"Dad, if we can just explain the movie to you…"

"How much money have you raised for this already?"

The two boys looked at each other.

"As an investor, you can't expect me to invest in something that nobody else has given any money to."

"Yeah, but, Dad, I mean, if you were the first person to give money, then we could get some from other people."

"Here's the way it works," Henry said. "I am not an expert in film. So I can't assess whether this is a good, moneymaking film or not. That's why your initial funding should be from film people. Send it to Hollywood. Your mother's cousin knows people there. Or people here in New York. Get a response. If they invest…" he looked at the budget now. "You say you need five million. If you can get two million from Hollywood, I'll kick in the last three million, how about that?"

"But what if—what about—" Peter fished for words, "what about investing in it for art's sake? Because you like the script, and you believe in independent film and want to support it?"

"As a hobby?" Henry asked. "Let me ask this. Has anything in my past behavior led you to think I enjoy independent film as a hobby? You are welcome to go out there and research and find people who want to spend their money that way, but if you'd done your research you'd know that I am not one of them."

Cal looked at Peter, hoping Peter would pull a miracle, but Peter seemed nonplussed.

"Does that just about cover it?" said Henry. "Don't be upset, Cal. You just got a commitment for three million dollars. That's pretty good for your first business meeting. If you're smart, that should provide you with leverage to get the rest of the money."

"But we wanted to shoot it this summer."

"Well, that doesn't seem to be a viable plan. Why did you wait until almost August to start your fundraising, then?"

"Because I wanted to show you I did well on my SATs, and then it took a long time for us to schedule a meeting with you…"

"Cal. This is a great start. A great start. You're on your way."

The boys were silent.

"On your way out, tell Bella I'll need ten minutes before my next meeting." Henry Bolt rose and put out his hand, and they both shook it.

The two boys left the office and rode down the elevator together in silence. Then Cal said, "So you're seriously sleeping with her? Since when?"

"That's not important. Here's the important part. Julie's father has a big church Upstate, and they may want to finance our movie. I don't think he's going to give two million, though. Julie said more like a few thousand dollars. But you know what? It's fine. It's good. I could just sell a painting or something if we need more money."

"No, don't," Cal said. "That's the whole thing with my dad. He wants to see that we can raise the money ourselves. So if Julie's dad could seriously pay for it, that'd give us more evidence to show him we're serious for our next film. Like, if we raised the money for this one ourselves…"

"Yeah, exactly. Anyway, this movie is supposed to be made on a budget. That's really what we're going for. We make an awesome first film, we can shop it around Hollywood, maybe next summer, after you graduate, we can make one for five million dollars, like your dad said. So all you need to do is to tell your dad you won't be going with the family to Paris next week, and we'll get the money from Julie's dad and shoot it while your parents are gone."

"Oh, shoot." Cal realized. "My tutor."

"What?"

"She's telling my dad about the SAT soon. Which means they'll never let me stay home from Paris."

"Can't you put her off?"

"I don't think so."

Peter considered. "Well, we'll just have to do something."

21

REASONS WHY THIS FILM WILL MAKE MONEY:

- **Appeals to a young audience.**
- **Controversial enough to gain wide media attention (we expect lots of interviews on major media outlets like the Daily Show and the Colbert Report).**
- **Never been done.**
- **Other similar films like *Pulp Fiction* have been successful.**
- **Has that Je Ne Sais Quoi.**

—Snuff, A Business Proposal,
Peter Wicka and Calvin Bolt

IN THE SUMMER OF 2008, TWENTY-EIGHT PERCENT OF NEW Yorkers were spending at least half their incomes on rent, and two days before he was laid off, Clyde Upson had joined their number, signing a lease on a studio apartment in Nolita that went for $1950/month. For the right to live in those four hundred and fifty square feet, he had paid Robert Blodnieks a broker's fee of close to three thousand dollars.

Now he sat on the floor of the tiny apartment, his eyes fixed on the single set of windows on the far wall through which the afternoon light entered, dimmed by a fire escape, and he wondered what he was going to do. He had nothing here, no stuff yet, nothing but the keys and a cardboard box that contained the contents of his desk at Bolt Corporation. He didn't have the heart to go home and tell his mother.

After releasing a slow sigh, he rose and began to stalk the room. "What are my options? What are my options, here?" He spoke aloud, as he did when nervous or alone. "Okay, okay,

okay. Find another job, that's the first thing. What other job, what am I going to do, here? My figures were good."

One of the strangest things about his "exit interview" only occurred to him now—Todd's insistence on the company confidentiality agreement, their brief discussion about how people could come after him "to the fullest extent of the law" if he discussed any of the Bolt company secrets.

"As if I would," he said. And he sat and thought.

Clyde had always been a good student and an optimist. He had always enjoyed the idea of living in the United States, liked and enjoyed capitalism because to him, capitalism was nothing, if not fair. If you had a good idea, you made it big. You became an entrepreneur. If your idea was not so good, or you ran your company poorly, you went under. Those with the best sales figures got the raises, the bonuses, the promotions. Those with poor sales figures didn't. He had listened without sympathy when his former colleague, Colleen, had complained about sexism in the workplace. It seemed to Clyde that women wanted the workplace to be about relationships. And it wasn't. It was about numbers. Which made it fair. Which was what Clyde liked about it.

"The best numbers in my department..."

It was Henry Bolt. It was the money-laundering implication. It was spite. He'd hurt Mr. Bolt's feelings, even though feelings had no place in business. "No place in business," Clyde muttered. "I never said he was a money launderer. He just—maybe I can apologize. That's what I can do. If I could just tell him he misunderstood..."

Clyde stood in the center of the room, his hands clasped together. It was a habit developed during his mother's late nights working when he was a child, that he unabashedly talked to himself.

"Mr. Bolt," he said aloud. "You totally misunderstood me. I just need—sir, wait, before you get in that car, I just need five minutes of your time. Wait! I am so sorry. I just want to apologize. I've put together a list of my sales numbers..."

161

He looked around the room, confident that at last he knew what to do. He dialed a number on his cell phone.

"Hey, Ma," he said, "Guess what? I got two tickets to tomorrow's Yankees game."

Cal Bolt had asked Lillian to meet him under the huge statue of King Jagiello of Poland in Central Park, and Lillian sat there at 7:49 p.m., poised under the vast crossed swords of the dead Polish king, watching joggers go by in the lazy evening breeze. She had left her computer at home and was trying to enjoy the evening for a change. The air was thick and warm.

Her cell phone rang.

"Hey," Nadya said. "I need to talk to you. Just a hypothetical question."

"Okay."

"How would you feel if I moved out?"

"Moved out?"

"I was just talking to this guy about moving somewhere else, maybe."

"Where?"

"To Europe. I was talking with Colin at Alligator Bar last night, and he's thinking of going back over there, so…"

"When would this be?"

"Right away. But it's just an idea. Would you be okay for August rent?"

"No."

"Well, it was just an idea."

There was a long silence. Then, "The thing is," Nadya began, "that my credit cards won't actually give me any more cash advances, so unless I open another credit card, I don't have the money."

"If you don't have rent, then how can you go to Europe?"

"Colin would pay for my ticket."

"What about your job?"

"What if I find you another roommate, between now and August first? That would work."

"I don't want another roommate. Nadya, how about this? I'm about to get myself fired anyway from this tutoring thing, so… why don't you and I both just find jobs? You know, unsexy, boring, pay-the-rent kind of jobs? If we did it together…"

"I can't."

"Well, just temporarily. Some forty-hour-a-week office thing."

"I'm going to Europe. This is what I need to do. I'm sorry. I'm—I've been blocked up all summer, worrying about my student loans. I haven't been writing."

"You said you weren't thinking about your loans."

"Well I was trying not to, but…I'm sorry, Lillian, okay? I just need to do this for myself. Start writing again. This will get me creatively ready to work again. I'm an artist. I can't wear a suit and answer a phone."

"Oh, yeah, sounds rough."

"No, I mean…See, that's the difference between us. You're strong, and I'm not. You can handle a real job. If I could, I would, but I can't."

"What about your writing jobs?"

"I got fired, okay?"

"From all of them?"

"I'm a fuck-up, okay? Forget it. I'm going to the bar."

"Don't go to the bar. We'll talk when I get home."

"I'm going. I'm meeting Colin."

"Okay, fine. Go to Europe. Fine. Have fun."

"I'm sorry."

"I just—it's rent, you know? I mean, what if I just walked out? What if I just stopped paying the rent and went and lived with—I don't know, some guy in Spain? How would you like it?"

"Maybe you should. Maybe that's what you need. You haven't been doing any writing either."

"Because I've been working!"

"Why don't you just ask Chris for the money? Or were you not going to tell me about that?"

"We broke up."

"You're lying."

"I'm not lying, Nadya, for God's sake…"

Nadya hung up. Lillian looked up to see Cal standing a few feet away.

"Sorry to interrupt," he said. He sat down next to her.

"Cal, what do you want?"

"What if I gave you ten thousand dollars?"

Lillian just looked at him and shook her head.

"I am completely serious. Look."

He opened his messenger bag, showed her a few bills, then closed it.

"You mean," she stammered, "you have ten thou—" She looked around. "You have that in your bag?"

"And I could get more. In a couple of weeks. My friend is going to sell some of his paintings."

"I'm going to tell your parents."

"They already know. They wanted me to pay you."

"Then I'm going to the police."

"No, wait a second. They don't know, okay, but I'll tell them. I'll tell them."

Lillian shook her head and started walking away. Cal caught up with her. "Hey, wait," he said. "I'll tell them tonight. I swear. Just, please, give me three hours. One hour. Half an hour. I'll tell them. I want to tell them. Don't do this. Please wait, Lillian, please wait."

"No, Cal."

"I swear to God. You can come tomorrow and talk to them, just let me tell them."

"Why should I do that?"

"But are you sure you don't want the money? It'd really help you out. You told me you had student loans."

His mention of student loans sent her over the edge. So he thought she could be bought. That was what these people did. They bought everyone. "I'm going to the police. Now."

"No!" he cried, his voice anguished. "No! Please! Give me two hours! I'll have my dad call you! Please? Please? Please. I promise. Please."

He fell on his knees.

"Please? Two hours."

"Two hours," she said, and walked away, leaving him kneeling in front of the statue of the dead king.

For once, a rich kid was going to have to do the hard thing. And she was going home, to the apartment she was going to have to pay for by herself. One hour later, after delays on the L train and the 4-5-6, she at last arrived on her street in Brooklyn, where she stopped for just a moment to look at the sky—far off lightning, the air heavy with humidity starting to turn into droplets of rain. It reminded her of something, of a summer night once when she lay in a car with a high school boyfriend she was terribly in love with. After kissing for hours they stopped and listened to the sound of distant thunder rolling towards them, and she felt as large and important as the sky, her heart as full of mystery as the thunder. She had spent all the years since then searching for something in her adult life that would live up to that moment of portent, and had ended up chasing a dream that now felt empty and narcissistic and had led only to self-pity and debt.

There was a van in front of her house and a nervous young man in a hoodie leaning across the iron fence that separated her building from the street. As she approached, the man turned and she saw that he was wearing a ski mask. He said, "If you scream I'll shoot you."

She noticed a gun in his hand, pointed at her. She stopped walking, confused, part of her brain still walking up to the apartment building and unlocking the door.

Someone came from behind and thrust tape over her mouth and then hands were grabbing her and shoving her into a van.

165

She thought of Nadya, maybe if she kicked hard enough Nadya could see her from the window above, but Nadya had already gone to the bar, and then there was a gun to the side of her face cutting into her temple, and a slender man shoving her to the floor of the van.

"Lie down," he said, waving a gun. His voice sounded polished, intelligent, not particularly thuggish at all. Almost bored. She couldn't respond. Her mouth was covered with duct tape and she lay down.

❧

At exactly nine o'clock, Henry Bolt placed his laptop in his briefcase and walked past his assistant's office to the elevator banks. At 9:04, Bella was on the phone with the residence, telling the housekeeper to start reheating his dinner for a 9:30 arrival. At 9:07, Henry walked toward the town car that had been waiting since 6:40, but a recently fired employee approached him.

"Mr. Bolt. Hey, wait a minute. I just wanted to apologize. Mr. Bolt. Wait a second, please?"

Henry turned to see the young man, and signaled to the security guard to remove him from the grounds. The guard didn't hesitate.

At 9:08 p.m., Henry's town car departed, and at 9:14 p.m., an ambulance was called for Clyde Upson, who had not revived after being knocked down and held to the ground for six minutes by the security guard.

"I didn't do it that hard," said Paolo Cincotti. "He was threatening Mr. Bolt."

Unfortunately for Paolo, one of the first people interviewed by the police about the incident was Bella Pointer, who mentioned that Paolo had been demonstrating strange, violent tendencies and had tried to drag her into a dark alley. Paolo was fired.

22

LILLIAN'S FIRST IMPRESSION OF HER MAKESHIFT PRISON
cell was that she was in a warehouse in New Jersey. She wasn't
sure why she thought she was there. Based on the driving time
from Williamsburg, she could just as easily be in Long Island or
Westchester County, but she thought she'd heard a tunnel, and
anyway, Jersey just felt like Jersey, even from inside a small,
windowless room. She could smell gasoline and hear the rumble
of distant traffic, and the ceiling of her cell was made of greasy,
rain-damaged two-foot square speckled tiles. She might have
been able to escape through the ceiling if she weren't handcuffed
to a heavy metal bed. Or if she didn't have a camera pointed at
her in the corner of the room—a fancy Sony that must have been
installed for the occasion.

The bed made her wonder about rape, and the camera made
her wonder about whom they would contact seeking a ransom,
when there was absolutely no one to pay. If they thought she was
affiliated with the Bolt family, if they had taken her because of
that, they'd be in for a disappointment.

Self-pity is the cheapest indulgence, and for that reason the
most popular. It requires only a small sacrifice of dignity, which
most people are more willing to part with than money. Lillian
sank into a long moment of certainty that she was going to die,
raped, unloved, with no family to care about her and no accomplishments to mark her short time on earth. She had not felt so
lonely since her parents' death, and she wondered whether she
would feel loved again in death. Then she made a note to herself
to write something sometime (assuming she didn't die) about the
aching loneliness of the crime victim.

A moment later, footsteps approached and a man entered the room wearing a ski mask. He dropped a paper plate with two slices of pizza and a can of root beer on the bed next to her, and left.

She stared at it for a moment.

The root beer—the almost embarrassed indifference of her captor—made her think that she might actually make it through this. If she had been given Coke or Pepsi, she would have been certain of impending death, but root beer suggested something human in her adversary. While she ate, she had the following thoughts, in order:

Nadya would call the police.

Maybe someone had seen something in the neighborhood. Someone looking out a window might have gotten the license plate of the van. There would be police looking for her already.

The pizza wasn't too bad.

She was going to be late on her student loan payments this month, and if you missed even one late payment, your interest rate went up. So if nothing else, this kidnapping was costing her thousands of dollars in late fees. Could she talk to Bolt Corporation about her special circumstances?

It didn't matter. Who cares about interest rates?

And then she returned, in self-pity, to the subject of her self-pity. She had spent the last few months obsessing about her student loans, using them as a measure of how much she had failed as a writer. Now she saw how much that had been a manufactured anxiety. Those could have been her last months on earth—and she had been healthy, well-fed, well-educated, young, and capable, living in New York City, and holding down a job that more or less paid her bills. She had, in short, been fine. But she had spent that time wrapping herself in a blanket of misery and writing a depressing book. If the only thing she had to complain about was the lack of a publishing deal, she'd been pretty well off—one hundred thousand dollars in debt notwithstanding.

It occurred to her then that if she managed to survive this experience, she might even be able to get a book deal out of it. If she was kidnapped, and wrote about it, surely that was worth a twenty-five-thousand-dollar advance. If she got raped, that should bring the advance up to fifty. That thought would keep her strong, if she were raped. She could focus on taking notes. "He smelled like garlic pizza." And if she were raped and tortured (assuming, of course, that she survived), she could count on a hundred-thousand-dollar advance—especially if she made the cover of the *New York Post*. Fingers crossed. Perhaps that was the solution to the growing burden of student loans in America—young people should all just work harder to find a quick path to fame. Like almost getting murdered, or appearing on reality TV.

But while clinging to the irony that is the last refuge of a frightened intellectual, she remembered that she had just told Nadya, while they were having their fight, that she wanted to leave, to walk out on her responsibilities and not pay her rent either. And Nadya had dared her to do it.

Nadya wouldn't be calling the police at all.

☙

It is one of the dark truths of families that children are generally destined to be as happy, on average, as their parents are. One sibling or another may beat the curve, but genetics and upbringing make it likely that the nervous parent will have a nervous child, and the upbeat, laidback parent will have a child who floats along the river of life. Even those children who try to avoid their parents' fate—the young painter who avoids the monotony of his father's office job—are likely to discover monotony in painting after painting, and turn to drugs the way their father turned to alcohol.

But in this grim economy of happiness, Clyde Upson had always been an outlier. He was far and away a happier person than his mother had ever been. He had always believed in good luck, in the uphill climb of human history. He had come back in sixth grade after learning about the Middle Ages and told his mother, "They only bathed once a year!" and he had spent the next week looking closely at his toothbrush and Sony Playstation, thrilled at the conveniences of modern life. He liked to imagine, when talking with his mother, what future years would bring them in terms of ease and pleasure, and he'd spent time identifying the chief disadvantages that people might invent a way out of—many of which she didn't have the heart to tell him had already been solved, just not for the poor.

Now Celia Upson sat next to her son's bed at Lenox Hill Hospital in Manhattan, listening to the steady rhythm of his heartbeat on the monitor. The nurse had told her that she could turn down the volume if she wanted, but instead she turned it up, whenever there was no doctor in the room to answer her questions, and she rocked slowly to the beat that told her there was still a rush of platelets coursing through her only child's heart.

He was in a coma. She had watched *Days of Our Lives* and *Guiding Light* for over twenty years, and she knew the soap opera coma well. It lasted a week or two, and then the patient made a complete recovery, just in time to utter a shocking pronouncement to addle the lives of family and friends. In movies, a coma could be shaken off by the words "I love you." But she told Clyde she loved him again and again. She held his hand. She kissed his forehead. She took the business cards and information of the forty-two lawyers who wanted to take her case.

She decided that she wanted to gamble. No more scratch tickets. No more visits to casinos. She wanted to take the big risk.

"Clyde," she whispered, "when we get out of this, I'm going to tell you about your father. Your real father."

"Hello, Celia." She looked up and saw Ivan Bulowski in her doorway, his long scarred face seeming to melt in the long afternoon light from the window. "I wouldn't do that if I were you."

"Then where am I going to get the money for these medical bills, Ivan? How am I supposed to pay for this?"

Ivan said, "I'll give you a few thousand bucks, Celia. But if you say anything to anybody, you'll both end up dead."

Marcus put it like this to Ronelle when she arrived at 6:02 a.m. for what would have been the beginning of Paolo's shift:

"It was that underground wrestling, man. He couldn't let it go."

Ronelle shrugged and pointed out that this was why you needed a union. If the security guards were part of a union, Paolo would not have been fired. "He'd be on leave."

"Union, shit. That guy was tying barbed wire around himself. That stuff will mess with your head."

But Paolo would have disagreed, as he drove down to Atlantic City several hours later. It wasn't the wrestling that had driven him over the edge. When he'd grabbed Clyde, he had been counting the hits.

The secret to succeeding at any job was that you had to like it. And while Paolo wasn't bad at collecting money for Ivan, he didn't really enjoy it, not like Kevin did. He just went through the motions. But if Ivan offered him a full-time job, what was he going to say? How was he going to pay for his apartment, his truck? How could he get any job in the security business again, now that his attack of Clyde Upson had made the second page of the *New York Post* under the headline "Nuts and Bolts"?

"Come on in," said Ivan when he knocked on the door. "Let's discuss your future."

Paolo shuffled into the leather sofa in the corner of Ivan's office. The *Post* was open on Ivan's desk.

"So you're free to work for me full time, is that right?"

"I'm free."

"'Cause I need you to go check in on a woman who's threatened to blackmail a favorite client of mine. I don't want you to speak to her. Not at all. I just want you to scare her. Show her you're watching her. Can you handle that?"

"Sure."

"'Sure,' he says. Here is my problem with you. From my perspective, it goes like this. I give you and Kev a list of places to go, money to collect, you do it. Great. But what I don't know is, if you saw some guy around town, and you knew he owed me money, would you go after him? Would you show initiative?"

"Probably."

"Probably. You got to see people as money, you understand me? Everyone is an income stream. That's what I want you to understand."

"I understand."

"So here's the story. Kevin's been shot in the head. Dead. His own damn fault, some lady he was bothering. But it got the police interested in my operations. They want to know, was he collecting for me, was he violent? I tell them, I never told anyone to be violent. Isn't that right? Isn't that what I said to you?"

"That's right, yeah."

"But to avoid any situations, I've had to take some money that I had stored at different locations, safe deposit box at the bank, I've moved it to my home so I don't get any of that tax evasion bullshit."

"All right."

"Which means I need some extra protection. I got guns, alarms, but there's people'd send an army after me, if they knew what I had stored up in here. And the police—they'd come after it, take half for themselves. Atlantic City Police are greedy little bastards."

"Sure."

"I like you, you don't seem greedy. I like loyalty. I'll pay you better, twice what I was giving you, but I want you to stay close. I see some police cars parked outside, I want you to get over here to back me up, you understand?"

"Of course."

"Or if I have meetings, business meetings. Anyone shows up here, like that, right?"

"Sure."

"You better be sure. Because when you're not out collecting for me, you're now my bodyguard."

23

NADYA LOVED LILLIAN. NADYA LOVED SURROUNDING
herself with people who weren't like her, and Lillian had been
the perfect roommate in that regard: kind, reliable, smarter than
Nadya in just about every way that mattered. Nadya was aware
of her limits, even though she liked to romanticize her shortcom-
ings, and she had made a habit of finding people who could
compensate for them. It was Lillian who knew when the gas bill
was due, Lillian who knew how much cab fare would cost from
the East Village, and who might even have the cash on hand,
Lillian who knew how to get a job, how to hold a job, how to
date someone for more than two months at a time. Lillian had
cushioned the blow of adulthood for Nadya, who had never
really paid her own rent, without assistance from her parents, in
her entire twenty-seven years.

Nadya had tried to repay her friend with romantic advice,
sexual advice, advice for living as an artist—but she'd expected
to be found out one day or another, to have Lillian point out that
Lillian was the better writer, that Nadya wasn't serious, that
Nadya knew nothing about anything, had nothing to write about.
But Lillian hadn't done so, and Nadya had been grateful for it,
and then Lillian was gone.

Nadya suddenly wanted to see Chris, that pillar of stability.
But she had to start the conversation with the fact that Lillian
was missing.

"Did you call the police?" he asked.

"Yes, I called the police twice, because you can't report
someone officially missing until it's been twenty-four hours." It
was true. She'd called the police after returning from Colin's
house early in the morning to an empty apartment. But she'd

been hesitant to do it, because calling the police meant it was serious, and serious things scared her.

"She didn't pack a bag, or leave a note?"

"No."

"Do you know her last known whereabouts?"

"Here. She went out, though. I don't track her movements, okay?"

"I know. I'm just wondering what we can do."

"Can you come over?"

"Sure. We could go look for her together."

"Okay."

While she waited for Chris to come over, Nadya walked into Lillian's room. The police had already come through to investigate and taken Lillian's computer as evidence. They had written down information about Lillian's job, her graduate school, her professors. They had asked whether she and Nadya had been fighting, and whether Lillian had any boyfriends. A young officer told her, "You could put up posters, if you're looking for something to do," but Nadya felt that once you put up missing posters, you doomed the person to a horrible death. It was better to stay light, light and easy, and things would work out. Now she sat on Lillian's bed and stroked the blanket, trying to intuit something.

"Lillian, come on," she said, willing her friend to provide a mental image of her whereabouts, the way a psychic might.

She lay down for a moment, utterly still. If things got bad enough, she could always commit suicide. It was a favorite idea of hers, a thought she'd had since she was a teenager, although she rarely said it aloud. If things got bad enough, she could always kill herself. She had tried it before.

Until Nadya was fourteen years old, she had trained quite seriously to be a professional ballerina, but her mother's obsessive fixation with Nadya's weight had sent her into a spiral of anorexia, bringing her down to ninety-four pounds at five foot eight by her fourteenth birthday. At the mental hospital, Nadya decided the other anorexics were tedious Valley girls and gravi-

174

tated instead toward the grunge-loving depressives. She dyed her hair black and traded in her ballet lessons for an obsession with Soundgarden and particularly its lead singer, Chris Cornell, whom she finally met and made out with years later at a party in the Hollywood Hills in 2004 in the middle of his divorce. Nadya had not conquered her anorexia in the mental ward, however. Instead, her return to normal eating had coincided with her separation from her mother, who split briefly from Nadya's father during Nadya's last years of high school to move in with a yoga-instructor boyfriend. Nadya managed to return to eating bread products by the time she got her high school diploma, but she continued to suffer from depression, which she self-treated with a cocktail of pot and gin, on which she could bubble along quite nicely between three-day stretches of not leaving her bed.

She thought about Colin, who had almost become a boyfriend, who only two hours after she told him that Lillian had gone missing had gotten on a flight to Europe, leaving her alone in this city where people got hurt, or disappeared, or died.

"Where was the last place anybody saw her?" Chris asked when he arrived.

"No one knows. She exchanged a couple of cell phone calls with this kid she was tutoring. He told the police he didn't see her, though. But she thought—she thought he was cheating on his SATs. Not that that has anything to do with it."

"Can I have his name?"

"Cal Bolt."

"Not the Bolts of Bolt Bank?"

"I think so."

Chris put down his BlackBerry and was silent, thinking.

"Chris?" she said.

"Yeah?"

"You were dating her, right?"

"No. She didn't want…She didn't want to. She didn't want me."

"Then will you sleep with me?"

"What?"

"Before I stab something?"

"Nadya."

"Before I just cut myself to pieces or something. I'm just—freaking out."

Chris put his arms around Nadya and gave her a hug.

"It's going to be okay," he said, "They'll find her. She probably just went away on a writer's retreat or something."

"No. You know her. She always knew when the rent check was due, you know? I don't think she had it in her to just hurt everyone like this."

He nodded.

"I know I shouldn't have asked you about—going to bed, I just—it hurts." Nadya leaned her head against him.

"I know."

"I was just asking for pity sex, that's all."

Chris smiled. "I would, but…We've been friends forever, and nothing ever happened before, so at this point, maybe it's a bad idea."

"Of course it's a bad idea. You've known me for ten years. When have I done something that was a good idea?"

They were silent for a long moment while he stroked her hair.

He nodded. "Okay," he said.

"Okay?"

In the morning, Chris would ask himself whether he'd slept with Nadya because he was angry with Lillian and wanted revenge on her somehow. Or perhaps knowing he couldn't help Lillian, he was simply trying his hardest to be of use.

Early the next morning, Cal Bolt and Peter Wicka were sitting in Peter's father's BMW at the back entrance of the Heavenly Alliance Church in Cohoes, New York.

Peter was buzzing with a strange energy Cal had never seen before. "Can I show you the footage of her? It's fucking amazing. We have to use it. In our movie."

"Use it? We can't use it. Are you insane?"

"Why do you think I filmed it?" asked Peter. "It's the real deal. The real deal."

For Peter, who had grown up in the sheltered bubble of the Upper East Side, doing anything real was a fixation, and the riskier the better. Peter's nannies had made sure he didn't get a single scrape or bruise until he was nine years old, and he had responded by trying cocaine at his first party when he was fourteen.

"But she's okay. She hasn't been, the guy hasn't..."

"No. Dude," Peter said. "The guy who's watching her went to Harvard, okay?"

"We'll get caught."

"The only reason criminals get caught is 'cause they're morons, okay? We're smart people from smart families. People like us don't get caught, and if we do, we walk away from it, right? That's what lawyers are for."

"How can we—this is stupid. You said it would—you said it would just be for the weekend, while Frank cleared all the stuff off his hard drive."

"Well, no harm in waiting until your parents get out of town."

"Is he going to let her go?"

"Of course. He just wanted to make sure there was nothing incriminating. It's only going to be for a couple of days. Let's just shoot our movie. Right? Isn't that our goal, here? You wanted to—you want be a filmmaker, right? So we shoot our film."

"If that footage gets out..."

"Dude. She is not going to think you were involved. I mean, we could use that footage in our film and no one would ever even suspect."

"I hate this. Why did you even tell Frank? You know he's a jerk. He could talk about the whole thing, the SATs, everything. He could blackmail us."

"We could blackmail him."

"I should tell my dad."

"Go ahead."

There was a long silence in the car. Cal's relationship with his dad was an unspoken fact between them. Cal could feel it sitting on his shoulders. Some part of him was enjoying doing something that would totally appall his father. It freed him. And anyway, the guy watching her had gone to Harvard.

"It's going to be fine," Peter said. "Watch and see."

Cal said nothing.

"Come on," Peter said, opening his car door. "Let's go be Christian."

Julie's father was a tall, slender man whose long face carried the pockmarks of a painful adolescence. He wore a white sweatshirt blazoned with the logo of "Pudding Hollow Bible Camp" and talked with slow deliberation, his chin bobbing downward for emphasis.

"New York City," he said. "I have been in New York City exactly once. Let me ask you something. If you don't mind, how much do you pay for rent?"

"Um...We both kind of live with our parents, right now..." Cal began.

Pastor Presley Walsh looked disappointed. Like many Upstate New Yorkers, he made a habit of asking New York City residents the details of their finances. Cal and Peter were too young to know that their role in this game was to provide some astronomical rent figure, so that the smiling local could demand of them how they could possibly live there, while touting the obvious advantages of Cooperstown or Oneida.

When Cal and Peter didn't take the bait, Mr. Walsh pressed on. "Let me tell you what I think of New York. Let me tell you my impression of the Big Apple." Here he slowed down even further and tucked in his chin to designate that he was waxing philosophical.

"Big cities..." he began, "are impressive. You see all these buildings, and people, and you think, this is a pretty impressive place. But then you look around at the faces of the people, and you know what you see?"

"They aren't happy," Peter supplied, irritating the pastor. New Yorkers weren't supposed to be aware of their own misery. That was the job of simple country folk—to point it out to them.

"But what you don't know is why." And the pastor launched into what was clearly a sermon, or at least a sermon-to-be.

There are several varieties of successful preachers, the kind who expand their flock into the thousands. Some are flashy preachers, all fire and charisma, who build multimillion-dollar compounds from the donations of their congregants. They drive Mercedes Benz cars and promise their congregation they will be able to do the same once they square themselves with God. Then there are the fear mongers—angry, lonely men with one eye on the Apocalypse and a reflexive hatred of gays, who are eventually caught with a male prostitute in a hotel room while their wives are birthing their ninth child. The angry preachers seem to enjoy their downfall even more than their rise, as it gives them a chance to strive for redemption.

But Pastor Walsh was a different variety—the folksy preacher. All of his sermons began with a set of truisms that his congregants were sure to agree upon. Family is important. Government and politicians can't be trusted. God asks for things from you, but he gives you even more in return. Once he had the flock nodding in agreement, he began to expound on his own particular philosophy. And no matter what he said, he made it sound as if he were only being reasonable, as if all his wisdom grew out of the simple wisdom of simple folks. "I am just a simple man," is his refrain. "I am just a simple man. And people, my congregation, they have wanted to put that on T-shirts, to make T-shirts that say 'Pastor Walsh is just a simple man,' but I say, no, don't do it. Don't do it. Because you aren't here to worship me, and I know that, and you know that. You are here to worship the light of the Lord your God Jesus Christ."

The sermon he touched upon now was called "No Shortcuts."

179

"You know, there are no shortcuts in life. You know that? People are always looking for a fast way to get somewhere. A fast buck. But God does not deliver success to people who rush. He doesn't open the gates of heaven to people who sin their whole lives and then make an apology right at the end, "Oh, wait, I'm sorry." No. Because that is not a sincere apology. It costs you nothing. Now I'm not talking about forgiveness. God will forgive. But he is going to reserve his greatest reward to the people who have spent their whole lives doing right. Day after day. Let me tell you something. I have enough money to retire already. At fifty-three. And you know why? Because I saved up. Ten percent of my income. Every year of my life I put ten percent of my income into savings. Investments. Mutual funds. Paid my daughter's college. None of these student loans, credit cards. And my investments—there were people telling me I could make a quicker turnaround with these—whatchamacallit—futures, and nonsense like that. But there are no quick ways to success."

"Absolutely, sir," Peter agreed.

"I read your script, and that's what I think your script is about. These so-called artists who are looking for a shortcut. They want to be famous, you see, and they think they would do anything to get there, but they don't put in the time to actually get good at their art."

This rang a bit too true for Peter and Cal, who nodded while avoiding each other's eyes.

"Now here's another question. I read your budget," he went on. "I saw you want twenty thousand dollars to make a movie. Now, maybe in New York City, that isn't a lot of money. But up here, that is a whole lot of money."

"It's just to cover basic…" Peter began.

Cal spoke up. "Most films cost more than that. Like, millions of dollars."

"I understand that. And here's what I want to know," said the Pastor. "Why do you want to make this film? What's in it for you?"

"I guess," Peter said, "for me it's about getting closer to—exposing some of that misery in New York that you were talking about."

"But you don't understand that misery."

"No, I know, but I guess...I guess we could learn. If you wanted to—to donate. To help."

"I'm afraid I just don't quite understand what you're talking about," said the Pastor. He had a nose for nonsense that was keener than Peter had anticipated. Peter struggled for a moment.

"It's a Christian movie, in a way."

"But why do you want to make it?"

"We want to express our vision of the world. Share it."

The Pastor looked unimpressed.

But then Peter had his masterstroke, without even meaning to. He looked at Cal, then at Mr. Walsh. "We figured you probably wouldn't have that much to give, of course. Being an Upstate church and all ..."

Pastor Walsh pointed out that his church had five thousand members, and that they showed his sermons on video screens at six other local churches, and that an estimated forty thousand people watched him on TV each week. Not that he was bragging about that.

"I'll tell you what," Pastor Walsh said. "I will do this for you. I will allow you the use of our cameras, our editing facility. But you have to make the movie right here. Right here in Albany."

Peter and Cal looked at each other, considering.

"With me, looking out for you, looking over this process," the Pastor added. "I want to learn about this, this filmmaking business."

Peter thought about it for a moment. "What kind of camera is it? Is it HD?"

Bronnie Bolt had not packed her own bags for a trip in five years, but she took very seriously the job of overseeing the packing, which was usually done by the household's nanny. This evening, she sat with her laptop perched in front of her on her bed, reading an email while Julie folded a linen skirt into a Goyard luggage bag no more than three feet away.

"That wrinkles," Bronnie commented when she glanced up for a moment.

"We can get it steamed at the hotel."

"You can't trust a hotel. They don't know how to take care of linen."

Julie nodded, taking in this information as if it were a valuable piece of wisdom. The family was staying in a suite at the George V in Paris that cost twenty-two hundred dollars a night, but Julie didn't want to quibble over whether or not the hotel was likely to steam skirts to Bronnie's satisfaction. (One reason, perhaps, that people of Bronnie's income bracket develop an exaggerated sense of their own wisdom is because everybody employed by them adopts the convenient habit of never arguing with anything they say. Celebrities develop the same weakness. Anyone who is always listened to will sooner or later conclude that they have something fascinating to say.)

"I need to talk to Bella before we go," Bronnie added. Although she loved shopping in Paris, trips with the family made Bronnie nervous. It was where she felt most exposed to the flaws in her life and her marriage. She compared herself to the other happy families on vacation—the dads carrying their children on their shoulders—and felt envious, and bought thousand dollar bags to bring home as gifts for her friends.

"Do you want me to try to reach her now?"

"No, I'll try her later. I just wanted a reminder."

Bronnie returned to her email. She was writing Canella again, to ask again for the names of possible ghostwriters for her blog. Canella had promised to get back to her, but was away in a villa she owned in Lloret del Mar on the coast of Spain.

"Do you think Cal is mad at me?" Bronnie continued after a moment.

"No, why?"

182

"This whole refusing to go on vacation thing. There's almost no point in going if he's not going to go."

"Oh, he just wants to work on his movie. He's a teenager. They like their independence."

"But there's no point in having a family vacation if we're not even going to have the whole family."

"Well, he's going away to college in a year. Maybe he's getting ready for that."

"I think maybe he's punishing me because I told him he had to keep taking tennis."

"Well, you and Henry can spend some nice time together, just the two of you. I can watch Amy, if you want to go out for a night."

Bronnie threw Julie a quick glance, to see if she was kidding. She wasn't. "Amy would feel left out if we went out, just the two of us." The truth was that Bronnie and Henry seldom went out to dinner together unless it was to a benefit where other couples could break the tension.

Julie let the issue drop. "Speaking of Cal's movie, I was actually going to ask...Cal asked if I could stay here and act for them. I was thinking. Maybe the week that we get back from France, I could take a couple of days off and do that?"

"I don't understand. Who would cover for you?"

"I'd find someone. Or, it's not such a bad time, Amy isn't in school, she really isn't doing that much. Maybe you'd want to spend a day or two with her. I could arrange stuff for you guys."

"But that's your job. You aren't just doing childcare, Julie, you're keeping this household running. I mean, I could watch Amy for a few days, but that isn't—the point is we need you to help us keep things going. This household is a very complicated operation. That's why we pay you very well. To help us keep things going. So if you want a break, you have to give me more than two weeks notice."

"I know. It's just for a day or two. I just thought, if it helps Cal..."

"Cal doesn't need help. He can find someone else."

"Okay, sure."

It was of course Peter Wicka who had asked Julie to take a minor role in the film. He had asked Julie to skip the Paris trip, to be the star of his movie, but Julie had been reluctant. She felt responsible to Bronnie, to Amy. She didn't want to let them down. "You should quit that job," said Peter, who had never held a job. "You can do better."

"Did Lillian get back to you about why she missed her writing session with Amy?" Bronnie asked.

"No. I left her two messages."

"Well, leave her three. And get Bella on the phone for me. Now, please."

Julie could see she'd upset Bronnie by asking for days off. She padded over to the phone that sat two feet from Bronnie on the nightstand and dialed Henry's office number. Julie thought about the joy of quitting, or even better, being fired. Maybe she would just not show up those days. Lillian, their tutor, had stopped showing up, answering phone calls. It was kind of inspiring to see someone totally ignoring the Bolts. But then there was Amy, who couldn't go to sleep without her.

"Hi, Bella, it's Julie," she said. "I have Bronnie on the phone for you."

Julie handed the phone to Bronnie.

"And you can leave," Bronnie added.

Bella Pointer was surprised Bronnie was calling for her, and she almost out of reflex transferred the phone call to Henry, who was in a late-night meeting.

"How can I help you, Bronnie?"

"Bella, I know Henry's been giving you some of my blogs to edit, and I wanted to tell you that you've been doing a terrific job."

"Oh, thank you, but it wasn't just me…"

"It wasn't? I thought he gave them to you to check for anything that would damage the company."

"Oh, yes, but he did have—has he discussed the polishing?"

"Oh, he didn't tell me. Who else worked on it?"

"Um…" Bella knew better than to get between the Bolts. "I think Mr. Bolt would have the complete information."

"Well, whoever it is, I want them to do a new addition to the blog tonight. Can you do that for me?"

"Sure. What do—"

"Take this down. I want to write that I am outraged, really outraged that Lillian—you can just say my daughter's writing tutor—didn't show up for a writing session with Amy today, and didn't even call. And now we are going to go on a trip, and my son isn't coming, and I just feel like everything is falling apart."

"Everything is falling apart," Bella repeated, scribbling down notes.

"Just everything. It's a disaster. Anyway, you get the idea. Make that into something good. Something that sounds better than that. But I really want the stuff about the tutor to go up tonight. Because if she reads it, I want her to know that my daughter cried all day because she didn't show up."

"Okay, but do you know where her writing tutor is?"

"Obviously no, or I wouldn't be posting this. Thank you, Bella."

Bronnie hung up the phone.

Bella's first response was to dial Lillian, to tell her that she ought to give the Bolts a quick call to explain her absence if she wanted to keep her job. But Lillian's cell phone mailbox was full.

So Lillian had gone AWOL. Bella would have to mention to Henry, as he departed the office, the little conundrum that had arisen from Henry deciding to not divulge who was writing Bronnie's blog.

Henry's solution, on hearing the problem, was simple: "Find somebody who can write like Lillian." For tonight, he added, Bella was just going to have to do her best to write the blog the way Bronnie had requested.

Bella's first draft was the result of her years of experience in corporate letter writing, and it read as follows:

> I am writing to express my severe disappointment in one of our employees (technically a 1099-MISC independent contractor), who was scheduled for an appointment with my daughter for a writing tutoring session. The employee did not arrive for the session and also failed to provide any kind of notification of absence. As a result, my daughter suffered severe emotional distress. This kind of behavior is not acceptable and is possibly subject to litigation. In addition, my son has chosen not to accompany us on the family vacation, leading me to the conclusion that everything is falling apart.

Bella read what she'd written. She knew she had the tone wrong. She knew she had to do something else to embody Bronnie, to adopt a voice. She pulled up her files and found the photo slideshow put together the year before for Bronnie's fortieth birthday party. It tracked the course of Bronnie's life— from her beautiful white girlhood in St. Louis, to her somewhat less white college years at Scripps College, to her brief stint as a television newscaster in New Jersey and then as a junior TV producer doing lifestyle segments for the *Today Show*. The last photograph from her single years showed her laughing, a cranberry wreath placed in jest on her head, standing with Jane Pauley on the set of *Today*.

After the wedding, Bella noticed that in not one of the photographs was Bronnie smiling. Something was missing from the young woman who had once placed a cranberry wreath on her head. Bella pondered the series of half-frowning photos, feeling a certain recognition in them.

Like many very attractive women, Bella and Bronnie shared a remarkably low set of expectations about relationships. Their high cheekboned beauty meant that they attracted men for all the wrong reasons, so they both had experienced love as a series of blazing courtships followed by tepid relationships with men who weren't actually interested in them. As a result, both women viewed romance as a kind of elaborate con. Bella's response had been to avoid the issue by throwing herself into work, while Bronnie's had been to settle for a "best offer," without a clear notion of what "best" might actually mean.

Bella looked over the blog one more time and then put her head down in despair. She knew, right then, that she was never going to return to her personal, secret dream of fiction writing, the one she'd shared with Lillian once over mojitos. She had lost it—she had lost the ability to use her imagination in that way.

But she couldn't explain the problem to Henry Bolt, either. So she pulled herself together and borrowed sentence structures from Lillian's previous entries—a reference here, a phrase there, until she had cobbled together a reasonable copy of the writing style of the missing MFA graduate. Her work done and posted, she sat back and wondered what was going on. Lillian had been almost a friend, and it occurred to Bella only then to try the police and see if Lillian had been reported missing. It turned out that they were about to call Henry's office to ask Mr. Bolt what he knew.

Dan Marrone, former NYPD Detective Squad Commander and current private security expert, had two rules for dealing with his wealthy private clients. The first was that you never referred to them as wealthy clients. "High-net-worth individuals" was Dan's preferred terminology, if he had to mention money at all, as in, "High-net-worth individuals run into their biggest security problems through employees who have had direct contact with the family."

Dan's second rule was that you had to give all of your advice without hesitation. Not "You might want to get a bodyguard for your daughter when she goes to Russia," but, "Get a bodyguard for her. No question." He had learned that the wealthier a client was, the more the person enjoyed being bullied. ("It's like what the fashion designers do," he explained to his ex-wife. "They

187

don't say, 'Maybe you should wear red this season.' They say, 'Wear red.' That's what makes the rich people listen.")

Dan was a big guy, burly in the shoulders, with a striped gray mustache that resembled the front grill of an old-fashioned steam locomotive. He always wore a blue or black suit with a striped tie, and his favorite part of his job was telling anecdotes about former perps he'd apprehended. ("We had one guy was sending this actress his sperm in a can...") He enjoyed storytelling so much that it could plausibly have been the sole reason he had opened his own security company—though it didn't hurt that he now pulled in over a quarter million a year on top of his police pension.

He had been on retainer as a security consultant for the Bolts since 2002, when Henry first joined the ranks of the *Forbes* "400 Wealthiest Americans" and decided to evaluate the kidnapping risk to his wife and children. Dan had helped the Bolts install a new security system for their country home in Sands Point, had recommended that Henry's regular chauffeur be replaced by a rotating car service, and had suggested that the family adopt a fake name during travel. (Henry had selected "Bulowski.") Dan had trained all the nannies in how to tell if they were being followed, and had given a star-struck Cal some basic training in kidnapping evasion, which had led Cal to consider, briefly, a career in law enforcement.

Now Dan sat in Henry's office at close to nine p.m., trying to ascertain the appropriate approach.

"You want me to find her?"

"Oh, well, I'm sure the police are doing a good job with that. No, my concern is that—Cal is at a sensitive point right now. He's working on his college applications. And the police have been asking about—I guess this girl wasn't quite certain that Cal's SAT scores were legitimate. That's what her roommate told the police."

"But Lillian was the SAT tutor, wasn't she?"

"What I'm concerned about is that this could all reflect badly on Cal, say if it got into the press, something about Cal possibly cheating on his SATs, and the girl…she goes missing…you see how this could be spun."

"Yeah, sure."

"And it could influence his chances of getting into college."

At last Dan saw the angle. "All right. Here's what we're going to do. I'm going to talk to the guys who are in charge of the investigation, tell them not to leak that bit to the press, this is a teenage kid here, we want to do the right thing."

"Thank you."

"I'll grease the wheels if I have to."

"If you have to."

"And if it gets into the press, say it gets out there…"

"But you just assured me it won't," Henry interjected.

"Right. It won't. I'll just make sure that it doesn't. I probably know the guys—I mean, I'm sure I know the guys working on this case, I'll talk to them."

"I'd appreciate that."

"So you don't want me to do any of my own investigating, here?" Rule number three in dealing with wealthy clients was that you should always look to expand your job, especially when you billed by the hour.

"No, that won't be necessary at this point."

"Because if it comes down to it, I can always get a couple of guys…"

"I know. That won't be necessary, thank you."

"Because if you—"

"Tell my assistant on your way out that I should be heading back to the residence in about fifteen minutes, would you?"

"Yeah, sure."

"I'm leaving for Paris in the morning, so if you have any questions, you'll have to reach me there."

Dan rose, shook Mr. Bolt's hand, and then paused at the door.

"Mr. Bolt," he said. "I've never told you this, because it's never really been relevant, but if you ever—if your kid was ever involved in something not quite legit, or anyone in your—I just want you to know that my first priority is to protect the family."

Henry looked steadily at Dan for a long moment. "That's good to know. But I don't think it's relevant."

"No, neither do I. I'll talk to you soon, Mr. Bolt."

Julie lay on Amy's bed with her young charge's head on her belly and her eyes focused on the glow of a Spongebob Squarepants sticker that one of Amy's friends had stuck to the underside of her desk. Amy had awakened at 10:45 p.m. that night and called out to Julie over the intercom, and Julie had spent the next half hour trying to lull the child in whispers so that Bronnie wouldn't know she was up and scold Julie for not establishing a better bedtime routine. Now Amy was at last asleep again, and Julie was preparing to make the first move in a familiar maneuver—first sliding Amy's head from her belly to her right arm, and then onto the pillow, and then in a series of slow moves lifting herself from Amy's bed, so she could sleep a few short hours before waking to spend the day preparing the family for their flight to Paris.

Her thoughts were on Peter. She was in love with him. In love! They had spent a delirious, stupid afternoon together last Sunday. She thought about it and felt guilty and crazy and overjoyed. She had lied to her father about her whereabouts that day, and she hadn't lied to her father since she was thirteen and snuck out to see *The Mummy* at the local multiplex. She was wondering if she was going to marry Peter, and he was going to take her away to Los Angeles, and she was going to be an actress. Or maybe they'd have kids together, and her kids would be child actors.

With this thought in her head, she made an error in stage two of her maneuver—the part where she moved Amy from her arm to the bed. Amy hit the bed just a little too hard, and her eyes popped open. She looked up at Julie.

"Don't go."

"I won't go." It was what Julie always said. Julie lay back down, with infinite patience, and let Amy return her head to its preferred position on her belly again.

Amy spoke into the half-dark. "I wrote a story about you."

"You did?" Julie whispered, hoping Amy would follow suit and whisper as well.

"It's about a horse named Julie."

"Oh. Really?"

"It's about how you're a horse in Argentina, and I get to ride you."

"Wow."

"Yeah, because I get to be on top of you now like you're my horsey."

"Oh, okay."

Amy sighed.

"And my daddy buys the horse for me, just like my daddy buys you."

The words caused Julie to take in a breath, but Amy didn't notice. She couldn't see, in the dark, that Julie had grown pale.

Julie slid Amy's head off her belly twenty minutes later and returned to her room, where she packed all her belongings into two small suitcases, placed her apartment keys on the desk just below the video intercom, and wrote the following note on a Post-It on top of Amy's Sleep Schedule: "I quit. Tell Amy I'm sorry."

If Lillian could quit and walk out on the Bolts, then so could she.

She walked out the doorway of the building and onto Park Avenue, smiled at the doorman, and started the walk to the subway, to the Port Authority bus terminal, to the bus back home. She would call Peter tomorrow, perhaps, but not yet. Right now, she just wanted to feel free. It was a cool summer night, and she felt good.

24

Don't do it for your future. Do it for hers.
—ADVERTISEMENT FOR XAVERIAN FUNDS, ACCOMPANIED
BY A PICTURE OF A THREE-YEAR-OLD GIRL FINGER PAINTING.

CHRIS AND WES SCHOTT SAT IN CHRIS'S CONVERTIBLE outside Frank's building, casing out the Starbucks. They had been sitting there for two hours and Wes was bored.

"Can I go pick up a copy of the *New York Times*?"

"I need a second pair of eyes, here, man."

"I just want to do the crossword." Wes leaned his head against his seat. "Are you sure he had something to do with it?"

"I don't know. Is he dangerous? Do you think he could be dangerous?"

"Nah, not really," said Wes. "You really think he kidnapped her?"

"I don't know."

"He's an asshole," Wes commented. "If that counts."

Chris had been doing his own little investigation of Lillian's kidnapping. It was, for him, a strange kind of penance for sleeping with her roommate in her absence. Sure, Chris knew that he didn't owe anything to Lillian, that she had in fact broken up with him, that it was over. But finding her gone—really gone— had left him brokenhearted. He had been hoping, somehow, in the back of his mind, to redeem himself to her—to prove that he wasn't selfish, which was what she'd been saying, he understood that, without her quite saying it. He had been hoping that maybe he could save a whale, or cure cancer, or something like that, he hoped, right in front of her, and he hadn't gotten the chance. So now he was determined to save her instead.

After deciding this (while lying in Nadya's arms Friday night), he had spent last Saturday outside the Bolts' apartment building waiting for someone who looked like the young man Lillian had said looked like Cal Bolt. It had taken him three attempts to pick out the correct boy-with-tennis-racket, but at last he'd found him.

"Cal Bolt?"

Cal had stopped and looked at him. They were at the corner, half a block from the apartment, where Chris wouldn't attract the attention of the doorman.

"Hi, my name's Chris. I'm a friend of Lillian's, your tutor?"

"Oh, hi."

"Hi," Chris said.

"So she disappeared, right?" There. It was at that moment that Cal had shifted his eyes from left to right, like a bad liar. It was that moment that told Chris how to proceed.

"Yeah, she did."

"Yeah, I heard about that. I'm sorry."

"The police talked to you. And your parents."

"Yeah. I guess, uh, Lillian had this idea I might have cheated on my SAT." There was a long pause. "But I didn't, so..."

"Why did she think that?"

"I don't know. I guess because my scores jumped so much, but that was just—I was really motivated that day."

"How did she think you cheated?"

"I don't know," Cal said.

"I just wondered when was the last time you saw her."

"Who are you?"

"My name's Chris."

"Okay. She was—I don't know when I saw her." Cal waited for Chris to say something.

"If you think of anything, will you call me?"

"Yeah, sure." Cal said this with kindness, making Chris doubt himself. Cal didn't seem like a brutal kid.

Walking away, Chris tried to recall how much Cal looked like the kid in the Starbucks, remembering that he and Lillian had no hard proof of anything.

Yet here he was a few days later, waiting to track Frank again, hoping to know more, hoping there was more to the story. Somehow. Going on instinct. Feeling like an ass.

After another fifteen minutes, Wes got out of the car and walked up to Frank's doorway before Chris could stop him. He spoke to Frank's building security guard, then returned to the car.

"What—Wes, what the hell was…"

"I just asked if Frank was around. And the doorman told me he thought he might be in Atlantic City for the weekend."

"Atlantic City?"

"Yeah. He's kind of—he used to be into poker, so maybe he's been doing that, now that he has some money. He used to talk about how he was learning poker."

"Atlantic City."

Wes looked over, smiled. "I'd be a good detective, right?"

"Yeah, you would, Wes."

"We could try this again next weekend, if you want. I should go back to school now, get some work done…"

"No, thanks a lot, man. It's okay. I'm just being an idiot, here. I don't know what I'm doing."

Wes nodded. "You like her."

"Yeah, kind of."

"If it was me, I'd go for Nadya. She's hot."

Chris started up the car and didn't reply.

"Punch it. Punch it. Punch it harder. Pull your arm back before you throw a punch. That's right."

Paolo watched as Vanessa's son Tyler tried to balance in his wheelchair while pulling his arm back as far as it would go. With a jerking movement, Tyler slammed his hand as hard as he could against Paolo's open hand, causing Paolo to wince a little.

"Better, man," Paolo said. "That was about a million times better."

"I really wish you wouldn't teach him that stuff," Vanessa said.

"What? It's a job skill. He wants to be a wrestler," Paolo replied.

"Is it a job skill for you, too?"

Paolo didn't reply. This was the fourth time he'd stopped by Vanessa's house, and they'd developed a strange kind of routine: first he would pull up to the curb and wait in his truck, breathing heavily for ten long breaths. Then with a single, fluid motion he would exit the vehicle and walk up to the door.

"What?" she would say, each time, before she let him inside and he sat down next to her son's wheelchair in her living room, breathing, silent, head in his hands.

"I think this is the wrong line of work for you," Vanessa would say. And then, when Paolo nodded in agreement, she would ask him if he would have a look at a leaking pipe, or help her start up her washing machine. And, without a word, Paolo would oblige.

After Paolo helped Vanessa with some household chore or another, he would sit down with Tyler and chat with him. Sometimes they would practice arm wrestling. After his second visit, he started bringing Tyler some of his old wrestling T-shirts to wear. Stone Cold Steve Austin, circa 1998. The Undertaker circa 2003. Sometimes they would listen to Pastor Walsh's television sermon together.

Tyler was obsessed with two things: professional wrestling and God. He wanted to be a minister, he said. And he wanted to wrestle, too, as "The Reverend." After he became famous for his wrestling and spiritual exploits, he would write self-help novels about overcoming his disease. He was frank and realistic about

195

his illness but also certain (in the way that children can be) that he was going to succeed in everything he hoped for. He had already written Chapters One and Two of his Autobiography and was saving the rest of the chapters for, in sequence: High School, College, Career, and Family. Then he would be ready to publish, if, he said, he was still alive by then.

Tyler never spoke about Paolo's debt collecting, but Vanessa did.

"What are you telling Ivan when you come here and you don't get money? What do you say to him about that?"

Paolo shrugged, and Vanessa right away hit upon the truth. "Are you giving him money and saying it's from us?"

"Maybe."

"Who are you taking that money from? Some other broke people?"

"Maybe."

"How can you do that to people? Doesn't that make you feel bad?"

"Sure, but they owe the money."

"Yeah, but you're keeping food off their tables. You know that."

"It's not like I'm going to do this for a living forever," Paolo replied. "I just want to get myself set up, that's all."

Vanessa shook her head. "That's how I felt about stripping. I thought, 'I'll get out. I just got to get myself set up.' It doesn't work, honey."

"You got out, didn't you?"

"Do I look set up to you?"

Paolo shrugged. "There's not that many ways to make real money anymore," Paolo said. "You got to go to school, now. You got to get, like—a degree, and I can't—I mean, there's not a lot of jobs for people like me. If you're stupid, how're you supposed to make money?"

"You're not stupid."

"I wouldn't be too sure about that." He smiled at Vanessa and her son and stood up.

196

"You leaving?"

"Yeah."

"You're confused, honey."

"But I like you," he said. "That I'm not confused about."

"Get outta here," she said, shaking her head.

Paolo tipped an invisible hat to both of them and walked out the door.

25

LILLIAN HAD BEEN IN CAPTIVITY FOR EIGHT DAYS, AND she had made a mental list of what she knew about her new universe. She knew, for example, that she had one captor—at least the only one she saw, except during the kidnapping. He struck her as young, in his twenties or thirties, white (though he always wore a ski mask), and basically nonviolent by nature. He was very nervous, never met her eyes, and reminded her of one of Nadya's ex-boyfriends who did too much cocaine. Like many writers, she had a gift for observation and could intuit people's basic outlines, and she would have bet her left hand that her captor was just doing this for the money. She guessed he had a drug habit.

She knew that he came and went but was pretty much there 24/7. He seemed to get as bored and restless as she did. He'd take her to the bathroom, walking her down a small windowless hallway with a gun to her side. Then he'd bring her back to her room, handcuff her again and sometimes duck out for an hour or two. She could hear his car leave. But it didn't matter, because she hadn't found a way around the handcuffs, or the weird expensive video camera watching her every move.

She knew, also, that nothing had been said to her about her captivity or her release. Nobody had asked her to make a video pleading for mercy. Nobody had told her that her "family had refused to pay," or even noticed that she had no family. This had led her to assume one of two possible scenarios about her capture:

198

1. She was being held by some kind of twisted psycho for his personal twisted use. He would come in one day, tell her a weird story about his mother or grade school teacher, rape her, and then cut off her nose while her drug-addled guard ate pizza in the next room. But her room didn't have the feel of a personal dungeon. It was an old office from a trucking company and had a calendar from 2003 on the wall with faded photos of the Sierra Nevada.

2. She had been wrongly assumed to be part of the Bolt family, and kidnapped for money. The Bolts had refused to pay, and the kidnappers were confused about what to do and were stalling.

The second option seemed like the most likely scenario. Henry Bolt wasn't about to dish out untold millions to help his kid's tutor. Not when he could find another just like her on Craigslist—and this one would come with a Ph.D. Bolt was probably busy consulting with his lawyers. He might pay if the kidnapping was going to damage the family's credibility, but otherwise, why bother?

There was of course a third scenario: that Cal had arranged her kidnapping to dodge the SAT revelation. But somehow, she just didn't see it. He wasn't a violent kid. He might try to beg and plead his way out of things, just like his sister did, but he didn't seem capable of hurting anything or anybody. And he would never have the courage, either.

She spent her free time thinking about her book. There was nothing else to do. She realized, on the second day of her captivity, that she didn't even like her book and that she didn't expect anyone else to like it either. She realized she'd been writing it in a desperate attempt to imitate what she thought was important literature, which, for the most part, was not even the literature she liked. It came to her—a revelation. It was because her parents were dead, and she'd been looking for parents ever since, so she had tied herself into knots to write something that would appeal to her professors. And, after spending one hundred thousand dollars, she couldn't admit that it had all been a terrible mistake.

She realized with sudden clarity that she didn't have to finish it.

The book was a mistake. There, she'd said it.

And a vast weight lifted off her shoulders.

She didn't have to finish the book. Heck, she didn't have to be a writer. She could pay off her loans and find a real career. If she'd made a mistake in going to grad school, so be it. She could move on. She could overcome it. She would never write again. She sat down, satisfied, feeling free.

A few hours later, she got an idea for a pretty good short story. Something about the loneliness of a crime victim, and how you can realize important things at moments like that. She thought about asking for paper, and when her captor at last returned with a meatball sub and an orange soda, she worked up the courage.

"Excuse me," she said, and her captor stopped in his tracks, looking almost as scared as she was.

Being a writer has the same appeal as being a magician. A good writer can conjure a solid reality out of the mist and smoke of words. It was its own kind of addiction, the attempt to capture a fleeting perception and make it appear solid.

"I'm sorry," she said. "Can I borrow a pen or a pencil? I'm just bored, and I'm a writer…"

The jittery young man looked at her. He stood in the door, considering, and then turned and walked out without a word.

"Or even a notepad …" Lillian trailed off. She looked at the sandwich. She was getting to know the local takeout pretty well. She'd probably be able to triangulate her prison's position, if she ever got free, based on the relative locations of Subway, Dunkin' Donuts, and a pizza shop. But then again, if she was in New Jersey, perhaps not.

Ten minutes later, her captor reentered her room, his ski mask still in place. Seeing that he had no pen or paper, Lillian thought, "Oh, God, I'm going to be raped," and froze. Instead, he dragged an old desk over to her and pulled up a chair across from her. He

200

poured in front of them a small pile of pennies, pushed half in her direction, and dealt her and himself five cards.

He looked up at her, and she understood. "Poker?"

He nodded.

"You know Texas hold 'em?" she asked.

Under the mask, the man appeared to smile. He picked up the cards and reshuffled them, then dealt again. This time only two cards.

And Lillian smiled too. Because Texas hold 'em was a game she knew well.

Poker rose in popularity in the U.S. in the early 2000s, as online poker became a national hobby. The World Series of Poker became a major spectacle on ESPN, peaking in 2006 when the winner won a pool of twelve million dollars, the biggest prize for any winner of any event in sports or television history. In the past, TV viewers watched contestants win a prize because they were skilled athletes or knowledgeable trivia buffs. Now the nation gave its most spectacular reward to people who excelled only at collecting piles of cash. The same was true of the financial markets, though no one had realized it yet.

Within this apotheosis of the quick buck, Texas hold 'em was the star game. Hold 'em differs from traditional stud poker in that players can bet four times on each hand, rather than two. The value of money at stake in a single hand rises far beyond that of stud poker, and at the same time, the fate of a player can twist, as the hand progresses.

Lillian had been a fan of Texas hold 'em since June of 2006, when she was an executive assistant at a publishing company in Baltimore. She had already been accepted to grad school and was killing time working a day job for the summer, and every night she walked to a cheap bar across the street from her building on O'Donnell Street and watched the World Series of Poker with the night crowd. Mexican waiters, black cab drivers, Polish house painters sat around discussing strategy and the different personalities of the star players. Sometimes, they would play a hand. Sometimes, Lillian joined in. Never for big stakes, but one night, she went home with a hundred dollars. The thrill of the game, for her, was not in the money, not even in the colorful people who were sizing each other up over a beer. The thrill was in the plot twists. First you were high, and then you were low. Everything good or bad could change in an instant. But she was never a very good player. When she had a bad hand, she knew how to handle it. But she never bet high enough when she had a good one.

Her opponent now was the opposite. He knew how to bet high when he had a good hand. His problem was that he was also too optimistic when he had a bad one. He was always a little too sure that the next flop would deliver the cards he wanted.

"This isn't fair, you know," she said. "You can read my face, but I can't see yours."

Her captor spoke, for the first time in eight days.

"I'm going to teach you a poker tell," said Greg Miller. "Are you ready?"

After thirty minutes of play, he was up, but just a bit—sixteen cents. And that's when she did it. She cleaned him out. First came a pair of kings, a lucky flop, and then she cleaned him out in a single round. He stared at her in silence. For Greg Miller, it was as if his whole life was encapsulated in that moment.

"I guess that's that," Lillian said. "I have a buck forty. Here, I don't think I'm going to do a whole lot better."

Greg was too annoyed with himself to answer. But then she gave him one more chance.

"Want to play for something real?" she said.

"What?"

"My freedom."

26

"It's not about life or death, it's about something more important than that."

"What?"

"Art."

—Screenplay for *Snuff*, by Peter Wicka

The Bolts' four round-trip plane tickets to Paris totaled twenty-four thousand one hundred dollars, exactly half the average American's household income in 2008. Henry Bolt and his family always traveled with the same airplane seating arrangement: Henry sat two rows forward from his wife, so that he could get work done on the plane, while Bronnie and the nanny surrounded Amy, with the nanny next to Amy and Bronnie across the aisle. Cal, had he been along, would have been seated on Bronnie's other side, shifting around and flipping through the movie channels.

Now Bronnie sat next to her daughter, her husband two rows ahead, without a nanny, without anybody but her daughter, feeling lonely. She had asked Henry to sit with her, just for this trip, just this one time to fill Julie's empty seat, but he had too much to do, he said. She watched him from her seat. She could just see the corner of his computer screen, and sure enough, he was working on business documents the whole way. He never once browsed the Internet or flipped through the SkyMall. He was an Important Man doing Important Things.

She had wanted to cancel the whole trip after Julie quit. She had suggested they postpone. But Henry had warned her that there was not going to be any time for him to take a vacation for at least another seven months, and they had agreed to go to Paris anyway. Several urgent phone calls to Amy's four former nannies had gone nowhere—two had other positions, one was eight months pregnant, and the other was planning her wedding for early September. An offer from Bronnie to pay for the wedding if it was postponed had been declined. And Amy would not accept a total stranger—Bronnie knew her daughter well enough to be sure of that.

So Bronnie was trying to make the best of things. She was trying to see Cal's absence and Julie's betrayal as a time to re-connect with her husband and daughter. How hard could it be to travel without a nanny? She and Henry had traveled alone early in their marriage. And now they had drivers to help with the bags. They had a hotel with room service and maid service and a team of concierges.

But she now realized that having a nanny along on family vacations had served another purpose: it had masked how little Henry did with his family, how little he was involved with them. Having a nanny to chat with had hidden from her the conversations she wasn't having with Henry. Watching a silly kids' movie with the nanny and Amy had disguised the fact that Henry never sat through an entire film with his children.

The family nannies had served as a buffer for a thousand fights that Henry and Bronnie never had. When the kids interrupted Henry and he shouted at them, the nanny got scolded for letting the children into his office. When Henry was late for their anniversary dinner, Bronnie hadn't said a word, but she had spent the next day blaming the nanny for giving the children milk allergies and had fired one of the maids.

Now, without anyone along whom Bronnie had the power to fire, she was forced to look at her husband as an outsider might, to evaluate her situation without the filter of a go-between. She saw the flight attendant approach him and ask him if he was having a nice flight.

"Can I make a request?" she heard her husband say. "Can you not speak to me again unless you have something particular to ask, for the rest of the flight? To be clear, something that you are required to ask, and that I would be upset at you for not asking?"

Bronnie realized that she hated her husband. It seemed strange that she had never noticed it before.

27

Fashion Week is just around the corner, kiddies, and that means a whole new wave of temptations for this recovering brand-name lover. (But first, can I take a moment to say how much I loved Michelle Obama's Maria Pinto dress at the convention? I stopped by Maria's boutique last time I was in the Windy City. Edgy cuts, great colors. No wonder the Democrats are so fired up this year.)

So there I was, in the lobby of the Mandarin Oriental having tea with an old college friend and her daughter, when who should appear but my old friend the Junior Shopaholic? (Looking fabulous with her long dark hair and a new coat—she must have hit the Thai Yoga treatment at the spa.) She was checking a BlackBerry but seemed ready to chat about her shopping issues.

"Problem solved," she tells me. Nice boyfriend is helping her out.

"That's not really a solution, is it?"

"You want to know the solution? Stop the credit card companies. They're like supplying drugs to desperate addicts."

"So you're just a victim?"

"We're all steered by conventional wisdom. And conventional wisdom is steered by people with money. Look at this coat," she says. "Karl Lagerfeld. Now, do I like this coat, or am I just being made to think I like it by people trying to sell it to me? And if so, is it really my fault for buying it? Advertising is a multibillion-dollar industry. And they spend all that money on advertising because it works."

"But if you know all that, why did you buy it?"

"Because it's pretty," she says, and smiles. She does have a point. It's fabulous.

Almost as fabulous as this week's Miu Miu coat, which I picked up at Saks in '04 and have only worn twice. Find it on ebay, shoppers. You know where. Canella

—Shopacovery by Canella McBride, September 1, 2008

www.shopacovery.com

On Paolo's fifth visit to Vanessa's, there was a foreclosure notice on her table, and she told him that the next week she doubted she'd be there.

"Where are you going?"

"I don't know. They shut off the phone. I can't call anyone to ask if I can stay with them. I guess I could use a payphone, but I don't even know who to call."

"Where you going to go?"

"Homeless shelter."

"What about Tyler?"

"What about Tyler?" she said. "Of course he'll come with me."

"He's got doctors here."

"Yeah, so?" Vanessa shot him a disdainful look. He just wasn't getting it.

"You own this house?" he asked. "So can't you sell it?"

"Apparently I don't own it. Apparently the bank owns it. That's what they're saying. The bank owns it until you pay them back. You think you're making mortgage payments, you're really just paying rent to a different landlord."

"How much you need?"

"What does it matter? They want me out of the house, and they're going to get me out. They got the lawyers."

Vanessa was smart, but not educated, and when life turned bleak, she was quick with conspiracy theories. She was not the only poor person who had come to believe she had been lured into buying a house as an elaborate trick to bleed her into greater poverty. The very rich and the very poor share the same illusion: that rich people are smarter than everybody else and know what they're doing.

"Throwing money away," she said. "That's what they say, right? When you rent, you're throwing money away. Better to buy, right? That's how you get out of poverty. That's what they said when they gave me the loan for the house."

"Why'd you buy a house if you don't have a job?"

"I did have a job. I was working at a restaurant. Then Tyler got worse, and he needed me full time. It was easier to stay home than work just to pay for a nurse, you know? I couldn't work and afford the nurse, so what was I going to do, let him lie here on the floor?"

Vanessa sat down opposite Paolo. They were in her kitchen.

"When I bought the house, I didn't know that was going to happen. You don't expect your whole life to fall apart."

"I know."

"You know the landlord we used to have when we were in Camden," she went on in a quiet voice, "he would—you know the law says a landlord can't let the heat and hot water be off more than twenty-four hours, or they get a fine? So every few weeks when the building ran out of heating oil, he waited twenty-four hours before he refilled it. Middle of winter. We'd have no heat, no hot water in February. He would push it just to the limit, on purpose, wait twenty-four hours, every single time, just to save money, you know? What kind of person does that? To take money from people, and then it's the middle of February, they have no heat? So then my neighbor says he's leaving one day. He says he's buying a home, no money down. And I was like, where do I sign up? And now my payments go up to eighteen hundred dollars a month? From eight hundred? This was done on purpose. They just wanted to take people's homes away."

What "they" probably wanted, Paolo thought, was to make money on late fees. He had learned enough from Ivan to know that. Everyone is an income stream, until they are in jail or in the hospital, when if they are lucky, they can bleed some money out of the system again.

"I want to help," Paolo said.

"You got eighteen hundred dollars a month? I can't get a job, either. Who's going to take care of Tyler? Any care for him would cost more than I can make."

"I'm going to fix this."

"I don't want your money. That's just stealing from other poor people."

Paolo shrugged. "I'll get the money from somewhere else."

"Oh, really? Well, it better not be from robbing a bank 'cause I already had help from one of those, thank you. Where do you think his father is? Get rich quick. You men and your get-rich-quick schemes. Tyler's father wanted to help us, too. He says, 'Baby, I'm going to do something about this. I'm going to get you the money. You and Tyler.' And what he gets is ten to fifteen years."

"You still love him?"

Vanessa shook her head. "No. I wish I did. Now I have nobody. He writes me, he's like he wants me to wait for him, and I can't. I just—I can't believe I owned my home, and I'm going to a homeless shelter."

"But you're not going to do that."

"Paolo, you're not my boyfriend."

"I know."

"Then what are you?"

"Well, do you—do you want me to be your boyfriend?"

"I can't move in with you just because I have no place. I can't do that to Tyler, and I won't, all right?"

"Can I just be your friend and help you out?"

"Not with money."

"Not with money," Paolo said, mulling over the words. He couldn't imagine what other help he could provide.

Paolo stayed for dinner that night. It wasn't much, just red beans and rice with a couple of hot dogs chopped into pieces. Vanessa's mother had grown up in New Orleans, though, so Vanessa knew how to create a meal out of strong spices and hope. They sat together afterwards, plates empty, watching the fading light come through the kitchen window. A cockroach ran across the floor and paused within sight of them, waving its little antennae, trying to get a reading on the best place to go.

"This is my home," Vanessa said.

Greg Miller's great-great grandfather worked for a wealthy family in England as a valet in the late 1800s. Hoping for a better life, that ancient Miller went into twenty years' debt to buy himself a place on a steamer that only took him as far as Newfoundland, where, while struggling to pay his passage, he married an Inuit woman, had a son, caught tuberculosis, and died at age forty.

Greg's great-grandfather was a fur trapper in Labrador. His workweek was three months long. From mid-September to mid-December and from January to March, he would drive off into the wilderness on a dog sled, then return to his wife and family months later with a load of furs, his fingers black from frostbite. The Hudson Bay Company held a monopoly on the Labrador fur trade back then, as well as a monopoly on the food and services the trappers needed, and he lost four toes while never quite managing to pay off the money he borrowed from the company for supplies, before he died prematurely at sixty-one from a lung infection.

Greg's grandfather fought with the Royal Canadian Air Force in World War II before settling with his family in Toronto to do construction work. He spent thirty years maintaining oil pipelines between Toronto and Montreal, but he managed to set aside enough money to own a home, and two of his three children completed college before he died of a heart attack at seventy.

Greg's father was an engineer who attended McGill University before moving to a nice home in the suburbs of Boston, Massachusetts, before his kids were born. He was still in good health (circa 2008, knock wood) but taking pills for high blood pressure because of the stress of the job. His financial health had been reasonable until he had to take out a second mortgage to send his kids to private colleges.

By the logic of onward and upward, Greg Miller should have done best of all: an eight-hour workday, no debt, owning a home, perhaps even sling-shotting his children into the ranks of the upper class. But Greg went to school in the middle of the dot-com boom and saw half his classmates making a quick buck off Internet startups. He had concluded that money could be had for nothing, for just the vague outlines of a good idea. He had spent his adult life looking for just such an idea, first investing in a friend's dot.com that sold DVDs over the Internet, then in a scheme to build solar-powered cars (into which he sank forty thousand of his sister's money), and finally into learning the art of poker.

Was he just lazy, a member of that infamous "younger generation," who'd never known hard work? Or was he buying into the same myth that everybody else was, missing the subtle tectonic shifts that were sending middle class life out of reach? The rising cost of college, of medical care, while the taxes on the wealthy had decreased, so that the middle class was now watching those above them race farther and farther away—so far away that the division of wealth had come to look much as it had in the 1890s, when that first Miller had traveled to the New World in an attempt at freedom.

It was his sister, Bella (Miller) Pointer, who was making good on the family promise of a better life, by doing just what her great-great grandfather had suffered and died to get away from. She was, in effect, a valet.

But Greg still held out hope he was going to make good. Which is why when Greg won the hand of poker from the captive he was guarding for Frank—when he watched her lose her freedom on a single hand—he had what he called an instinct. A gut feeling. He was on a winning streak. He had to go and do something about it.

Frank had already paid Greg six thousand to guard Lillian, enough to repay most of what Greg owed to Ivan, and that was good, right? But Frank was going to tell Greg to release Lillian soon, he'd hidden most of his incriminating SAT scam evidence already, and then the money would run out.

No. With a hand of poker at a real casino—with a good hand of poker—he could turn that six grand into eighty or a hundred grand and clear all his debts in one blow. And maybe even make a little for himself off the top, to start a life again.

With a hundred thousand dollars, he could pay back his sister.

He could start his own business—teaching people to play poker.

He could go to Vegas and turn it into a half a million dollars, or a million, or twenty million.

And with twenty million dollars, he could be pretty much set for life. He would never have to work again, and he could set up his sister so she wouldn't have to work anymore either. He could get married and have kids and buy the kids amazing toys. He could take his wife out on a sailboat off the shore of Cape Cod, and skiing in Canada every winter. He could be the perfect father with twenty million dollars. The perfect husband. His parents wouldn't think he was a failure. His classmates from Harvard would respect him. And the crazy part was that the potential was actually there. The money was there, already sitting there in his hands, just waiting to be used. That six thousand dollars was going to be his future.

With one good hand.

Chris Schott had once helped a friend find a missing bike, as he had told Lillian. He had lucked into an eyewitness account from a neighbor about the young man who had taken it. He had driven around the area looking for the right kid. And when they spotted the boy who had stolen the bike, Chris threatened to go to the police, and sure enough, the boy returned the bike, pretty much intact. And he and the boy started talking, and he realized the kid just needed some direction and got the boy an internship at Chris's college newspaper, where the boy worked for two months before he was fired for stealing office supplies.

That experience may have infected Chris with a certain cynicism about helping the poor, but it had given him a certain optimism about police work.

Looking for Lillian was proving to be different. Chris had at last recruited Nadya to put up missing person posters. They had contacted all the local TV stations. They had fielded endless phone calls from dirt-seeking reporters from the *New York Post*. But there were no leads.

And something had changed for Chris. Everything in his life seemed flat these days. He wasn't doing well at work. He was still sleeping with Nadya. She had come to stay at his place, but he woke up dreaming about what could have happened to Lillian. He knew what it meant when a young, attractive woman didn't reappear after four or five days. His last, best hope was that she had been sold into white slavery, was off working in a brothel somewhere, would reappear with a strange tattoo and some dark stories.

He could hear Lillian's voice, speaking about Nadya: "She's not a hooker."

He didn't love Nadya, but he felt that she needed him. Her nonchalance about Lillian had opened wide to reveal a chasm of horror beneath. She couldn't sleep in her own apartment, woke up four times a night, drank a lot. She had nightmares.

He was also experiencing a strange vertigo. He had never fallen in love, not really. He had enjoyed Lillian's company, but he probably would not have fallen so hard for her if she hadn't disappeared. But now it was as if losing her was the first real thing that had happened to him. His money and success had not been able to cushion the blow, as it had before when he lost out on jobs or girlfriends. She was simply gone.

So when he got a call from a hospital that there was a mysterious young woman in their coma wing, he walked out of a meeting at work to be there, to see her, although his manager looked stunned at his departure.

And when the girl was not Lillian, was overweight with dyed-black hair, he found himself sitting in the hospital hallway hours later, unable to will himself to leave. Nadya arrived (he had shared the news with her) and she sat with him while he restlessly ran his thumb over her knuckles.

"I'm sorry," he said. "I'm not very much fun right now."

"Who is?"

"I guess I'm feeling less optimistic."

"You gave up on the poker-playing guy?"

"The SAT thing? Yeah, I don't know. It seems unlikely. I mean, you really think the Bolt family would make Lillian disappear just because she was going to accuse their son of cheating on his SATs? It's so risky. And Henry Bolt has so much money."

"He could buy his son into any college in the country, so why bother?"

"Yeah, exactly."

"Come home."

"I will. I just need a minute. A few minutes."

Chris found the hospital, in an odd way, comforting, because no one in it was happy. It suited his state of mind.

"Do you want me to stay?"

"No, no," he said.

Nadya watched him for a moment, then nodded and kissed his cheek and got up and left. Chris found himself staring down the glassy eyes of a young male patient through an open doorway across the hall. After a few moments, it was too much for him, and he rose to look for a vending machine.

"Henry Bolt," came a faint voice.

Chris paused, uncertain of the origin of the voice. Then the voice said, "...has mob connections."

Chris backtracked two or three steps, looked through the open doorway again. There was a young, dark-haired man looking up at him.

"Did you...?"

"Henry Bolt has mob connections," repeated the young man.

There was a noise from the nurse's station, and a nurse came rushing down the corridor and stopped to look at the patient.

"Clyde," said the nurse. "How are you feeling?"

Clyde ignored the question. He and Chris were staring at each other, sizing each other up.

"Can you prove that?" Chris asked.

214

"I'm going to call your mother," the nurse continued. "Clyde? Clyde? Can you hear me?"

Clyde whispered, "Yes."

Paolo had been instructed not to speak to Celia Upson. His job, instead, was to follow her—to see where she went. His job was to make sure she didn't do anything suspicious. He followed her when she went out to the street and got into an old Chevy and started driving. He followed her when she pulled onto the highway and drove all the way to Connecticut, to Mohegan Sun Casino. He watched her at the slot machines, the mechanical way in which she fed in the quarters, one after another. After about a half hour, he stepped outside for a smoke. He called up Ivan on his cell phone and said, "She's not doing anything. She's just playing slots." Ivan said, "Then what the hell are you calling me for? Tell me something useful or don't bother me, you stupid asshole." Paolo hung up.

That was when he noticed the valet parking attendants.

He watched them opening car doors for people, holding out gloved hands to attractive ladies, and he realized, in a rush, that he felt jealous of them. Now there was some easy money. Just drive around pretty cars all day and wait until someone got lucky at the casino and handed you a fifty.

For the first time since he'd been the fat kid in grade school, he wanted out of his life. He wanted out so much that his imagination was leaping into someone else's life, dressing himself in a valet uniform, imagining accepting a tip. He wasn't a good gangster. He wasn't made for it. He kept waiting for it to get better, for something to get cool, and it hadn't. Instead he was just getting yelled at by his boss, like at any other job.

That was probably what put Paolo in a bad mood. A rotten mood. So bad that when he saw Greg Miller pulling up to the casino, getting out of his fancy rental car and clearly flush with cash, he didn't hold back. He walked right up behind Greg, pressed a gun into his back, and muttered into Greg's right shoulder: "You are a fucking dead man."

When Bella arrived in her office at 7:15 a.m. on Monday, September 8, 2008 (1:15 p.m. Paris time), there were two voicemails for her. In the days that followed, Bella would listen again to the two voicemails and second-guess her decision.

The first message was: "Hey, Bella? It's Greg. Call me. I need some advice. Okay?"

She would ask herself, later, whether she had detected the false nonchalance, the undercurrent of terror. But she was distracted by the second message:

"Bella. I'm going to need a meeting set up by phone with the managing directors for this afternoon, preferably around three p.m., my time. I would also like you to get the Board of Directors on the phone for a meeting to follow the MD meeting. I would estimate that the board meeting should take place at about six p.m. my time. Also, please arrange for a private jet to fly me back to New York tonight. I may not take it, but I'd like to have the option. If I don't leave tonight I may leave tomorrow morning, but nothing earlier than a ten a.m. flight, Paris time, since I'm still partly on New York time. See if you can arrange for a hotel tonight at the airport, in case I want to spend the night at the airport in Paris before the flight in the morning, but there's a good chance I'll want the flight tonight. If I have to take a commercial flight because no private jet is available, that's acceptable, but only if you can get first class, or BusinessFirst if it's Continental. Oh, and Carver should be on vacation in Venezuela but I'm sure his assistant has his number and I'd like him in both meetings, too, by phone if necessary. Thanks."

Bella decided to deal with Henry's call first. Later, she would remember that she didn't think much about her brother's message and planned to call him at the end of the day.

28

CAL BOLT WAS OFFICIALLY THE DIRECTOR OF THE MOVIE *Snuff,* and Peter Wicka was officially the star, but things had grown a little more complicated on set. Peter wanted to check the camera angle and lighting for every shot, particularly those that included him, so they had recruited a teenage volunteer named Obadiah from the Heavenly Alliance Church youth group to act as Peter's stand-in.

On the Saturday of Labor Day weekend, on their eighth shooting day out of ten, Obadiah, feeling awkward, was standing at the edge of the set with a hypodermic needle in his pocket, while Julie and Peter carried out the following debate:

"I don't understand why I say, 'Do it!'" Julie was asking.

"Because you want to die," Peter replied.

"Yeah, but how do I know you're there to kill me?"

"Because you see the look in my eye."

"But is the audience going to get that? Because the last time my character talked to your character, it was kind of happy. It was about our childhoods and stuff."

"Yeah, but the audience knows that I'm there to kill you."

"But will they know that I know you want to kill me?"

Peter sighed. "Julie, just—say the line, please? Trust me. This is my vision."

Peter often talked about his vision during the shoot, particularly when people pointed out small logical gaps in the script. He did, in fact, have a vision. Immersed as he was in Andy Warhol's Factory days films, Peter believed that rough, unpolished acting by nonprofessionals was the best kind. It took away the artifice of the performer. Robert Bresson films were a secondary model. The problem (in Peter's mind) was that he had handed

217

over the crucial role of director to Cal, who didn't appreciate the value of such cultivated rough edges.

An impatient Cal spoke up, "Will you come look at the shot, Peter?"

"We're working on the acting first."

"Okay, but why don't we set up the shot and work on the acting right before we shoot it."

"Okay, fine."

Obadiah sat down next to Julie. "I thought it was a good question," he said.

Julie's problem was that she immersed herself in everything she did. She had received the highest GPA out of 265 undergraduate education majors at SUNY Oneonta. Having quit her job to act in this film, she was serious about her role—but her earnestness, intensity, and willingness to cry on cue were spoiling the "wooden" acting quality Peter had been hoping for. There was little chance that Julie would spark ironic detachment in the audience, and rather than appreciating what he had discovered—a natural actress—Peter was busy mourning the detached-cool-art-house film he saw in his head.

"Hey Obie," Peter said, looking up from the video monitor, "can you raise that needle so I can see how it looks when I hold it up?"

"Sure thing." Obadiah stepped forward and raised the hypodermic needle. While he did, he chatted with Julie.

"You went to Maple Hill High School, right?"

"Yeah."

"Yeah, me too. Who'd you have for English?"

Cal spoke up, "Hold up the needle a little higher, and, like, hold it above her neck."

"Okay."

Their soundman, a round-shouldered guy who worked as a local substitute teacher when he wasn't doing audio for Pastor Walsh's sermons, spoke up. "Hey, Obie, can I get a line so I can set volume?"

"Stay still!"

218

"Do it!" Julie replied.

"I can't! I love you!"

"You don't love me! No one can! Just kill me! Kill me!" Tears leapt to Julie's eyes.

"Okay, thanks," said the soundman.

Peter turned from the camera to face Julie. "Can I talk to you outside for a minute?"

"Sure," said Julie. "I'm sorry, I'm just trying to get it right…"

Julie and Peter walked into the hallway, where they began talking in earnest. Cal rubbed his hands together, embarrassed and uncertain. He picked up his iPhone and opened his email. He glanced toward the door. He thought this film was a disaster, that it was never going anywhere, that it was not going to impress his dad or anyone in Hollywood.

At the end of each day, they had to sit with the Pastor, talk about how things were going, and discuss possible script revisions. Pastor Walsh had suggested a coda in which the main characters talked about their lives and their regrets from beyond the grave, to drive home the Christian message. Peter was trying to say that this shouldn't be in the cut that went to film festivals. It was a hot debate.

Cal missed his mother and sister. He wasn't having fun. He wondered if Peter had just used him to try to get money out of his father. He wondered how Lillian was doing, and he felt anxious and sick and guilty. He had to tell his father that they knew about the kidnapping, even if it was Frank's idea. But if he did, he'd lose his dad's respect forever.

"How could you have been so stupid?" his father would say. How were you supposed to answer a question like that?

What if she got hurt? Every scene they shot with Julie as the kidnapped captive, it haunted him. He wanted his life to fall apart, and was terrified it would, and felt himself approaching the edge, and felt excited and sick and dull.

He watched Peter kissing Julie's cheek, her ear, out in the hallway. He looked down, and, on a whim, decided to check his mother's blog on his iPhone. He'd been avoiding reading it because it might include something embarrassing, but now he was hoping for a Paris update, for something that would make him feel closer to his family again.

He read: "So now I find that our nanny has deliberately allowed Amy to not learn to sleep on her own, even though I told her that Amy must must must learn to sleep on her own. And Henry left for New York and now I've been up for thirty-six hours with Amy and she won't sleep. And I'm tired and I want a divorce."

29

I have an aching memory somewhere of what it was like before all this. One big step across the floor as a child and my small hand on the round door handle and then opening the door to see my mom and dad in bed. I knew I wasn't supposed to be in their room, yet I'd done it somehow, and there they were, together, not making love or anything, just smiling at me across the endless expanse of covers. I wish they'd scolded me that day. It would have prepared me better for what was to come. Instead they took me into bed with them and held me and smiled, and I came to believe that across each forbidden boundary was something wonderful.
—"The Field Trip" by Lillian Fitzgerald, *The Antioch Review*

SOMETHING HAD CHANGED IN LILLIAN AFTER THREE weeks in captivity. A feral will to live had begun to emerge, an animal cleverness. She was almost sure that her sense of smell had grown stronger. And she had decided to make a break for it the next time her captor left. Her first conclusion was that the video camera was, in effect, meaningless. Whoever was watching was not responsive. The handcuffs were the challenge, but she had come up with a theory on how to disassemble the bed. Now all she had to do was wait until her poker friend took off.

Barely a half hour after he wiped her out in Texas hold 'em and she lost her chance at freedom, he was out the door. She heard a car start up and drive away. And then she took action.

First step: bang the bed against the wall and see if anyone responds. She pulled at the bed with her wrists, slamming it against the wall. No response. She made a dent in the wall, and that could be trouble if she didn't get free.

Next step: identify a weak joint in the bed and go to work at it. Slamming. It wasn't easy. Every time she slammed, she had to stop and listen. Had he come back? Would this mean murder? She slammed the bed against the wall. Listened. Nothing. She slammed the bed against the wall again. Listened. Nothing. The bed didn't seem to be falling apart in the way she'd imagined, but it did loosen up, a little at a time, becoming wobblier, and then after more effort she was able to wrench it apart somewhat. There was no changing her mind—she was standing there connected by handcuffs to the metal headboard.

She decided on a new strategy—banging open the door and dragging the bed behind her. (She could see the news report in her head: "Woman found dragging bed by side of New Jersey Turnpike.") She set to work at the door. Banging with the headboard. It was a heavy metal door, she discovered. She was stuck.

Hours passed without headway, and she was growing more frantic, hungrier, more determined but less clear-headed about what to try next. She wondered if this was how military pilots felt while they were under enemy fire, or how animals felt fleeing from predators. There was joy in being focused, desperate, playing for your life like that. Her reckless joy dulled in an instant when she heard a car pull up and two car doors close.

She stepped away from the door, ready to fight, ready for anything.

"In here?"

Someone shot at the door handle with a gun, and she pressed against the wall. Five messy shots and the door opened.

An elderly man with a shock of white hair and a scarred face stepped inside, accompanied by a large, dull-eyed man with traces of blood on his hands. Lillian watched them both, silent. She had seen Paolo before, but she couldn't remember where. His bloody hands made him unrecognizable to her, made him only a creature of terror. The old man nodded his head at her a few times. He examined the wrecked bed, then pulled up a chair while the tall, bloody gunman stood at the door, glancing outside.

"Hi." said Ivan. Thick Jersey accent. It sounded like "Hoi."

Lillian said nothing.

"What, you don't speak English?"

Lillian shrugged, unwilling to commit to understanding him.

"Here's the way this works," said the elderly man. "The man who was holding you captive, he owes us money, so now you belong to us. He says he was holding you for somebody. Who was he holding you for?"

"I don't know."

"How long you been here?"

"Three weeks."

"All right, let's get her outta here," said the old man to the large bodyguard. The bodyguard, frowning, looked at her handcuffs, then pulled out a set of keys and flipped through them, searching for the right one. He unlocked her hands.

Henry couldn't have told you, for certain, whether he loved his wife. He knew that it had seemed like a good idea to marry her. He knew that she had certain desirable qualities in a wife and other qualities that he simply enjoyed: the smell of her long dark hair, the acid twinge of her perfume. She was a sharp woman, angled, but the base of her neck had a dent tinged with blue. She was also from money, spoiled from childhood, and had at first seemed happy to be possessed by someone who could keep up the buffer between her and real life.

But if you had asked him whether he loved her, he would said "of course," while thinking that you were wasting his time. Whether he loved his wife in no way affected how he was going to behave toward her. A business required what it required—and anyone who thought otherwise was not going to succeed in business. If this meant he lost his wife, if she was too shortsighted to recognize that everything he did was for his family, then so be it.

223

If he allowed that kind of worry to creep into decisions, he would be paralyzed.

The truth was—and Henry didn't tell this to anyone—that he'd only loved one woman in his life. There'd been an original sin moment for Henry, after which he had no longer believed in love. It had been when Celia, his girlfriend many years ago, had taken money to break up with him and had taken his kid with her. Ivan had told Henry he could buy her off, and Henry hadn't believed him, but sure enough, she'd taken the money.

When she walked out on him, he'd lost the ability to care about anyone. He loved his kids, he supposed. And he loved that he could control them, so they would never leave him.

Now Ivan said Celia had resurfaced, that his other son was out there somewhere. Henry hadn't wanted to know who the kid was. He just wanted to know how to keep her away from him. He didn't like that there was a part of him that still felt hurt.

Henry had decided to take the evening jet from Paris, so he was in his office the next day when Bella called him on his office phone. It was an hour before his next meeting with the Board of Directors.

"Henry," she said. "I'm very sorry to interrupt, but there's something I think you should see."

"How urgent is it?"

"I'm not sure."

"Does it require my decision right now?"

"I just thought you should know about it as soon as it happened."

"Go ahead."

"I've sent you an email with the web link," she replied.

Henry rolled his chair to his computer and opened the email, then clicked on a web link to Bronnie's blog. He read the news of his possible impending divorce with Bella on the line.

"Okay, thank you," he said.

Bella waited, hesitating, wondering if there was more she should do.

224

"I was just wondering..." she began, "if you'd like me to contact the web hosting service and have that taken down."

"No, that won't be necessary."

"Okay," she said.

"For the record," Henry said, "that wasn't urgent."

"Okay. I'm sorry."

Bella hung up the phone and called the catering company to confirm that there would be at least two vegan options for that day's Board of Director's meeting, as one of the board members was on a no-cholesterol diet.

Henry sat at his desk going through a mental list of what had prompted Bronnie's announcement. She had been quiet, in Paris, when he said that he needed to go back to the city. She hadn't protested. Maybe being without a nanny had just been too much for her. Then he dismissed it from his thoughts. There was too much else to focus on. Bolt Bank's stock had declined in the last forty-eight hours because of bad news at Lehman. He needed to discuss with the board how he could transfer his devalued stock options into a new compensation package while maintaining the public perception that the company was going strong.

Making money required what it required. Even if that meant breaking up with someone. And that was what he'd learned from Celia.

Lillian got her first glance of her former poker-playing captor without his mask when Paolo shoved her into a Lincoln Town Car. Greg Miller was beaten and bloody and unable to speak. He looked at her, wordless, his eyes glowing through a blue mask of bruises. She could tell he had been handsome, was handsome. He looked kinder than she had expected, but on edge, and as frightened as she was.

She turned and stared forward. The large man who she assumed had delivered these blows got into the driver's seat while the elderly man took the passenger seat.

"I'll tell you what I think," said Ivan. "I think that you are a very attractive young lady."

"Oh. Thanks."

"You could make some good money, you know. If we set you up to work for me."

"You mean? For you? What would I do?"

"What I tell you. I don't ask girls what they want to do. They do as they're told."

Lillian looked at the bloodied man next to her and said nothing. After a few moments, she attempted a dodge. "Well, I just—I don't think I'd be very good at...some things."

"You don't have to be good at it." He chuckled. "You think anyone cares? Now shut up. I'm tired of you talking." He waved a gun over his shoulder to emphasize the point. Lillian was silent, tears running down her face. Through most of her captivity, she hadn't cried. Now she found herself breaking down, sobbing. The men in the front seat ignored her.

"I'm really—I'm a writer. If you need anything written..." The last, desperate attempt.

"Written? What would I need written? Listen to this, do you hear this?" he asked his silent associate.

"I don't know," Lillian said. The only person who'd asked for her to write something was Bronnie, so she ran with that. "Your autobiography? Have you thought about writing about your life?"

Ivan laughed. "I tell you, if I ever wrote that, nobody would believe a goddamn word."

"You could—you know—it would be like that guy who wrote the book for *Goodfellas*."

"That guy was a snitch. If you snitch, you can write your autobiography. Otherwise, they'd arrest you."

"Anonymously, you could."

"Jesus, are you listening to this?" Ivan asked his strong man. "The nerve of this one."

"I'm sorry. I'm just offering."

"That's—huh," said the man. "And you think you could write it so it sounds like me?"

"That's what writers do. We're good at pretending to be other people. I could make it sound exactly like you."

"It would be a hell of a lot more exciting than *Goodfellas*, if I ever wrote one."

"I'm sure it would," said Lillian. For the first time, she had a glimmer of hope.

"What a crazy idea," he said.

"Why not? I mean, someday you're going to die, right? Not anytime soon. But you could have this record to leave behind you, you know, of who you were, and what you thought about things."

"I do have my own way of doing stuff, this is true."

"I bet you do," Lillian said.

"Are you listening to this?" Ivan said to the silent heavy.

Paolo shrugged.

The older man reached over the back of his seat with the hand that wasn't holding the gun. "My name is Ivan."

"I'm Lillian."

"Lillian. You can write my book. We got a deal, okay? But if you try to turn me into the police I'll put a bullet in your skull."

"Okay. I'll do a great job."

"And if I don't kill you, this guy will."

"I understand." Lillian nodded. Then she said, "That sounds like a good opening line to your book."

"What?"

"If you turn me in to the police, I'll put a bullet in your skull."

"You think we could open a book with that?"

"Yeah, it'd be great. Wouldn't that suck you in, if you were reading it?"

"Yeah, sure, why not?"

"Does he need to go to the hospital?" she ventured, looking at the man next to her.

"Good point," said Ivan. "Dump him."

The car screeched to the curb, and the large man grabbed Lillian's poker-playing captor.

"What do we want to tell this guy, Ivan?" asked Paolo.

"Just tell him 'Don't come back.'"

Paolo reinforced the words by kicking at Greg Miller's stomach (once, and mostly for Ivan's benefit) before leaving Greg by the side of the road. Lillian wasn't able to see for certain whether her former captor was still alive before the door closed and the car sped away.

30

THE *SNUFF* SHOOT WAS BEHIND SCHEDULE, BUT PETER HAD a plan. Two more weekends in September should do the trick. They really only needed four more shoot days to get a few more key scenes, like Julie's kidnapping. In the meantime, Peter planned on editing what they'd already shot, along with starting his freshman year at Fortuna.

Julie was looking forward to the end of the shoot. Things had been growing tense with her father, who had developed an antagonistic relationship with Peter's "vision." It distressed her to see the two of them upset with each other. She also hadn't explained to her father that she had walked out on her job as a nanny, and she knew she would have to sooner or later. She had nowhere else to stay but home. When the shoot was over, she was going to have to 'fess up. There would be a lot of prayers involved, and possibly some yard work.

The Sunday night before shooting was to wrap, she stood outside her father's office, watching him write his thoughts following the day's sermon. He kept a diary, and although he said he never planned to publish it, he seemed to expect that she would read it someday, possibly after his death. It was like a long letter he was writing to her future self.

"Dad."

He turned and looked at her. She felt, had always felt, that she was in some way a disappointment to her father, though she couldn't identify her crime. She used to think he had wanted a son, but now she wondered if she hadn't given him enough to do. She hadn't given him enough teenage rebellion. He was an active man, and he liked to have a problem to work on.

"How's the shooting going?" he asked.

"It's okay. I wanted to talk to you about that, actually. About the ending."

"Okay. Come in, sit down."

She sat down in the chair designated for his parishioners and said, "I think maybe you should let Peter do the film his way."

"Why do you say that?"

"I don't know. Just because—it's his film. And Cal's. I mean, there's no way it will be the sort of film it would be if you were directing it."

"I have no interest in directing a film."

"I know." She sighed, twisting her hands together.

"Julie, has this been a good experience for you? Have you been having a good experience? Acting?"

"Oh, yeah, I guess. It's not what I thought it would be."

"Why not?"

"Because I thought it would all be about feeling your way into a character. But it's really about trying to make the director happy. Which is okay, you know. It's not that it's...I mean, I've had a good experience."

"And you wrap up soon."

"We aren't going to get the whole movie done by tomorrow, I think. I think maybe they'll have to come back up for a couple of weekends."

"And that's okay with your job?"

Julie leaned forward. "I don't think I'm going back to my job. I kind of quit to do this movie."

There was a long silence in the room, while her father waited for some kind of explanation and Julie waited for some kind of judgment.

"I see," he said after a moment.

"Dad," she said. "Will you trust me?"

"I'm not very good at trusting anyone. It's one of the things that happens when you do my job. You see all the ways people can err."

"I know. I know that. But I don't want you to trust people. I want you to trust me."

230

"You mean, because I love you?"

"Yes. I want you to trust me about the job. And Peter and Cal, and the film. And all of it."

He sighed. "Then I will do that. They can do the film their way."

Julie nodded and started to cry.

"What are you crying for?"

She shook her head. She couldn't say it was because he'd never relaxed the rules for her, not ever, not in her whole life. To point that out to him would have been cruel.

Thirty minutes later, Julie stood outside Peter's motel room, clutching a thin gray sweater over her shoulders. The Sundown Motel had agreed to donate rooms for the purpose of supporting Pastor Walsh's film, and Cal and Peter were in the rooms at the end of the motel closest to Route 4. Julie wasn't sure why she was nervous. She was bringing good news. But something about standing outside Peter's room in the dark, with the breeze hinting of early fall, made her feel ultra-alert, hesitant. She raised a hand to knock when she heard voices arguing. Cal might be there, or maybe it was the TV. She listened at the door to be sure.

"Oh my fucking God." It was Cal, and he sounded anguished. "Jesus Christ."

"She could be fine, man."

"She's—this is a disaster. This is going to ruin my life. We can't keep going like this."

Julie looked down, ashamed. She was certain the disastrous "she" referred to Julie.

"It's just—the kidnapper is gone. He's just gone. That's what Frank said."

The kidnapping scene?

"But if she got hurt—or killed –"

"Repeat after me. Not our problem."

"She is our problem. She's a fucking human being."

"Who is not our problem."

"Yes, she…"

"Lillian is not our problem."

Julie stood still, feeling that old cliché occur in fact—the blood had drained from her face. The world seemed to turn to black and white.

Peter went on. "I'm sorry, okay? I didn't expect anything to happen. But now the best thing is for us to just act like we know nothing about it. Because if she turns up dead—"

"Don't say that."

"I'm sorry."

"You're sorry! I fucking hate you, man. You're not my friend. You use people. You're only friends with me for my father's money."

"That's not true."

"Bullshit."

"You need to calm down!"

"No. I'm going to tell my father!"

"Don't you leave this room."

"I'm leaving. Watch me."

The volume of the words increased until the door was opened, but still Julie didn't move. She just stood there as Cal stared at her. He had been in the process of storming out.

She glanced at the two of them. Both boys had identical blank expressions on their faces. Then Peter roused.

"Hey, Julie," Peter said, half-ironic, with an undertone of warning to Cal. All her illusions about him, about how he was going to marry her, about the good man underneath who was going to be transformed, fell away and piled on top of her feet, so that she couldn't move.

"Did you need something?" Peter went on.

Julie looked at Cal, his misery combined with fear of being caught, and she felt pity. She and Cal had both been seduced.

"Peter," she said in a soft voice. "You have to go to the police."

"About what?"

"I heard you talking. If you know something about Lillian…"

"Lillian who?"

Cal looked even more miserable. He couldn't meet Julie's eyes.

"Then I'll go to the police."

"You don't want to do that," Peter said. "Julie, come on." Cal was still keeping his eyes to the floor. "Julie, come on." Peter walked up and put his arms around her. "It was just a joke. We don't know where Lillian is. We were pretending. For the script."

Julie looked at Cal. "Cal," she said, without meeting Peter's eyes, "you have to go to the police."

"I can't," he wailed, reminding Julie of his sister: the same begging for help, begging for someone else to do the hard stuff that he'd never been asked to do.

"Cal."

"I'll tell my dad," he said. "I'll tell him, tomorrow. I'll tell him in a couple of days. I just need forty-eight hours to fix this."

"I have to call the police."

"No. Julie, my dad could—my dad knows security people, stuff like that. He could—they could—don't report it, Julie, please? Please? I could go to jail and—I didn't even know about this until tonight."

Julie said, "I have to tell someone."

"Julie," began Peter.

"Shut up," said Cal. "Julie, I'll tell my dad tonight. I promise. I will. You can go with me. Please just give me a chance to tell my dad, please?" Cal knew how to wheedle with nannies. It was what he'd spent his entire childhood doing.

Julie nodded. "If you don't tell him…"

"I will."

Peter said, "What about our movie?"

Julie looked at him and started walking to the car.

"Julie," he called after her, "I'm not saying we should shoot tomorrow, I'm just asking."

"Cal, call me when it's done."

Julie got into her father's car and drove away without a word.

"Okay," said Peter. "Well, so we're fucked."

Cal nodded.

"You know what?" said Peter. "We should just use the kidnapping footage. I mean, Frank's been shooting Lillian the whole time, right? I mean, we could—if they did actually kill her, the guys—we'd have an actual snuff film."

"What?"

"We could have an actual snuff film. In our snuff film."

Cal just stood staring at him.

"Which is kind of—I'm not saying it's cool—" Peter began. "I mean, look, I'm just saying if we can't finish our movie—if Julie won't do it…It's just an option."

"I'm going home and telling my father."

"You want to be an artist, right? We should be willing to do anything for art. Anything. I mean, if this—if we did this, we'd be fucking famous. Forever."

"I don't want to be an artist."

"You said…"

"I just want to go home."

They drove together in Peter's father's BMW down I-87. Every few minutes, Peter tried to put a positive spin on something, but Cal continued to ignore him, so he decided not to bother.

"I'm not a bad person," Peter said after a while. "It's not like…"

And he trailed off, unable to think of what it wasn't like he was.

Julie drove off into the silent night of Upstate New York, under a sky pierced with stars. After a mile of driving, she started weeping. It came on so strong that she had to pull over, her body wracked with sobs, wrenching her forward over the steering wheel. It was almost exciting to be so wretched, to have fallen so low, to have been so deceived. She had loved him. And she had let him seduce her—she had fallen into evil—had lost her virginity—had made an evil film, and acted in it, and done it all for him. She had given up her God, everything, for Peter.

She had left her home, had gone to New York City without knowing why, had turned on her family and church to take a job without knowing why, or what she was doing, and now, in some deep spiral of despair, her saintly face strained forward through the tears in peace and clarity. She knew why she'd done it.

She had, at last, something worthwhile to confess to her father.

When Cal arrived at home, he went to his father's study, hoping that Henry was in bed early for once. But his father was working, as always.

Henry looked up as he entered. "I thought you were with your mother at the country house." Bronnie had retreated there after Paris. She hadn't said a word to Henry about the divorce. He hadn't called her, either. Maybe after his meetings. When he had the time.

"No," said Cal. "I was up in Albany doing the film, remember?"

"Right. Of course."

Cal pawed the door handle, swaying it forward and back like a child.

"Did you need something?" his father asked.

"Oh, yeah. I mean, I just need to talk to you."

"Okay," Henry said.

A long moment passed.

There it was. Even Henry felt it, who had trained himself not to feel. The long shadow of silence between father and son. Neither of them knew how it had gotten there, or how the world would have looked if things were any other way.

"Dad, that thing—about me cheating on the SAT? Well, Peter, my friend, he knew this guy who could—who could help arrange something like that, and so I said that you know, if I really wanted to go to Fortuna, it might be a good—it might be something… anyway…"

Cal paused to make sure his father was picking up on the subtleties of the situation. Henry nodded his chin for Cal to go on.

"But this friend of…of Peter's, he got upset when he found out that Lillian started to suspect something—because she was going to turn him in, and he thought, like, maybe his whole thing, like he was running it like a business, and—anyway, so I guess Peter just told me, like, tonight, I didn't know about it before, but I guess that Peter says this guy had something maybe to do with Lillian, my tutor. And how she was kidnapped."

"I see."

"So I thought I should tell you, because I didn't know, and I didn't have anything to do with it, but it could come back to look like I did, or, you know? And it could … "

"So you cheated on your SAT, and Lillian realized it, and the person who helped you cheat kidnapped her?"

"No. Not exactly, I mean, I did all the tutoring and stuff, but you know, I did have contact with the guy who—who helped some people cheat."

"You had someone take the test for you."

"Well, Peter said that a lot of people do that now, that it's sort of part of what students do to be competitive."

"Peter Wicka."

"Yeah."

"Who you were making the film with."

"I realize—he's not my friend anymore. He gives pretty bad ad…advice."

Henry rose from his seat and walked to the window that looked out on 68th Street. He sighed. He didn't look at Cal for a long time. Cal was relieved. He had never confessed anything like this, and he hadn't been sure if his father would cast him out.

"I'm sorry," Cal said.

"What?"

"I said I'm sorry. I know you've never done anything illegal."

Henry took in this assertion. "You're sorry?"

"I screwed everything up."

Henry nodded. He sat down again.

"Well," he said, "it sounds like we ought to give Dan Marrone a call."

"He's a police officer, though, right?"

"Not anymore."

236

Cal had expected a lecture, a discussion of moral failings. But his father was a fixer, a closer, a problem solver, and Cal had presented him with a complicated problem.

"That sounds okay," Cal offered.

"I'll talk to him first, but he may have some questions for you."

"Okay."

"You can go to bed. It's just as well your mother isn't home. Don't tell her about this."

"I won't."

"You can close the door on your way out."

Cal closed his father's study door on the way out.

That was the first night that Cal understood how glad he was to have a father with all the money in the world, a father who could protect him from everything. The absence of his father during most of his childhood suddenly seemed worth it—if it meant that his father could now keep him out of jail, get him into college, fix this one massive, life-shattering mistake.

31

Lillian had been laboring for years under the assumption that it was hard to make a living as a writer. She now understood, sitting handcuffed to her chair in a tiny locked room in Ivan's house, that making a living as a writer was pretty easy. All you had to do was be willing to give up any credit for your work. If you wrote somebody else's story, you could make a decent living. That was what she'd done for Bronnie, right?

Without noticing, she had actually been doing it! She had been doing it for weeks! She had been earning her living as a writer! Living her dream career! She wondered if she should have accepted Ivan's offer to be a hooker, instead.

Ivan was discussing his third wife, Nancy.

"Nancy was—she was a little high strung. Very pretty woman. A little high strung. She started to do cocaine, I told her I'd divorce her if she did any more, so when I caught her again I divorced her."

"All right."

"That's pretty much Nancy. What else do you want to know?"

"So, no kids?" Lillian asked.

"Nah, no kids."

"Why not?"

"Never wanted them, not when I was young anyway. And then later…"

Lillian waited a long time for him to go on.

"So here's a story. I met this young kid once, about twenty-five years old. I used to go to this Wally's Donuts, right? You know them?"

"Not really."

"Donut shop. I'd meet some guys there, we'd talk about business. It was our regular meeting place. And I catch the kid behind the counter listening to us. The owner, but a young guy, right? He knows I'm doing, you know, some not-so-legal stuff. But we become friendly. So one day the kid comes to me, wants a gun. Thinks I can get him a gun. Of course I want to know why, you know. I make him explain. Turns out he wants to kill himself. He's driven this little donut shop into the ground, and he met this girl, and now she's pregnant. Whoops, bam, he's broke, she's knocked up, he hates his life, feels trapped, you know? And you know what I tell him? I say, 'Kid, I'll tell you about business. Here's how to run a business.' I say it's all about perception, you know? So I gave him a few grand, told him how to doctor the books so it looked like he'd made a huge profit, then sell the business to somebody else who'd take the hit. Had him run some money for me at the same time, you know? We had people thinking it was the most profitable donut shop in Jersey for a while. Then he sells it for a lot more than he bought it for."

"That worked, then."

"Yeah, sure it worked. And he still runs his business like that today. He's successful now, so I won't tell you his name, but you better believe that when he says he's making a profit—well, maybe he is and maybe he isn't, but his shareholders think he is. That's what success means, right?"

"His shareholders?"

"I got rid of the girlfriend and the baby for him, too."

"You got rid of them?"

"Yeah. So she found out about the money laundering, and was making a fuss, so I told Henry I was going to pay her off, right? Get rid of her. Pay her to have an abortion or something. Henry said she wouldn't take the money, and I said, 'Well, you'd be surprised.' Turns out he was right, and she wouldn't do it."

"Henry?"

"Maybe I'm making up his name, don't put that in the book. But anyway, I had a few friends in the Mob back then. I took a couple of 'em and went to her, right after she had her baby, and

239

my guys told her that if she didn't leave Henry alone, she'd get shot in the head. And if she ever talked to him, she'd get shot in the head. And even if he tried to contact her, she'd get shot in the head. I never told Henry I did that."

"So he never saw his kid?"

"Well, yeah, because he never wanted that kid. I rescued him from this life that was making him want to kill himself. But the point is, now he is a successful guy. Because I taught him the first principle of business. It's all perception. Anyway. That's all I'm gonna say. But I'll tell you something else. The girlfriend shows up at my place a few weeks ago. She tells me her son has ended up working for Henry. She wants to know if it's okay to tell Henry about his son now."

"And what did you say?"

"I said, you do that, I shoot you in the head."

"And Henry didn't mind?"

"I told him I paid her off again. I was doing him a favor whether he knew it or not." Ivan shrugged. "You know I had this room built as a safe, in case I ever needed to hide money in here?"

Lillian looked around. "So let's get back to your third wife," Lillian said.

Frank Wheeler had built his business on his ability to recognize desperation. It was an instinct that told him which SAT students to help and which ones not to, which test takers to hire and which ones might have a crisis of conscience. He hadn't agreed to help Cal Bolt until he'd met Cal in person, until he'd seen the young man's expression, his hopefulness, his terror. Cal didn't just want SAT help—he was already half-living in that glorious, perfect world after he got his perfect score. This was reassuring to Frank. Frank needed those around him to surrender any sense of power. He sometimes mulled over the fact that most people seeking his help were wealthier, better looking, more privileged than he was. But it was just those sorts of people that fell into the trap of promising more than they could deliver.

When Frank first sought out Greg Miller, Frank was seeking a tutor to help him train for the World Series of Poker. Greg had made a name for himself as a poker player—in the circuit back in 2005 before he crashed and burned ahead of the finals—and Frank was pleased to have a coach who'd actually played the circuit. But when Frank saw Greg getting beat up in the back room of the Trump Taj Mahal, he recognized something more essential—Greg was desperate, and desperate people came in handy. Desperate people would help with a messy situation. And they might do it cheap.

The trouble was, desperate people could also do stupid things. They could get themselves beat up, and hand the captive over to a gangster, and come crawling to your apartment in Manhattan looking like a fucking truck had run over them.

And then what the hell were you supposed to do?

"You do realize you could have been followed here," Frank snarled when he met a near-dead Greg Miller outside the back entrance to his building. "Let's go up the freight elevator."

But Frank didn't know that it was he himself who was being followed. It was his apartment that was being watched. By a couple of good guys, a couple of old friends of Dan Marrone. Former, but not present, NYPD.

Chris and his coworker Darren were sitting in Chris's office on the ninth floor of the Xaverian Fund offices, located on two floors of a glorious old building built in the 1930s out of marble slab and cheap labor.

"It's all about perception," Darren was saying. "Henry Bolt has managed to create the illusion that his firm is immune to the subprime mortgage crisis. But it's going to crack. You're telling me they aren't exposed to any of those mortgages? Come on."

"Yeah, but Bolt's always had strong fundamentals. They're much less heavily leveraged than Citibank. They shifted some of their debt before the real estate crash."

"That's a temporary fix."

"I don't think it matters. It'll get them through the next couple of quarters, and by then the economy could pick up…"

A cough at the doorway. Chris looked up to see a dark-haired young man holding onto the doorframe. Clyde Upson hadn't bothered to get a haircut since he'd been in the hospital. His face was unshaven, and his eyes had the wary look of someone who thought he was being followed.

"Hey, come in," said Chris. He got up. "Here, take my chair."

Darren took the cue and stood up. "Well, I'll see you at the meeting."

"I'll make a decision by the end of the day. I'm just waiting for a few more numbers," Chris said.

"Just don't miss that meeting," Darren said. "You walked out on one already, and Jim is pissed. We have to make some big decisions today. If you're not there, you're going to be in trouble, man."

Clyde sat down in the seat Darren had vacated and shivered as if from cold. "So what's it like to work here?" he said in a quiet voice, quavering with just a hint of his restless energy. "I'm l-looking for a j-job."

"Oh, it's all right," said Chris. "It's good, it's fine. So what did you bring?"

Clyde lifted up a cardboard box and placed in on Chris's desk.

"I guess I wasn't even thinking when I took it with me," Clyde said. "I probably shouldn't have this stuff. But—you know, most people keep everything on email now, so they didn't even search this when I got fired. But I'd made photocopies of this stuff when I was out in Jersey researching the early history of the Bolt Corporation. Just because I didn't want to remove any files. I was afraid of losing them. Here, look at this."

Clyde opened a folder and handed it to Chris.

"See? Wally's Donuts makes thirty thousand dollars in profit each year for the three years before Henry Bolt buys it. Then the year Henry has it, it makes one hundred and two thousand dollars in profit. And then Henry sells it, and the next year…"

"Sixteen thousand dollars?"

"So Henry builds his career on this. He gets investors when he starts Bolt, which was just a little local bank and credit card company in New Jersey at first, because they think he's such a good businessman. I used to be really impressed by that. Only, there's no way that could be right. If—say Henry had really drawn in three times as many donut customers, then don't you think some of them would have stuck around at least a little while after he sold the company?"

"I hear you."

"So I'm thinking—maybe it's money laundering. Because it all appears to have come in just a few deposits. Most are cash, but the first one is from a guy. Ivan Bulowski. Google him."

Chris typed a few words in his computer and read aloud. "Small business owner from Atlantic City best known for testifying for the defense in the trials of two accused Mob members in the 1980s, Bruno Lestacchi and Tino Krauer. Both were acquitted, but Lestacchi went on to be convicted of the murder of Howard Manslo in 1992."

"Ivan's small business is debt collection." Clyde folded his arms. "It's cold in here."

"I'm sorry. Can I get you a cup of coffee?"

"Yeah, that'd be great."

The two of them walked together down the hallway to the espresso machine next to the elevator lobby.

Clyde lowered his voice and said, "So you think Henry could have asked one of these mob guys to kidnap the tutor so it wouldn't get in the way of his son getting into college? Or rub her out?" Then Clyde saw the expression on Chris's face, and added, "I'm sure it's not that. I mean, this guy Ivan co-owns a strip club in New Jersey, so she could be there. She might be in like, white slavery or something."

243

"Maybe."

"Look, if you want to go to the police…"

"No," said Chris. "I have no proof. It just seems so unlikely. Bolt Bank is so solid now. You really think he was involved in money laundering?"

"Solid?" Clyde smiled. "Some of Bolt Bank's departments are leveraged up to four thousand percent."

"You mean four hundred," said Chris.

"I mean four thousand. I got that figure from Eduardo. My co-worker. He's a statistics nut. He's never wrong."

Darren, walking by to get a coffee, stared at Chris. "Who is this?" Darren had heard their whole conversation.

"Nobody," said Chris. "Nothing. I have to go."

"The meeting."

"I'll be back."

Darren watched as Chris shook Clyde's hand and walked him outside. Then Darren made himself an espresso and stood staring at the gray cabinets for a long time. So Bolt was four thousand percent leveraged? This was not common knowledge.

Xaverian Funds made a complicated series of moves during the next twenty-four hours, which were far too complex (and intended this way) for the layperson to understand. Translated into normal, everyday terms, what they did looked like this:

> Xaverian had already purchased a form of insurance that guaranteed them money if Bolt Bank collapsed. This form of insurance was intended for firms with a financial stake in Bolt, but Xaverian had purchased the insurance simply to collect on it if Bolt went under.
>
> Xaverian sold a large number of shares of stock in Bolt Bank— shares they didn't own, but had promised to buy at a later date. This helped set off a selling panic among Bolt shareholders nervous about the ongoing Lehman Brothers collapse.
>
> Xaverian prepared to collect on the value of the "insurance" they had taken out against Bolt Bank collapsing.

All of this was perfectly legal. The value of Bolt Bank stock dropped from $3.51 a share to $0.73 a share in the next forty-eight hours. A half a million people nationwide who'd had significant portions of their 401k invested in Bolt Bank lost, all told, a billion dollars in retirement funds—including Pastor Walsh, who lost half the value of his retirement as the stock market collapsed within the following ten days.

Paolo Cincotti sat next to Vanessa. Tyler had missed school that day because of a problem with his breathing, and the boy now lay on the sofa between them, taking heavy breaths, one arched foot lying on Vanessa's leg. He seemed, at last, to be asleep, and Paolo was listening to a frantic message on his phone from Ivan. Something about a business meeting. Someone was coming to see Ivan about the girl.

"I have to go to work," Paolo whispered.

"So go."

"I hate that fucking job."

"Why do you do it, then?"

Paolo shrugged. He was silent for a long moment. Beating up Greg had changed him. He'd done it, first out of anger, then because he knew he had to do it—to prove himself to Ivan, to prove his worth. And it was that second beating, the "showing off for the boss" beating that stuck in his gut and made him feel sick.

He had never imagined, when he took the job, that he'd have to beat up somebody whom he knew and liked. He'd never imagined he'd beat up anybody who didn't have it coming, just to show off for the boss. And now that he'd done it, now that he knew he was capable of that, everything had changed. He didn't like himself much anymore. He worried that when he pushed Greg out of the car, Greg hadn't been strong enough to get to the hospital. But he'd been too afraid of Ivan to speak up. He'd been too afraid.

"Will you take some money, at least?" he said.

"No."

"Then will you—will you consider taking me, then?"

"What do you mean?"

"I mean come live with me. Be my girl. You know."

Vanessa sighed and flicked her eyes back to the television.

"And my daughter and I prayed," Pastor Walsh was saying from the screen.

"Well?" Paolo asked.

Vanessa shook her head.

"That a no?"

"That's a no. I'm sorry, Paolo."

The TV pastor continued. "We think that what we need is money, or fame, when all that we really need is God. And he's already in us. Already in here."

"You just don't like me?"

"I just can't," Vanessa said. "I can't take your money."

"... not what you owe to yourself, but what do you owe to your God."

Paolo stood up and walked to the window.

"I'll quit," said Paolo. "Is that what you want?"

"When?"

"Today."

"What are you going to do, then? For work?"

"I don't know. I guess I'll just go be a doorman somewhere. Maybe a valet parking attendant, like at a casino or a hotel or somewhere. You think I could get a job like that?"

"Yeah," said Vanessa. "Yeah, I do."

"I'm not even going to pick up my phone, okay? I'm quitting Ivan, as of right now."

"Then I'll come live with you."

"Really?"

"Where do you live?"

"Queens. I gotta one bedroom but we could make up the living room for Tyler, for now, you know. And we'll get a bigger place."

"I guess that'd be okay."

246

Paolo gave her a huge hug, so huge that it woke up Tyler in time to see Paolo kiss his mother full on the lips and then hug him, delighted.

"What's going on?" Tyler asked, letting out a yawn.

But Paolo just stood up and looked out the window. He didn't answer his phone, when it rang and rang and rang. He knew he was never going to go back to Ivan's again.

32

"I'VE NEVER KILLED A MAN. THAT MAY BE MY ONE regret. It's a rite of passage, you know. I've seen it in the wise-guys I've known, the way it makes them sure of themselves. I can respect that, but I've never done it. Maybe that's the secret of my success. Killing is like anything else. You get an appetite for it. Guys lose control, they get addicted to it. They end up in jail.

"The only thing I ever got addicted to was money. I wanted the biggest car, the nicest house, the fastest boat. But I didn't know how to hold onto money. At the beginning, back in the sixties, I made some dough on horses, but then I turned around and lost it all. We're talking sixty, seventy grand. Dug myself into a real hole. Then a friend, casino owner—he pulls me aside and says, 'What are you doing, Ivan?'

"I should mention that this was after some of his guys beat the shit out of me for a debt I owed. I got this big scar on my face from the beating, so I guess he felt bad about it.

"I said, 'What do you mean, what am I doing? I want to get rich.' He says, 'You want to get rich?' 'Yeah, I want to get rich.' He says, 'You know how you get rich? You get rich by taking money from other people, not by betting on fucking horses.' He says, 'You got two choices: take money from rich people or poor people. Now, the rich got a lot of money, but it's hard to take it from them. But the poor don't have much money, but it's easy to take it from them.' He says, 'Ivan. Take my advice. You're never going to be smart enough to take money from rich people. But with that scar, you can scare the hell out of poor people.' So I became a heavy. I worked for this guy, Marty Rhodes. I did debt collection for his bookie operation. And eventually I had my own heavies doing the work for me."

After reading this section, Lillian looked up and waited for Ivan's response.

"Wow," he said. "You're good."

"No."

"Yeah, really."

"It's all stuff you said yourself. I just strung it together."

"But you put it together in a way that sounds good, which I sure as hell can't do," Ivan said. "You know what I think? I think it's going to be a bestseller."

"That'd be great, but…"

"Now I got to tell you, I was skeptical," Ivan went on. "I thought, Fortuna graduate, what the fuck's she know about debt collection. But you really—you got into my head there."

Lillian stammered. "Well, that's—I mean, that's what writers do."

"No, but you're good at it. You're good at it," Ivan said.

Something in Lillian relaxed at the words. It had been a long time since anyone had said that.

"Thanks," she said.

That was when somebody rang the doorbell.

"Jesus," Ivan said. "Paolo's fucking late. He's fucking late. I got a meeting, I got no fucking protection here."

And he pulled a gun out of a holster under his arm, cocked it, and slid it into his pocket before pushing open the door and walking outside into the garage. Lillian heard him say, "Hi. You here about the girl?"

"Uh—look, no, I'm sorry, I'm lost, and I…" Lillian recognized the voice, but couldn't place it. Then she realized who it was, and her breath caught.

"You from the police?"

"No. No. Wait. Please don't… don't shoot, I'm sorry."

"Get inside," Ivan told him.

Chris walked into the room, his hands up, and looked at Lillian. Ivan shoved him onto the floor face first.

"Oh, Jesus Christ, who is that?" said Ivan. Another car was arriving. Ivan tucked the gun out of sight and closed the door. They heard him lock it.

Chris looked at Lillian.

"Hi," he said.

"Hi."

"You okay?"

"Yes. What are you doing here?"

"Attempting a rescue."

"Chris."

"It was dumb."

"It was sweet, but..."

"Let's go. He's distracted."

"I'm handcuffed."

"Okay, um...Let's do something about that."

He raised up the laptop to try to smash it against her handcuffs.

"Not that!" Lillian cried. "Anything else!"

Chris spun around, looking.

"Ivan Bulowski?" Frank spoke in a slow drawl, one hand on the driver's door of a car.

"You here about the girl?"

"I am," Frank said. He seemed unwilling to move from the door handle of his car. Ivan glanced inside the car and saw Greg sitting there, glaring at him through bruises.

"Okay," Ivan began, "what I want to know is, what the fuck kind of racket is this? Greg tells me you were only giving him two G a week to hold her. What the fuck kind of money is that?"

Frank replied, "I pay the going rate."

"I want ten grand a day."

"I don't need her held any more. We were about to let her go."

Ivan said, "What the fuck kind of racket is this? Come inside. I want to talk to you."

250

Frank sighed, looking over his shoulder as if he wished he were already driving away. "Look, I don't really have time for this, okay? I've got a tournament this afternoon. Can you just let her go? I'll pay you for it."

"Come inside the house. This is fucking ridiculous." Ivan, without a bodyguard, was suddenly suspicious of being kept outside. Exposed. And then—right then, behind Frank, Ivan saw a car drive by. He saw two distinctive men—cops, he could tell. Big, burly types. Bulletproof glass.

"What the fuck is this?"

"What the fuck is what?" Frank shrugged, which pissed off Ivan even more. Ivan, with no protection, on his own at last, pulled out his gun, shot at Frank, shot at Greg, and started shooting at the passing car.

Six gunshots fired, the satisfying warmth heating up Ivan's hand. Six shots fired back from the passing car. In the moment before he died, Ivan managed to resolve his one regret: he killed two men before he was shot to death by the two former NYPD who were trailing Frank.

In the coming days, the funerals would be paid for as follows:

Greg Miller's corpse would be driven to Boston. His parents would ask Bella why she hadn't told them that he was in trouble and then ask her for money to help pay for the funeral. She would pay the entire sixty-seven hundred dollars herself.

Frank Wheeler's parents would bury him near their home in the Bronx at a cost of thirty-eight hundred dollars and not speak of him for the next three years, until one of his cousins was caught selling pot outside school and was asked whether he wanted to end up like his cousin Frank.

Ivan Bulowski's funeral would be paid for by the money from a life insurance policy he'd left in the hands of his fourth ex-wife. He had prearranged the whole funeral, which cost a total of twenty-eight thousand dollars, but the funeral director—a personal friend of Ivan's—did a last minute swap of the coffin and put him in a cheaper wooden one, pocketing the forty-five hundred dollar difference.

Back at Ivan's house, before the shooting began, Chris was trying to use an old stapler to attack the desk where Lillian was handcuffed when they heard shouting outside. Then gunfire. They both dropped to the floor, and a handful of bullets popped through the walls in ugly puffs. Chris lay next to her.

"Thanks for coming to get me."

"Are you okay?"

"Yes. I'm sorry I was so mean to you. I was being stupid."

Chris smiled. "Don't worry about it."

"Don't get shot, okay?"

"Okay."

They listened as the gunfire got louder, then stopped. Lillian and Chris looked at each other for a moment, then looked around.

Hundred dollar bills were raining from boxes lining the walls. Bills were floating through the air, drifting onto the furniture, sweeping across the carpet.

"Jesus," said Lillian.

It had grown very quiet.

Then a bang at the door.

"Open the fuck—open the fuck—"

Neither of them moved. Ivan unlocked the door at last and pushed inside, badly wounded, blood coming from his neck. He looked around at the bills fluttering through the air.

"My money," he said.

Then he fell. Frank's car was on fire, and the heat caused something in the garage to explode, pushing a fireball along the hallway, lighting the money in the air on fire, lighting the room with it.

Lillian tried crawling toward Ivan's body but her handcuffs and the heavy desk made it impossible for her to reach him.

"The keys to the handcuffs—he has the keys, Chris."

Chris crawled to Ivan's burning body below the waves of smoke and searched him. He found a set of keys in Ivan's hand and crawled back to Lillian. She was coughing, wiping her eyes. And then he was searching for keys, and testing them, blind in the smoke, until he had the right key. She felt his hands on hers.

Chris grabbed Lillian and helped her crawl out the door. As she left, she turned for one more look. There was money everywhere, drifting through the air, pooling into the blood, burning. She saw a hundred-dollar bill waft before her eyes. Lillian hesitated, then grabbed the laptop with the rough draft of the novel to take with her.

33

DAN MARRONE ARRIVED AT HENRY'S OFFICE EARLY THE next day with a report labeled "Confidential."

"I need to give this to Henry."

Bella had arrived at 6:30 a.m. The precipitous stock decline had made for a busy day yesterday, and she was expecting more of the same.

"That's fine," said Bella, distracted. "You can leave that with me."

"I'd rather do it in person. He's still at his residence?"

"Yes, but he should be in by 8:15. Would you like to wait?"

"Yeah, I would."

Dan sat down in the waiting area, the packet in his hands. Thirty minutes passed. It was 8:21.

"He said he'd be in today, right?"

"He said so, but I really can't guarantee exactly when. Did you have an appointment?"

"No, but I need to see him."

"He must be running late. It's been a busy week."

"I got another appointment. Don't open that, okay?" Dan handed the package to Bella. "Keep that very secure until he gets here. Don't leave your desk, okay?"

"Of course."

Bella nodded. To make Dan feel better, she placed the packet in the far corner of her desk. She waited until he'd left, when— as she always did with Henry's mail, even the confidential mail—she took it out of the packet and walked into Henry's office to place it in the appropriate spot on Henry's desk.

Her phone rang.

"Hello, Bella, it's Mom."

"Hi, Mom." They hadn't spoken in months.

"Someone left a message on our phone this morning while we were out, and it sounds like something happened to your brother. Have you heard anything about this?"

"No. What happened?"

"They said someone shot him. The police spoke to us from Atlantic City."

"I'm sorry, what?"

"We don't know if it's true or not. They found our number on his cell phone. They want someone to go down. Listen, can you go down there? Can you drive down?"

"Of course, but…"

"Let me give you the information."

When she hung up the phone, Bella sat very still for a long moment, until a few words caught her eye on the "Confidential" document on Henry's desk.

"Greg Miller was among the deceased. Mr. Miller was a friend of Frank's and apparently an active participant in the kidnapping. He was in the back seat of Frank's car when we tailed it from New York to New Jersey. Greg is believed to have been killed in the crossfire when our guards engaged."

Bella sat down and read the report.

"…was persuaded by Greg to go to the kidnapping victim, which is how we located…we have arranged with the local Atlantic City police…your name will not be in the papers…your son will be represented as a victim…Lillian and her associate Chris Schott spoke to local police, and we persuaded her we were on a rescue mission…unlikely to cause you any future embarrassment…please burn this copy, and all other copies will be destroyed except one that is kept in our…"

Bella put down the confidential document. She placed it in the proper inbox in Henry's office and walked out into the hallway. Then, she went back and, with the deliberateness of a murderer, took the document to the photocopier and made a copy.

As she completed the action, Henry walked into his office. Without a word, she walked in, placed the document in his inbox, and walked to her desk. She called Henry on his office phone.

"I'm not feeling well," she said. "I'm going to ask Therese to cover for the rest of the day. There's a confidential report in your inbox, and you have a conference call at ten-thirty."

"This is a bad day for you not to be here."

"I'm very sorry, Mr. Bolt. This is my first sick day in four years."

"Well, get me Jason Hegeman on the line before you go," said Henry. He went back to reading an email.

Bella got Jason Hegeman from Legal on the line, and then put on her coat. She caught a taxicab. She took her photocopied document to the *Daily News* and left it at the front desk with a note addressed to the Metro Department. Then she went home.

When she got home, she called her work voicemail to listen to her brother's message again, to hear his beloved voice one more time, before she got in her car and drove down to the Atlantic City morgue.

After giving their stories to the police until close to eight p.m., Lillian let Chris drive her to his apartment.

"Nadya's been staying with me for a while," he blurted out, and Lillian knew everything.

"The two of you…"

"Yeah, we were—just, you know."

"You're dating."

"You and I weren't together."

"I know. It's okay."

Chris glanced at Lillian and saw her staring out the window, avoiding meeting his eye. He was surprised to see that she might care. His rescue mission, until then, had been for himself. He had not pictured a happy ending for Lillian and himself, and now, suspecting she might like him, he was flustered.

"No," Chris said. "I don't know. I think we just..." He thought of saying "we were just worried about you," but couldn't say it, because it sounded too strange.

Chris hadn't called Nadya to give her the news, and Nadya dropped a bowl of carrot ginger soup when she saw Lillian come in the doorway. Then she rushed to hug her.

Chris explained how he had found her and what had happened, and then he stood back and watched. The girls sat together on the sofa, Nadya's hand grasping Lillian's. They spoke in short questions and one-word answers, putting their lives back together. Lillian told her story in detail, but tried to make light of it, breathing out relief. Chris and Nadya were horrified.

"That little shit," was all Nadya said, meaning Cal. Lillian was still unsure whether Cal had anything to do with it, but Chris told her he suspected otherwise. And her first thought was to pity that poor, desperate kid whose imagination went no farther than to hide all evidence of his misdeeds.

"So how's your search for an agent going?" Lillian nudged Nadya.

Nadya shook her head. "Oh, goddamnit, I don't care. Anyway, I need to get a job. I've been living off Chris."

"You guys are together now."

"Well, yeah," said Nadya. "Kind of. But he's really in love with you. Aren't you, Chris?"

Chris said, "Nadya."

"No, it's fine, though," Nadya said.

"It's okay that you guys are together," Lillian began.

Chris said, "I'm going to go get us some takeout for dinner..."

Nadya said, "No, I'll go. I'll go, Chris. You guys talk."

"Nadya, come on," he said.

"You want Thai food, what?" said Nadya. She looked at the two of them. "Don't worry about me. You guys can talk about getting married or whatever."

Lillian said, "Stop it."

"No, it's fine," Nadya said. "I knew. I always knew," she said to Chris.

"Nadya, wait a second," Chris began.

Nadya shook her head. She didn't want Chris to mess up this moment for her, because she found that she enjoyed giving away a boyfriend to Lillian. It made her feel a slender sense of hope for herself. Maybe she wasn't such an artist after all. She could be nice, even, from time to time.

"Don't worry," Nadya said with a smile. "I'm going to go have a cigarette. This is what cigarettes are made for."

The three of them ate Thai food and homemade mojitos, and then Nadya insisted on taking a taxi back to her Brooklyn apartment by herself, where she stepped onto a pile of unopened credit card bills and threatening letters from her student loan company. For a moment, she considered suicide. She walked to the bathroom and looked at her pills, her antidepressants, her razors, and then she sat down on her toilet seat and stared at the modernist print on her bathroom towels, and she started to laugh.

And then she realized, with a strange sense of loss, that she was not going to commit suicide, not actually going to do it, not ever. It was like saying farewell to an old friend. Instead, she was going to grow up. She considered her career prospects and then lit a joint, took one drag, stamped it out, and walked to her bedroom and flipped open her Mac laptop, where she started to work on her most neglected piece of creative writing: her resume.

Chris and Lillian stood looking out the window in Chris's apartment.

"Nadya and I just happened."

"It's okay. You and I weren't together."

"You thought I was a jerk."

"No, never. I liked you. I just didn't know how we could ever work."

"With Nadya, it was just—I think we were both so worried about you."

"It's okay," she said. "I wasn't raped, I wasn't tortured. I was lucky."

He put his head on top of hers and sighed. "Thank you for making it out alive."

"I wouldn't have made it out alive without you. I couldn't have reached those keys. I would have died there."

Chris had been useful after all. He had proof of it, now. The thought disturbed him. It had really been that close, and she would have died in the fire if he'd been a few minutes later. He didn't like the feeling of being a hero as much as he'd expected. His arrival, just in time, felt so arbitrary that he knew that luck, not courage, had won the day.

"I love you," he said.

"I love you, too."

His cell phone buzzed in his pocket. Once, twice. He glanced at it.

"It's a message from work. I'll get it later."

"No, go ahead."

He listened to the message, one arm still around her, looking out at the darkening sky.

"What is it?"

"Nothing major. I just got fired."

It was on the cover of the *Daily News*. It was on the cover of the *Post*. It was referred to in a Maureen Dowd column of the *New York Times* and snarkily hashed out on gawker.com. Cal's SAT plot—and his involvement in the ensuing disastrous kidnapping—were mocked, parsed, dissected. And Bronnie, now in the heat of a divorce and with plenty of problems to write about, was informed by her lawyer that she couldn't blog anymore.

Bronnie had pulled Cal and Amy from school because of the scandal and was living in the family's country house on Long Island, where both kids were being home schooled by a revolving series of Ivy League tutors, who had been instructed not to mention anything about the family's circumstances and who were only too happy to oblige. Their Long Island neighborhood was the kind with houses so far apart that the concept of "neighborhood" was theoretical, and each residence was in effect its own gated community. Cal upped his tennis training to five hours a week and did an additional five hours of practice on the family's tennis court each weekend with a young tennis pro from the local club who had become Cal's entire social circle now that Cal had dropped off Facebook. It would be nice to say that Cal did a lot of thinking about truth, responsibility, and his future while on the tennis court ten hours a week, but it would be inaccurate.

Peter Wicka's comeuppance, if he had one, existed only in the negative. He started college as a tabloid footnote, remembered only for putting Cal in touch with Frank's tutoring scam. Cleared of any criminal charges, he hoped at least for a certain notoriety, a conversation-starter with the ladies, but no one seemed to care. And Peter, whose fledgling film career might have benefited from a certain Roman Polanski-esque bad-boy sheen, found himself relegated to the role of second-tier supporting player to Cal's leading man depravity.

The incomplete footage for *Snuff* met a more interesting fate, as the forty-one digital video tapes the boys had shot were lying in a storage box for duplication in Pastor Walsh's audiovisual office when Julie went to her father to confess her wickedness—including some footage of Lillian's actual kidnapping, which Peter had hoped to sneak in as B-roll. Pastor Walsh saw no reason to return the footage to Peter (who in any case, by the terms of their contract, did not own it), and he also saw no reason to throw it away. It was handed over to Obadiah, who edited it all together on the Holy Alliance Church's editing software. Obadiah added a voice-over to cover the plot holes and shortened it to a 45-minute film, and it became a minor hit at Christian film festivals and Bible camps, primarily because a lot of thirteen-to-seventeen-year-old Christian boys decided that Julie was "hot."

Peter tracked these events from his Fortuna dorm room, and concluded that perhaps he might not go into filmmaking after all.

Henry, at first glance, seemed almost unaffected. He continued to go to work each day, although the collapse and impending bankruptcy of Bolt Bank meant that his day was booked front to back with meetings. In a strange twist, the leak of Cal's betrayal was never traced back to Bella, because an Atlantic City police officer tried to sell part of the story to the press. So after three days of calling in sick, Bella found herself back in Henry's office, answering phones for the man whose life she had attempted to destroy. In secret, she was also sending out resumes. She would never have come back to work for Henry at all, but real estate values had dropped so much that she was now forty thousand dollars underwater on her Hoboken townhouse. There was no point in getting herself fired until she could land another job somewhere else. And perhaps more important, she wanted to see Henry suffer firsthand.

Henry's finances were insulated from the collapse of his company. He had insured himself against bankruptcy by transferring his stock options to cash a short time before the company collapsed, and he was due to get a salary of seventy million dollars and a bonus of forty million dollars that year, which he had lobbied the Board to guarantee him, even if the company went under.

Henry had also received three calls in the last week from senators asking if there was a way Washington could help his company. Bolt Bank was a big employer. It deserved to succeed. It was a vital part of the economy, and they were here for him, if there was anything they could do. And they were running for reelection, in case he was curious.

With wife and kids gone, with meetings day and night, he seemed efficient—waking, sleeping, and eating. But he moved like a man in slow motion. He was late for his cars in the morning. He went home from work at eleven or twelve at night. He ate the wrong foods, and when he asked Bella to order him a cheeseburger, it shocked her more than anything he had done. He ignored the photographers from the press. He looked older, but there was no one around him who cared enough to notice.

261

About a week later, Bella called him on his office phone to say a woman was in the lobby asking to see him. She didn't have an appointment, but she'd left her name. Celia DiMaio Upson.

"Send her in."

Celia had dressed for the occasion in a pale pink suit. She walked in and stood at the door.

"Hi, Harry."

"Close the door."

She closed the door.

"What can I do for you, Celia?"

Celia sat down opposite him. "The last time I saw you I was about to have the baby. Remember?"

"I remember."

"I bet you do. So when did you decide to send him? Was it then? When I said I hoped you'd be a good father?"

"You mean when did I send Ivan?"

"Yes. Ivan and then the other men who came to me and said to stay away from you or they'd kill me."

"What men?"

"Real nice way to get rid of me…"

"Ivan said he offered you money."

"Yeah, and I wouldn't take it."

"You did take it!"

"What the hell are you talking about, Henry? I didn't take the money."

"What are *you* talking about?" asked Henry, panicking.

"Your friend Ivan and his buddies said he'd kill me if I contacted you. And that you didn't want to see me again. And if I tried to talk to you again, he'd kill me."

"He wasn't supposed to!" Henry was stunned. He thought he knew everything.

"Your own son. I never understood how you could do that. And why."

"I didn't tell Ivan to threaten you," said Henry.

"Sure you did. He was your friend, wasn't he? You were running money for him. I knew that."

"Celia…"

"And then when Clyde came to work for you, I was so scared for him, that Ivan would hurt him. But I hoped maybe you'd changed, maybe you'd help him out."

"Celia, Ivan told me that my son had come to work here, but I told Ivan not to tell me who it was. I told Ivan just to—to pay you off again, like he did before."

"You just by accident put your son in a coma?"

"A coma? What are you talking about?"

"He worked so hard for you. And you had your people beat him to the ground. I didn't know you were even capable of that. Your own son."

"Clyde Upson."

"He would have been Clyde Bolt if you'd done the right thing. And he is so smart, too. Ambitious. Just like his dad."

Henry rose and walked to the window.

"I didn't know Ivan threatened you, Celia, I swear. He wasn't supposed to."

"Stop lying to me."

Henry was paralyzed. The moment that had destroyed his life hadn't happened. Celia had never betrayed him at all. That meant that he had betrayed her for money, not the reverse.

"Your security guard almost killed your son and you're saying it was an accident?"

"Clyde Upson." He tried to remember the young man from that one, brief moment at the company barbecue, but all he remembered was intensity, eagerness, and an almost painful innocence that Henry had misread as cynical plotting.

"What do you want me to do? What do you want from me? What do you want, here?"

She looked up at him. "I never wanted money from you. I wanted you to be a father. But you become a father to somebody else. And then you screwed that up, too. I read it in the papers. You're a terrible father."

"I know I am."

"I just wanted to see for myself what kind of a man you are. Now that that monster Ivan isn't there anymore to threaten me."

"I tell you what," Henry said. "Let me give you money. To help you out. Anything you need."

"Go to hell." She rose. She was the only woman he had ever loved. And this was why—because she couldn't be bought.

His office phone rang. Bella's line.

"Mr. Bolt, I have Penny Danner from Fortuna on the line."

"Just a moment," he said. He looked up at Celia, and he saw her pause in her tracks.

"We've got medical bills, Harry," she said.

"Of course I'll pay those. You want cash?"

"I just need help." And Henry realized she was going to take the money.

Henry nodded. "That's what we'll do, then. I'll send something to you. I have to take this call."

"Harry, wait."

"What about a thousand dollars a week for life?"

Celia looked at him, stunned. The sad part, to Henry, was that she had no idea that wasn't a lot of money to him.

"Just leave your number and address with my assistant."

"I loved you so much."

"Just leave your number and address with my assistant," he said, and he saw her face grow pale, trying to connect with him as he looked straight through her. It took her a moment to realize she would get nowhere. No one ever could. She turned to go.

To the extent that Henry still had a heart, it broke. She had taken the money. His billions made it too easy to put a distance between him and everyone he loved. And it would, forever. It was impossible to get really close to anyone without the money tainting it, somehow. He hated that. Except for its one advantage: that you never had to get really close to anyone.

"Put the woman from Fortuna through," he said.

A soft, warm voice came over the receiver.

"Henry, it's Penny. I just wanted to update you on Cal's application."

264

"You don't have to soft-pedal," Henry replied. "I know what's been in the papers. Just tell me the truth."

"The thing is, I love Cal. He is such an talented young man, and he has such a bright future. But right now, it's just been—I've been doing everything in my power to convince the admissions office to see this for what it is, he's so obviously a victim, but they just seem to feel that—well, they're being stubborn."

"I see."

"And I just wanted you to know that—that of course I understand if you don't wish to—and because of your company's troubles, and the stock market, if you just can't make the kind of commitment you had in mind."

"I appreciate that."

"And I am just—I wanted to tell you what a pleasure it has been to meet a man like you. Even by phone. You are a good man, Henry. You have such wonderful goals for your children. And for this country."

"You don't have to sell me a bill of goods," said Henry.

"No, not at all," said Penny. And she used, at last, the ammunition she had been storing up for so long. "It's just that—seeing your son go through this, it must be so hard. It must feel almost like—almost like you're losing him. Like losing a child."

And Henry Bolt, the Self-made Man, began to cry. He nodded, thinking back to all those years ago, when Clyde was born, all those years when he'd believed Celia had abandoned him. "My wife left me," he said.

"I am so sorry," said Penny.

"I just feel so alone. Right now." The words choked out, one after the other, like stones.

Penny told Henry how sorry she was, and how she knew that a man like him must be isolated by work, but she reminded him that everything he did was for his family, and for others, at the end of the day. The nation had been built by men like him. His commitment. His vision. He represented the best of America. And his family was going to see that someday. They were going to see how much he loved them, and they were going to become the kinds of people he wanted them to be. His son and his daughter both. Someday, they were going to be so proud of him. Because they would know that he stood for something.

By the end of the phone call, Henry had recommitted to the full one hundred and fifty million dollars. Even though his son was not going to Fortuna. Even though nobody in his family had any connection to the school at all.

34

LILLIAN WAS ASLEEP IN THE LIVING ROOM. SHE HAD COME over to Chris's place and they had made a long afternoon of watching television and doing nothing in particular on their laptops. Lillian's laptop was the one she had stolen from Ivan. She decided not to turn it in to the authorities after learning that the NYPD had lost her laptop—along with all her writing, every single draft of her thesis novel, which she'd never quite gotten around to backing up elsewhere—when they confiscated her laptop to search for evidence relevant to her kidnapping. What Lillian didn't know was that the young officer assigned to read her book had to take time off to be treated for depression.

When Lillian dropped off to sleep on the sofa, safe at last, it was the closest Chris had known to peace in weeks.

He had spent a lot of time thinking about the job he'd lost. If he had been at work that day instead of attempting to rescue Lillian, he would have participated in the decision to short the Bolt stock, and he would have cleared a bonus of eight million dollars that year. Instead, he was sitting in his gym shorts on a twelve thousand dollar sofa trying to work out how he was going to pay his mortgage. He had put all his money into his apartment, which he had purchased for 1.7 million, and which his broker had told him was now worth 1.2. So that ate up his savings. He had thought that half a million in savings was pretty good, but now he was worth just about zero.

He didn't want to be a private detective. That much had become clear when he was trying, over and over, to wrench Lillian's hand from a handcuff. It hadn't felt like an adventure after all. He had always thought he was fascinated by the darker side of human nature, but in the full light of day, he realized he wasn't. It seemed to him that the great crimes of humanity were not perpetrated by masterminds, but by people who didn't seem to be thinking much at all.

He just wanted quiet and beauty. He thought about his favorite place in the world, the Hotel Villa d'Este in Italy. What had he loved about it so much, during that one time he visited? It was the quiet. The calm. The sound of waves lapping against a shore. It was the way that the hotel staff was not only competent, but they were also kind. They did their jobs as if it were a pleasure. It wasn't that they acted subservient before his money. It was that there was so much money floating around that everyone could pretend that money didn't exist.

That was what he wanted: to be rich enough to live in a world where everyone pretended that money didn't exist. But he also realized that people like him—people who just wanted to sit by a lake—weren't the people who really succeeded in business. The people who succeeded, the Henry Bolts, were those for whom no amount of money was ever enough. The people who couldn't stop. The people like Clyde Upson, who Chris learned had accepted a job at Xaverian Funds—just an entry-level spot in the trading department. They met for lunch a week later to discuss all that had changed since they'd first met in the hallway of a hospital.

"I don't have any time anymore," Clyde said. "You know, we've really been making a lot of money out of bundling some of these assets for the Asian market. I don't really understand it all, yet, but I—I've been getting home at one, two in the morning, I'm learning so much, you know?"

"I know."

"Stock market's going crazy. Going down, man. But I like it, though," said Clyde. "I'm learning so much, and you know what's crazy? If I'd still been at Bolt Bank, I'd probably be laid off right now anyway. Hedge funds are the safest place, right now, because they aren't restricted. It's the way capitalism is supposed to work, no one looking over your shoulder."

"I feel a little bad," Chris said, "about people who invested in Bolt Bank. I mean, Xaverian was responsible for taking down that company."

"It's not your fault, though. I mean, if Bolt was a strong company making good decisions, then Xaverian wouldn't have been able to take it down."

"But people put their retirement funds in it."

"That's temporary. It's just the way the stock market works," Clyde said. "Somebody's left holding the bag."

"Usually the average American."

"Well, that's why you have to work in the stock market."

Chris was silent for a moment, considering Clyde's remark. It was so accurate a description of the attitude of everyone at his job, and pretty much everyone he knew in finance (once you stripped away all the optimistic mumbo-jumbo about "spurring growth" and "trickle down" and the "invisible hand of the market") that Chris was a little taken aback. Perhaps Lillian had been right about those who worked in the financial markets. He couldn't think of a single person he worked with who would have disagreed with the personal and ethical assumptions underlying Clyde's statement.

When Chris later pinpointed the moment he decided for good that he was going to leave finance, that was it.

"Anyway, I gotta go." Clyde pulled out a BlackBerry. "Man," he said, "I have to be back at the office like, ten minutes ago. I've got no life anymore, I'm telling you." But Clyde looked happy. He was happy not to have a life.

Now Lillian shifted in his arms on the sofa and looked up at Chris. "What are you thinking about?"

"I'm just thinking about trying to sell my place and maybe going back to school or something."

"In what?"

"I don't know. Maybe study economics, get a Ph.D.? I don't know."

"You're just jealous of my unemployment and student loan debt," said Lillian with a smile. "Someone told me that debt is a sign of adulthood."

Chris smiled. "Don't believe him. He was probably hitting on you."

"Are you worried?"

"No," he said. "We're going to be fine."

Lillian loved him for saying it, even if she wasn't sure it was true. The great blessing of someone from Chris's background was that—whatever happened to him, whatever he was up against—he could say something like that and actually mean it. Even if his family lost all his money, he would still believe he could slog along and get somewhere fantastic by sheer effort and education. That might have been the greatest gift and curse of being born rich—becoming accustomed to the idea that you could get whatever you wanted. Lillian decided to borrow some of Chris's relentless optimism, at least for a while. She planned to approach some agents with a new idea for a book.

Three weeks later, Lillian had a fifteen-thousand-dollar offer for the true story of her kidnapping—with an emphasis on her relationship with Ivan, the would-be mobster who was shot dead in his garage by a couple of private security guards. Her book was tentatively titled *Autobiography of a Gangster*.

It took three months for her to write the first draft. Her agent loved the book, but proceeded to engage in a debate about the appropriateness of including Ivan's story about how he had helped a young businessman with a donut company—wondering whether it might seem like Henry Bolt, whether there was enough proof, and would they get sued for libel.

"Never mind," her agent said at last. "We'll just give it to the lawyers, see if they want to run it by Bolt's people."

Lillian got a phone call at home twenty-four hours later.

"Lillian, this is Henry Bolt."

"Hello, Mr. Bolt," Lillian said.

"I'd like to discuss your book. Can you meet me in my office, please?"

"I'd actually prefer that you meet me in my office," Lillian said. Later, she was never sure how she had the gall.

"I don't think I'm going to have time to do that."

"Your decision."

"Let me put Bella on," said Henry.

And Lillian and Bella had a brief, perfunctory conversation about scheduling, and where exactly Lillian lived in Brooklyn.

"Whatever," said Bella. "I really don't care anymore. I'll put it in his schedule, and he'll do it. He does whatever's in his schedule." She was leaving for Goldman Sachs the following week.

Henry Bolt showed up at Lillian's tiny apartment the following day and sat on her Ikea sofa next to Nadya's new cat, Mimi. Lillian had spent the morning wondering why Henry was bothering, how this could possibly hurt him, until she stumbled across a story about a possible government bailout of the banking industry, and decided Henry was trying to dodge the political cost of more bad press.

"I'd like to ask you not to publish that story about the donut shop," he said to her. "People might read that and get the wrong idea. You understand."

"I understand," Lillian said. "They would think it was you."

271

"I assume if you've called me here, you want something from me in exchange for not publishing this. What is it you want?"

"I'm not blackmailing you, Mr. Bolt. You contacted me."

"I understand that. What is it you want?"

For a brief moment, money flashed before Lillian's eyes. She could see it—that miracle she'd always hoped for. All her loans disappearing in a moment. And it would cost Henry next to nothing, just the amount he might spend on a two-week vacation rental in the Hamptons, or a new set of floor tiles for his kitchen.

And she would be free. Just like people were free when they graduated school back in the 1960s. Free to travel the world— playing guitar, doing drugs, finding themselves.

"I guess, what I want is this. I will agree to not publish that story, if in return, you agree that—at some point in the future— maybe I'll ask you for something. I'm not saying this with any- thing in particular in mind. But if I ask you, I will expect you to help."

Henry Bolt thought about it for a long moment.

"You have nothing particular in mind?"

"Not at this point."

He nodded, unsmiling. "I think I can agree to that."

They exchanged a stiff handshake, and he turned and walked out her door and down the narrow stairs to his waiting town car.

Lillian stood watching him from her window.

What she had wanted, at the end of it all, was not the money. It was to have Henry Bolt in her debt.

Her book came out, without the Wally's Donuts story, to de- cent reviews. But Lillian continued to struggle to make her rent payments. Her agent said there was much less money, always much less money than you expected, in a first book. But it was all right. She got another job working at an afterschool writing center for a public school. And she started another novel. A love story. Something to do with sailboats and the way a wealthy family wove in and out of a poor family's existence. Kind of like the Kennedys, maybe, but different. Somehow beautiful, and strange, and with an implausible, happy ending. Because that was part of the human experience, sometimes.

The same week that her book climbed to number nineteen on the *New York Times* nonfiction bestseller list, she discovered, in the top spot, a book co-written by Bronnie and Cal Bolt. It was entitled *Little Boy Lost: A True Story of Crime and Redemption on Park Avenue*, and Bronnie and Cal appeared on *The Today Show* and *Oprah* to explain what Cal had learned from his experiences, and how getting caught cheating on the SAT was the best thing that had ever happened to him, and all about the new charity that the two of them had started to help students get free SAT tutoring in poor neighborhoods. Bronnie's next book, Bronnie said, was going to be a parenting book. Cal had been accepted to Princeton for the following year.

Lillian later found out that Bronnie's and Cal's book had been ghostwritten by one of her Fortuna classmates, an earnest young man named Joel, whose thesis novel had been a fictionalized autobiography of Martin Heidegger wrestling on his deathbed with the consequences of Nazism. Joel confessed the Bolt connection to Lillian several months later when they were swapping writing stories at a party.

"I wrote about your kidnapping," he offered. "I hope I got it right. I wanted to call you, but I'd signed all these confidentiality agreements, so I couldn't really talk about it."

"Don't worry," Lillian said with a smile. "I'm sure it's fine. I didn't even read it."

She watched Joel staring out the window towards the distant Manhattan skyline.

"So how was it," she asked, "working with Cal and Bronnie? How is it, working for the Bolts?"

Joel considered the question for a long time.

"Well," he said finally, "It's a living."

ABOUT THE AUTHOR

RACHEL CAREY is a writer and filmmaker. She received an MFA in Film Directing from NYU, an M.Ed. from Harvard, and a BA in English from Yale. She currently lives with her family in New Jersey and teaches college film classes. *Debt* is her first novel.

www.ingramcontent.com/pod-product-compliance
Lightning Source LLC
Chambersburg PA
CBHW060307260626
47160CB00007B/2533